The Seeker's Storm

Silver Sagas Book 6

A sweet romance

By Lea Carter

Generations ago—no, before that, during a time so long ago that all they really knew about it came from the bedtime stories their great-great grandmothers spun—there was a great conflict between the five tribes. Eventually, peace had been their only option if they wanted to survive, so they separated, each tribe gathering in its own place... Only the Water Fairies had withdrawn completely, sealing their separation with a warning so dire that none but kings had spoken of it for millennia—that they would use their power to cause streams and rivers to dry up, or become foul and undrinkable. The whole of Fairydom was at their mercy in that respect.

"Yes," Kuntza nodded, his thoughts on the future rather than the past. He glanced about the room, at the fairies he had come to know so well in so short a time. He had been promised an entire winter by his tribal council, a season in which to collect information, to prepare a recommendation. Clearly, that was no longer to be trusted, for there was another Bullierd to be considered, a woman-fairy named Amber. Kuntza had been inclined to trust her when he first met her, then gradually found his suspicions growing. Just before his impetuous decision to visit the surface, he had gone so far as to sign papers restricting her to the capitol city of Cachora. What a fool he had been to ever allow her to travel freely through Water Fairy territory!

My thanks to all those who have contributed to the writing of this book. My friend, Thomas Barnett, for his valuable input on the design of the Sky Fairy windships. My father and brothers for listening to me and answering questions on Sunday evenings while I struggled to understand electricity and thunderstorms. My mother and sisters for their continuing support, including editing skills.

And especially to my readers, who remind me that they still want to know what happens next.

Chapter 1

As Prince Oliver followed his father from Arnold Mosley's elegant hotel suite, he saw a flicker of movement out of the corner of one eye. The long hallway was lined with statues and ornate paintings, and dotted with recessed doorways that lead to other suites. Curiousity getting the better of him, Oliver signaled for the marine behind him to continue flying forward no matter what. When they reached the next doorway, Oliver slid into it. Careful to stay hidden, Oliver turned back towards Mosley's suite and sank soundlessly into the plush carpet between the beautifully carved planks that framed the doorway. Dropping first to his knees, then down to lie flat, he stifled a chuckle at the idea of trying to explain himself to the hotel guest if the door beside him should abruptly open. Carefully, he inched his face towards the edge of the doorframe. The small party that had escorted him and his father to Mosley's hotel faded away, the sharp click of a window—locking behind them— the last sound he heard. One eye finally clear of the doorframe, Oliver held perfectly still. And waited. The hallway was so still that he thought he could hear the paint on the walls fading in the bright afternoon sunlight.

The motion he saw might have belonged to anyone—a chambermaid, another guest... Oliver was beginning to give in to the feeling of foolishness when a slightly built man-fairy peeked out from behind one of the statues at the far end of the hall. Mosley had dismissed his servants when the king first arrived, which meant the suite should still be empty, Mosley having also gone off to take care of personal business. Oliver's right eyebrow lifted fractionally when the man-fairy slipped over to Mosley's door and glanced furtively around before he produced something from the inner folds of his scribe's robe, *and let himself in through the locked door.*

More than curious now, Oliver came silently to his feet. Decades of playing hide and seek with his younger siblings contributed to his swift, but soundless flight down the length of the hallway, where he arrived just in time to slip between Mosley's door and its frame. He quickly dropped to his knees in a shadow before it swung shut behind him. From there, he was able to watch as the scribe began searching single-mindedly for something on Mosley's desk.

It was all so absurd that Oliver nearly gave in to the urge to laugh at himself. He had just assisted his father in interrogating Mosley—and unless Mosley was an even more masterful manipulator than the Wood Fairy Minister of the Interior, he had been telling the truth when he denied any involvement in the delay of the winter storms. Now he, Oliver Bijou, Crown Prince of the Sky Fairy Tribe, was hiding in the shadows? Sleuthing was the specialty of his younger brother, Prince

Cambrian. Still, Oliver could not shake the feeling that something was amiss here. Mosley might have given a scribe a key to his suites, but…*scribe!* Another piece of the puzzle fell into place, bringing Oliver to his feet precipitously. Cambrian had recently brought evidence to them that a scribe was involved in the conspiracy.

Startled by Oliver's movement, the scribe jerked to one side. His elbow struck one of the taller stacks, knocking it over in an avalanche of blue, white, and yellow papers that fluttered to the floor. Some fell quite a distance. Others struck the hem of the frozen scribe's robe and landed about his feet.

"Harold Scroggins," Oliver casually scooped up a small volume of poetry from the entryway table beside him, "I arrest you in the name of the crown." As he had expected, Harold flew towards the nearest window. Oliver's arm came up and snapped forward, hurling the hard-bound book towards Harold's back. "Well, that is a first," Oliver murmured to himself as he watched the scribe crumple to the floor, temporarily stunned. "I do not recall ever seeing a book drop a scribe before."

Tugging the window sashes free, Oliver bound his prisoner securely. As he was about to begin searching the desk himself, Harold stirred. Weak blue eyes stared up through his tousled blue bangs, full of unanswered questions for his assailant.

"A thousand pardons for interrupting your search." Oliver, eyeing the stacks of papers that

Harold had not yet begun to search, felt that the thousand pardons should be made to him, not Harold. If Oliver had just waited, Harold might have found whatever it was that he was looking for. Anyway, judging by Harold's glare, Oliver's humor was not appreciated. Which gave him an idea. Why not use Harold's expressive face against him? Mosley had already given whatever hard evidence he had to Captain Constance Kimberlite, who had in turn passed the documents on to the crown. That left…what?

"However, since the map has already been removed," Oliver shrugged with one hand towards the door while keeping both eyes on Harold, "your search was already a failure."

Harold blanched. "You have to protect me."

Oliver's false nonchalance melted away. "From whom?" He leaned forward.

"Does it matter?" Harold shot back. "If I do not return with that map…" Words failed him and he began simply shaking his head.

Oliver was accustomed to high pressure situations, but negotiating with criminals was well outside of his usual duties.

"Harold." Oliver waited briefly, then repeated, "Harold." When the scribe finally looked him in the eye, Oliver wasted no time on subtlety. "Your life is balanced on a knife blade. Tell me what I want to know," he nodded reassuringly, "and you will be protected."

Harold seemed to crumple even further into

his capacious robes.

"One problem at a time, Harold," Oliver recommended, folding his arms across his chest and taking a step forward. "If you are convicted of treason against the tribe, that map will be the least of your troubles." An imposing figure at his most casual, Prince Oliver Bijou straightened to his full height, despite the fact that he was holding his breath.

"What do you want to know?"

"Maps are easy to come by." Oliver chose the topic that was nearest Harold's fear, pretending ignorance of the fact that the maps had been subtly altered over the last few hundred years until they were dangerously inaccurate. "So you will tell me what makes this map so important."

Harold's inner wrestle was written in frown lines on his face. At last, he glanced up at the closed curtains and exhaled slowly.

"I could draw that map in my sleep," he said bitterly. "I made enough of them. But this copy," he lifted his bound hands as if to run his fingers through his hair, then dropped them back to his lap in frustration. "It is one of a kind, not meant to be given away." He hesitated, then unconsciously leaned closer. "It is not what you can see that makes it special; it is what is hidden in plain sight."

Oliver inhaled slowly, trying to mask his excitement. Carefully, he questioned Harold, wishing the whole time for a pageboy, or a marine, or anybody that he could send to bring his father and brother to him. The thought that Harold had dared make a secret copy of the treasonous master plan was mind boggling. Even Harold could not explain how it had gotten from his private files into Mosley's hands, but the important thing was that it had.

"Royal Marines!" bellowed a voice from outside the window. "Open in the name of the king!"

"No!" Harold reached for Oliver with both of his bound hands. When Oliver stopped, Harold continued in a whisper, "I know that voice. He is not a marine."

Oliver squatted beside Harold long enough to warn him. "If this is a trick, or you try to cry out to your friends," he jerked his head towards the window, "I will throw more than a book at you this time." Harold's wildly nodding head was all the answer he needed. While a trick was still possible, Oliver dared turn his back on Harold long enough to peer through the place where the closed curtains met. The whole of the outside world was tinged a painful shade of purple by the thousands of tiny fibers protruding from the curtain edges, but unless facemasks had been added to the marine uniform in the last five minutes, something was sorely amiss.

Seizing Harold by his collar, Oliver stuffed him under the desk, where the knees and feet normally went. Setting the chair back in its place, Oliver draped his jacket over it.

"Remember," he warned Harold in a hushed tone, "the map is well beyond reach." Scooping up the book of poetry he had used to stun Harold, Oliver sprawled on the nearest settee, with just enough time to muss his hair and close his eyes before the outer window splintered open.

"Wha…" Oliver nearly threw the book to one side, as if in an involuntary twitch of fright as three armed civilians stormed through the window. "How dare you!" Coming to his feet, he glared them down.

"Quiet, you!" The nearest of them put one huge hand in the middle of Oliver's chest and shoved him back on the settee. His smirk was evident even through the mask as he watched Oliver flop onto the cushion.

"Leave him," barked one of the others. "Scroggins is all we want."

"And the map," reminded the third, already scanning the room. "Keep an eye on him," she fluttered a hand in Oliver's direction, "but get busy. The sooner we find what we came for, the sooner we can leave Regalis."

Oliver's ears pricked at that. Regalis was in the path of a monster snowstorm, something they had learned just that morning. Nevertheless, the capital city was a much safer place to be than any village or town he could think of…unless they were headed for Aureus? If that was the case, then they might have considerably more time than any of them had guessed, for Aureus was nearly two days away by windship.

"I," Oliver found himself staring down the length of a highly-polished sword blade. Deciding in an instant that deception was his only choice, he swallowed visibly. "I say," he shrank back a little, "Mosley is not here right now. But if you would just tell me what you are looking for…"

"Never you mind," sneered the sword-wielding villain. "You sit," he tapped Oliver on the chest with the point of his sword, "quietly."

Looking wildly towards the one woman-fairy in the group, who was approaching the desk, Oliver pretended to think aloud. "Mosley has an entire book of maps in…" He stopped when the sword point settled firmly against his chest.

"Maybe you *can* help us." The woman-fairy did not look up from the stack of papers she was rapidly thumbing through. When she had finished scanning them, she dropped them on the floor. "What happened to those papers?" She pointed at the papers Harold had knocked over.

"I bumped into them." Oliver answered without hesitation.

"Tsk, tsk." The woman-fairy picked up another stack of papers and began flipping through them as she flew towards Oliver. "And you did not think to pick them up?" She allowed the papers in her hand to flutter down over Oliver, her eyes narrowing thoughtfully when he continued to meet her gaze. In her experience, fairies who were truly in the wrong place at the wrong time tended to exhibit fear. Spontaneously, and especially when their personal space was invaded. "Who are you?" she asked sharply.

Again Oliver gambled, aware that he had somehow given himself away.

"I am Prince Oliver Bijou, heir to the throne of the Sky Fairy Tribe." He relaxed back into the comfortable settee, sensing that his indifference added to her pique. "Princes," he smiled, "have servants to clean up after them." The thought of expressing that sentiment to even one of the household servants at the Crystal Castle made him smile even more broadly.

"Indeed? A prince, eh?" She sounded more annoyed than impressed. "What a pity that you will not live to inherit that throne."

"No?" Oliver held up one hand, palm towards the windows, as if examining his manicure. "Perhaps if I told you that the map you are looking for is even now being taken to the royal kitchen, to be read near a warm cooking fire," he smirked up at her, "you would not be so arrogant." This time the sword point pressed against his throat, so tightly that Oliver hardly dared breathe. "I assure you, you will never make it to Aureus."

"Overstepped yourself there," the man-fairy holding the sword growled triumphantly. "Why should we wait the winter out buried under snow?"

"Stupid," snapped the woman-fairy, crumpling the last few papers in her hands. "Stupid, stupid, stupid! What else would you like him to know?" By now even the third fairy had stopped searching and was watching the scene play out. "They obviously know about the map. Which means," she continued, her voice temperature dropping by the syllable, "that it is just a matter of time before the timetable, the routes, *and* the list of the council are in their hands."

"Well, tell him all about it, eh?" sulked the berated man-fairy beside her.

She did not even bother to look over at him, just kept staring at Oliver. "On the other hand, why should we keep secrets from our friend?" Her smile was cold, serpent-like. "Perhaps we can tell you where *you* will not be spending this winter."

"You mean take him with us?" The poor fool holding the sword opened his mouth to continue protesting, only to choke on air when she turned her icy glare on him.

It was possible that the woman-fairy was about to let loose with another string of derogatory remarks. Oliver did not wait to find out. Leaning back more firmly into the overstuffed settee, he removed his throat from imminent danger.

"Now!" With his left hand, he slapped the sword point away from his body. His right hand shot forward, grabbing the shocked man-fairy by his sword wrist while a squad of marines exploded into the room through the broken windows. Oliver pulled on the man-fairy just until he reflexively tried to jerk his hand free, then released him to stumble backwards into the waiting arms of two husky marines.

Oliver had no sooner completed the move than he realized that the woman-fairy on his left was coming towards him, dagger in hand. Rather than being sensible enough to dodge her attack, he snatched up a heavily upholstered pillow and lunged at her. The dagger, thrust hastily at his attacking form, became embedded in the pillow, allowing him to easily twist it free of her hand. He extended his wings, halting his forward rush in time to escape the force of an adrenaline-fueled marine who struck her from the side, taking her clear to the floor.

"Your Highness," the squad leader, a second lieutenant, confident that things were in hand, saluted him from the far side of the desk. "Reporting as ordered."

"And just in time," Oliver grinned back. He was going to have to remember to thank his father's escort for sending someone to check on things. Gesturing towards the prisoners, he commanded, "Separate them—and keep them separated. Absolutely no communication between them starting now."

It was just as well, he decided, that they were not going to be put in a single cell. The insults they were tossing about as the marines hauled them away would have singed the rust right off the cell bars. It was a waste of energy, too; Harold was the one they should have been blaming, not each other.

"Oh, Lieutenant," Oliver spoke up as the last prisoner approached the window. "Send a carriage back for me, if you would." He helped the prisoner along with a none-too-gentle shove and found himself alone in the room. Well, almost. "Hsst." He bent towards the back of the desk, hovering so that he would not get glass from the windows embedded in the soles of his shoes. "You can come out now."

Chapter 2

Oliver was about to pat himself on the back for successfully sneaking Harold into the castle when three pageboys descended on them all at once.

"Your Highness!" said one.

"King's respects," began another. They both stopped speaking when they saw each other.

"The king requests your presence in the library," finished the third pageboy, realizing quickly that they were all on the same errand.

"I…thank you." Keeping a firm grip on Harold's arm, which seemed even bonier now that he was without his robes, Oliver smiled at the pageboys and turned his course towards the library. At least now he would not have to hunt his father down.

The library door had barely come into view when he heard a sharp popping sound, followed by several frightened outcries. Recognizing his mother's voice in the midst of the chaos, he barged through the door without knocking. He got a vague sense of the fairies in the room—his parents, his brother, Cambrian, and two others—then realized they were standing in a loose semi-circle around a table in the center of the room. The table held a very strange contraption, something he would have dismissed as a sad attempt at art if there had not been a distinct sound emanating from it. He frowned, concentrating. It sounded like…water on hot metal. But there was hardly any metal present in…whatever it was. It looked remarkably like an empty glass bottle suspended between two wooden braces with a crank on one end.

"Hey!" Prince Cambrian, struck in the shoulder by the abruptly opening door, took several steps to one side before stretching his wings and righting himself. "Who in Fairydom…" His outrage evaporated when he recognized his brother in the doorway. "Quickly," he beckoned Oliver and whomever it was with him into the room, shutting the door firmly behind them.

"Is everyone alright?" Oliver asked. He was still getting answers to his question when he became aware that Harold was trying to pry himself loose.

"Let go of my arm!" Harold protested, scrabbling futilely at Oliver's much stronger hand. "Before you break it!"

Oliver relaxed his hold, but did not actually release Harold until he was planted in a convenient chair. Too late Oliver realized that Kuntza, the Water Fairy ambassador, or truth seeker, was in the room also. Kuntza's tribe had severed all ties with the world above the ocean eons ago and become the stuff of bedtime stories since. If pirates had not recently invaded their world, they might have gone on in their self-imposed exile forever. Oliver quickly stepped between Harold and Kuntza, who was already taking refuge under the deep hood of his cloak, no doubt to hide his distinctive pale pink hair and hazel eyes. Next to Kuntza, Jennings, Cambrian's valet, was hastily draping a sheet over the contraption on the table.

"Father," Oliver addressed the king, who was on the far side of the group from Kuntza, "permit me to introduce Harold Scroggins, royal scribe and toady to the traitors who have been illegally stormpiling the snow clouds."

Harold, exhausted from the events of the day thus far, did not even bother to look up from massaging his bruised upper arm.

"Hello." King Jasper cocked his head to one side while he surveyed the scribe. The last time Jasper had heard Harold's name—and the first time, too—had been a few short hours earlier, when Cambrian had asserted that there was some connection between Harold and the traitors. Jasper could only assume that Oliver had found something more substantial than similar handwriting, something worth dragging the poor man-fairy to the castle and into the heart of a top secret meeting. "What can I do for you?" Jasper noticed Oliver's quickly suppressed smile, but did not withdraw the question.

Harold, meanwhile, started in disbelief. "What…what can you do for me?" he eventually spluttered. "Well, that does it." He made a move as if to stand up, then changed his mind when he looked into Oliver's unblinking indigo eyes. Sinking back into the chair, he ran trembling fingers through his thinning blue hair. "If not for the glass cuts in my pants," he reached down to rub a sliced spot, "I could believe this has all been a dream. One very long, very bad, dream."

Oliver reached out to touch him lightly on the shoulder, his first effort towards reassuring Harold.

"It is almost over now," he promised. "Just rest there, alright?"

Harold nodded slowly, but could not help wondering if it would ever really be over.

The queen, seeing how pale Harold was, moved towards the nearest water pitcher. Pouring a glass, she took it over to him.

Confident that Harold was in good hands, Oliver gestured for Cambrian and Kuntza to join him near his father. That left Jennings, good man-fairy that he was, watching Harold like a hungry falcon.

"Father," Oliver's voice dropped to a whisper. "Where is the map that Mosley gave us?"

"Here," Cambrian drew it from an inner jacket pocket. Before he could ask what was going on, Oliver had lifted it free of his fingers.

The library was littered with tables, and each table was furnished with an oil lamp. Producing a match from one of his own inner pockets, Oliver struck it and lit the nearest lamp.

"Careful," Jasper warned as Oliver unfolded the map by the top of the lamp. "Those lamps can get surprisingly warm."

"Father." Cambrian could barely get the word out when he began seeing letters spring into view on the back of the map.

"I say!" Jasper leaned closer, his excitement focused on the front of the map.

Without another word, Cambrian snatched up a blank sheet of paper and a quill. Writing as quickly as he could and still produce legible words, he copied down everything he saw on the back of the map, committing it to memory as he went.

Oliver, as soon as he saw what Cambrian was doing, repositioned the map so that Cambrian could see the entire back of it.

"There," Cambrian tossed the quill aside and handed the paper to his father. "Now we not only know the basic timeline of this coup, we also know exactly who was behind the pirate buildup earlier this year, who convinced Major Layton to turn pirate, *and* who orchestrated the snowstorm: Bullierd, former count of the Silver Fairy Tribe."

Jasper felt the blood draining from his face as he scanned the rest of the names. While he never would have called those fairies his personal friends, it was a shock to find that they had participated in planning the annihilation of the nearly thirty villages between the snowstorm's last reported position and Regalis.

"Look here," Oliver reversed the map so that Cambrian could see it from the front.

"What," Cambrian squinted and leaned closer, "are those peculiar marks supposed to represent?"

"Portals." Kuntza said the word flatly, his entire being seeming to frown at the map.

Cambrian shot Kuntza a glance, then resumed examining the map. Could Kuntza possibly mean—Cambrian inhaled slowly as he leaned both fists on the table.

"Jennings," Jasper dredged a casual tone up from somewhere deep in his stores of strength. "Please escort Scroggins to…"

"No point," Harold interrupted heavily. "I could draw that map in my sleep. And, I hid the list on the back." Only after he had spoken did he realize he had basically confessed to treason. His mouth suddenly dry, he took another sip of water.

Oliver closed his eyes briefly as understanding struck him. Harold had said that back at Mosley's, also, about being able to draw it in his sleep. Apparently he had been speaking of the *entire* map, including the portals.

"What can you tell us," Oliver asked, setting the map on the table, "about these portals?"

Harold took yet another sip of water before he answered. "They lead to passageways under the sea."

"And go where?" Cambrian posed the question in a lowered voice, quite as if he were speaking to himself instead of subtly interrogating Harold. It was important to know just how far knowledge of the Water Fairy Tribe had spread.

"Where?" Harold shrugged. "Never told me that." Tipping his head back as far as it would go, he drained the glass. "Thank you," he said to the woman-fairy who had provided it to him. "That hit the spot."

"You are most welcome." Queen Marta smiled graciously at the young scribe as she accepted the glass back. While she understood what he had done in serving the traitors, she sensed no malice in him, just a regrettable lack of spine.

Kuntza stood silently by the table, studying the marks before they faded from view on the rapidly cooling map. His downturned mouth, and the way that his eyebrows gathered together, spoke volumes.

"Dan-gerous," he muttered to Cambrian when the last mark had disappeared. "The portals were our greatest se-cret."

Cambrian could well imagine. He had learned of the existence of the Water Fairy Tribe a few short weeks ago, while investigating Marine Major Layton. After the initial surprise of learning that Layton was also the infamous pirate Bane, Cambrian had been shocked to find himself escaping the pirate prison through a lava tube, guided by none other than Kuntza.

"The treaty," Cambrian thought aloud. Generations ago—no, before that, during a time so long ago that all they really knew about it came from the bedtime stories their great-great grandmothers spun—there was a great conflict between the five tribes. Eventually, peace had been their only option if they wanted to survive, so they separated, each tribe gathering in its own place. The Deep Woods to the east became the home of the Wood Fairies, with their brown hair and eyes, and their fabulous animal wrangling skills. Likewise, the Plant Fairies had retreated to the southern border of Fairydom, where they would have the best weather for the most time, and could devote themselves to their gardens. The Silver Fairies, diplomats even then, moved to the north, relinquishing all claim to the stark mountains of the west, where the Sky Fairies felt most at home. Only the Water Fairies had withdrawn completely, sealing their separation with a warning so dire that none but kings had spoken of it for millennia—that they would use their power to cause streams and rivers to dry up, or become foul and undrinkable. The whole of Fairydom was at their mercy in that respect.

"Yes," Kuntza nodded, his thoughts on the future rather than the past. He glanced about the room, at the fairies he had come to know so well in so short a time. He had been promised an entire winter by his tribal council, a season in which to collect information, to prepare a recommendation. Clearly, that was no longer to be trusted, for there was another Bullierd to be considered, a woman-fairy named Amber. Kuntza had been inclined to trust her when he first met her, then gradually found his suspicions growing. Just before his impetuous decision to visit the surface, he had gone so far as to sign papers restricting her to the capitol city of Cachora. What a fool he had been to ever allow her to travel freely through Water Fairy territory!

Jasper set the list by the map. He had been studying what little he could see of Kuntza for the last few minutes and had an idea that the tall Water Fairy had come to some sort of a decision.

"Kuntza." Jasper spread his empty hands before him, palms up. "Whatever we can do to help, we will do."

Kuntza felt a new wave of respect wash over him as the king's sons straightened beside their father, each of them binding themselves to their father's promise with solemn nods.

"My thanks," he bowed from the waist, as was the custom here. "Also, my apo-lo-gies. I must go home. Quickly."

Jasper frowned thoughtfully. "We have very few windships in port right now. Most of those are military vessels, here for the winter. Even the fastest of them would most likely be too slow for your needs." His frown deepened as his thoughts temporarily went to the docks, where Captain Constance Kimberlite was directing the refitting of every available cloud chaser.

"Of course," Cambrian's frown was slightly darker than his father's, "there are a few civilian yachts in port."

"Including," Oliver was quick to see where Cambrian was going, "the *Seeker's Wind*." She was a record-breaking yacht, once the pride and joy of the fairy who had built her. When he foolishly put her up for collateral, he lost her to one Arnold Mosley, whom Oliver and his father had just visited. A spectacularly wealthy business fairy, Arnold briefly joined forces with the very traitors responsible for this entire perilous situation. Even Captain Constance Kimberlite, Cambrian's intended, after coaxing Arnold into cooperating with the crown, found herself caught in Arnold's web of deceit—married to him, to be precise.

Cambrian straightened away from the table, determined not to lose his focus. Punching Arnold's teeth out was going to have to wait a bit longer.

"Do we know where Arnold is?" Jasper asked, well aware of the yacht's ownership.

"I will find him," Cambrian offered.

"Very well," Jasper agreed after holding his son's gaze for several seconds. "Bring him to the port captain's office. Intact."

Cambrian knew he should be hurt that his father felt the need to add that specification, but it was a point well-made. Bowing slightly, he left via a library window.

"Should I go with him?" Jennings volunteered without taking his eyes off of Harold.

"Good idea," Jasper agreed. "Two heads are better than one, after all." He smiled a shade grimly at Kuntza as Jennings vanished out the same window. The treaty might be in jeopardy, but at least he trusted Kuntza to be on their side. "We have very little time. You must pack your things while I arrange for a carriage."

"And I will settle Harold upstairs," Oliver inserted. "He is falling asleep over there." The rooms were smaller upstairs, but Oliver reasoned that would make it easier for the guard assigned to keep track of Harold. "Oh," he paused and looked between his father and Kuntza. "What is that thing under the cloth over there?"

Jasper exhaled slowly. "A lightning machine. And, our best hope for defeating this snowstorm." When Oliver looked down at the table, then sideways at him, Jasper chuckled and nodded. "It sounds crazy, I know. However, it is true. It can transfer lightning to metal objects." Since he did not understand how it worked, he skipped that part. "Kuntza believes that we can force the snowstorm to become a thundersnow storm by launching the treated metal into the cloud."

"Rather a large risk, I gather." Oliver looked intently at the cloth-covered device.

Jasper nodded once. "Rather." They were risking the lives of the windfairies who volunteered to crew the storm chasers. The towns between the storm and Regalis were also in peril. And, while this was not the time to explain it to Oliver, Kuntza had identified silver as the best metal for the task, so a significant portion of the tribe's finances was forfeit whether or not this plan worked.

Oliver nodded back. They were doing the best they could with what they had.

Once Oliver had taken Harold out, Marta flew over to where Kuntza and Jasper were standing.

"I will miss you," she said simply, proffering her right hand.

Kuntza took her hand in both of his, keeping them on either side of hers instead of placing one on top, in dominance, or one below, in deference.

"You have been the most per-fect hostess," he bowed. "My stay could have been more pleasant only if it were allowed to be long-er."

Marta blushed slightly, moved enough by his sincerity to forget herself and suggest, "Perhaps we can come visit you sometime."

Kuntza stiffened visibly. His eyes met Jasper's and held them. "Per-haps. This once," Kuntza breathed, causing Jasper and Marta to look at each other in alarm. "No. It is not possible." Releasing her hands, he took two long strides away from them, tapping his forehead with one hand while wrapping his other arm behind his back. "But, how else…" He kept muttering to himself under his breath, then returned even more quickly. "You are won-derful!" Wrapping his arms around Marta, Kuntza hugged her fiercely. "An idea! Such an idea." Releasing the startled queen, Kuntza caught Jasper by the shoulders. "My time here is too short. I cannot find all that I need for the questions my council will ask." His energy dissipated marginally as he continued, "You must send someone with me."

Jasper stared, open-mouthed, up at Kuntza. For any investigation, any task at all requiring the seal of the royal family, he had always sent Cambrian. But this? Send his son to winter beneath the sea with a tribe of unknown intent?

"Kuntza?" Marta placed one hand gently on the truth seeker's arm. "Let us discuss it?"

Kuntza smiled down at the beautiful queen. "Of course." Taking his hands from the king's shoulders, he began making his way towards the far wall. "I will pack my things and await your answer." With a bow and a flourish, he slipped out of sight behind a secret panel in the library wall.

Marta half-laughed, half-sobbed as she watched the panel close behind him. "We have trusted him with so much already." Like her husband, her reflexive answer to Kuntza's request had been Cambrian.

Jasper drew his wife close, pressed her head to his shoulder. The secret passageways were a closely guarded secret, known only to a select few. It had not been an easy decision to allow Ian, Jasper's personal bodyguard, to reveal them so that Kuntza's presence could be more easily hidden.

"I know," Jasper said emphatically, "that if it were up to Kuntza, Cambrian would return safely."

"But," Marta drew on their over five hundred years of marriage and her understanding of politics to finish his thought, "if Kuntza was in charge, Cambrian would not have to go."

"My love," Jasper kissed her forehead gently, "you are still as smart as you are beautiful."

She chuckled and cuddled a little closer. They both knew they were delaying the inevitable. Jasper would have to leave soon for the port master's office, where he would find a way to tell Cambrian about Kuntza's request. She assumed that Cambrian would volunteer. He always had.

"And you are our strength." It was a difficult thing to say. However, she knew he forgave her for leveraging his compliment, using it to wisely remind him of all who were all depending on him. She understood that if Jasper had to ask their son to take this awful risk simply because Jasper was the king, it would break his heart. She could only hope that she had eased his mind a little through thoughts of all those he would be protecting by taking this action.

"Oh." A startled voice, colored by intense embarrassment, spoke from the shadows by the far bookcase. "Forgive me, I," the young man-fairy apologized, his silver eyes semi-averted as he flew slowly towards the now-separated couple. "I did not mean to intrude."

Marta would have recognized the young historian even without his standard-issue leather boots and tiny quiver of fresh quills. He had his mother's friendly eyes and wavy silver hair, framed in his father's well-balanced face and settled firmly above squared shoulders.

"We accept your apology, Rolf," she answered with a faint smile.

"On one condition," Jasper intervened before the historian could relax. "You must tell us how long you have been there in the shadows."

"Why," Rolf blinked once, "only a moment or so." He looked longingly at the loaded bookshelves surrounding them. He was so close… "I was just going to do some reading before dinner."

"I see." Jasper knew it would be rude to doubt Rolf, who was his guest, an apprentice historian, *and* a member of the extended Silver Fairy royal family, but something still bothered him. "We did not, however, see you enter." Folding his arms, Jasper waited for Rolf to start fidgeting. Rolf had arrived earlier that day with copies of the latest history books. He could not have been in the castle for more than six hours. How could he possibly have found the obviously not-so-secret passageways that quickly?

"I imagine that is because I did not come in through the hallway door." Rolf briefly contemplated attempting to withhold his true objective until he had obtained the evidence he had been sent for, then discarded the idea. If even a shred of their suspicions were correct, there was no time to waste. "Your Majesties," his bow included them both, "there is something I must tell you."

Jasper had to work so hard to keep his eyebrows from shooting up towards his hairline that he was frowning before he realized it. His previous experience with sixty-something-year old boy-fairies had led him to expect a certain reluctance when it came to divulging ulterior motives.

"I did not come to Regalis," Rolf continued as if kings frowned at him every day, "merely to deliver an updated set of historical records from the other tribes. I am here at the special request of the king and queen of the Silver Fairy Tribe."

Jasper was perplexed enough that he began frowning in earnest.

Rolf was so close to fidgeting that he resorted to one of the relaxation techniques his uncle, Hugh Lawson, had taught him shortly after the coronation. Looking Queen Marta in the eyes, Rolf smiled. Then, with considerable effort, he repeated the maneuver on King Jasper. Having literally faced his fears, he was able to refocus and continue.

"There is a growing concern regarding random water fluctuations around Fairydom. We think we know how they are happening, but we would like to know why."

"Are we supposed to know the answer to that question?" Jasper asked evasively.

Rolf's heart beat a little faster. He knew a dodge when he heard one. But this was a lot more important than who took the last jelly roll or why someone had not finished their assignment for class.

"I should also tell you," he decided aloud, "that Ambassador Julene is the one who instructed me regarding the secret passageways."

"Why would she do that?" Jasper asked through clenched teeth.

"So that I could more easily find her great-great-grandfather's marriage certificate."

Jasper inhaled sharply. If Rolf knew about that, then there was very little he did not know.

"She seemed to think that I should take it with me when I go to visit the Water Fairies. Along with her personal letter of introduction."

Marta tried to loosen her death grip on Jasper's arm, but without success. Her brain and her body seemed oddly disconnected as she viewed the situation anew. Rolf was already planning to visit the Water Fairies. Even an apprentice historian could act as an intermediary between two tribes. Reason tapped her on the shoulder when Rolf looked at her, then back at her husband. Her best friend, Annabelle, would be devastated if anything happened to her son Rolf and Marta knew she would never be able to face her again if Cambrian stayed behind.

"Historical marriage records are stored in that corner," Jasper indicated the spot with a nod of his head. "Get what you need and then come with me." If Julene had seen fit to entrust Rolf with the truth about her recent Water Fairy ancestry, the situation was dire indeed.

Rolf was already by the shelf, counting over from the left. Ambassador Julene's directions to the certificate were precise, allowing him to find it quickly.

"I am ready, Your Majesty," he called as he slid the file back into place. Dropping a meticulously prepared square of soft leather on the nearest table, Rolf set the certificate in its center and folded the leather over it to protect the document during its travels. Securing it inside the pouch that always hung on his left side, Rolf followed the king into one of the secret passages.

Chapter 3

Arnold Mosley, blissfully unaware of all that had taken place after he left his suite, leaned casually against a chimney. From where he was standing on a warehouse rooftop, he could see everything that was happening on the docks below.

The cannons being removed from the cloud chasers were wheeled to the south end of the docks, where draft ants hauled them one by one out of the melee and through the narrow, twisting streets to the castle. Meanwhile stacks of ballista parts, recently removed from the castle defenses, were blocking the north end of the docks so that a caravan of ant carts was stopped cold. The shouting match that had commenced between the caravan's lead driver and the marine sergeant from the castle was rapidly increasing in volume and audience.

Towards the commotion flew Captain Constance Kimberlite. Arnold's gaze lingered on her as she made her leisurely approach. Her hair was up in the same braid that she had been wearing when they signed their marriage contract earlier that morning. Not too surprisingly, she had since changed out of her exercise uniform and into something a little more formal. It struck him as highly irregular that he found her to be just as fetching in either uniform as she had been in the formal gown she wore on their one and only date to the restaurant Do'tore.

Curious to see how she would handle the debacle, Arnold flew off the roof and slipped closer to the arguing fairies. To his utter delight, she ignored them outright.

"You there!" She pointed at the driver of the second cart, shouting just loud enough to be heard over the other two. To her relief, once they were no longer the center of attention, the argument quickly began to peter out. Still speaking to the other driver she asked conversationally, "Are you familiar with the street that runs just on the other side of these warehouses?" When he nodded, her manner changed instantly. "Then why are you all sitting here?" she bellowed. "Back that last cart up and swing it around the buildings. We need those carts unloaded onto the chasers today, not tomorrow!"

Turning abruptly, she came almost nose to nose with a rather smug-looking marine, the same sergeant who had failed to resolve the situation by swapping insults with the lead driver.

"As for you!" A mere captain in the royal fleet, she knew she had limited authority over the marine sergeant, but she stretched it as far as she dared when she icily inquired, "Who put you in charge of the ant carts? I should say you have your hands full getting these ballistae installed. Now everybody. Back to work and hurry up about it."

The ant cart drivers hastily passed her instructions along to the last cart, while the marines who had gathered to enjoy the argument began seizing ballistae parts—everything from the forward spring frames to the windlass handles—almost at random and hauling them away.

That was when Constance spotted Arnold. Her anger spent in reprimanding the others just now, she found herself curiously lacking in emotional response as she returned his gaze.

Arnold, sensing her indecision, took a slow step back into the shadows. He was relieved when she decided to follow him.

"Constance." Removing his hat, he tucked it under one arm. The rest of his speech stuck in his throat when the wind shifted and he got a nose-full of her scent. It was just ordinary soap for the most part, but there was that ineffable something special that reminded him of why he had wanted so badly to marry her. He had to clear his throat before he could proceed. "Constance, I manipulated you shamelessly this morning when I convinced you to marry me." Admitting that, and seeing the agreement on her lovely face, should have been the worst of it. "I…" Struggling with what should have come next, he took a less direct route. "Do you have our contract with you?"

Surprised, Constance was already reaching for it before it occurred to her to wonder why he wanted it.

"It all happened so quickly this morning, I just wanted to examine it." Arnold smiled faintly, understanding her hesitation. "Make sure it is filled out correctly."

Reluctantly, Constance handed their marriage contract over, her hope that it was somehow lacking, and therefore not binding, outweighing her distrust of him.

"Thank you," he said, accepting it. Opening it, he skipped the pre-filled legalities that occupied the top and middle of the document to inspect their signatures and those of the witnesses. "All there." He refolded it, keenly aware of the disappointment that flickered across her face at his announcement. "Perfectly legal contract." He held it out, but did not release it to her when she reached for it. "One that I will not hold you to," he managed to say with some effort. "Especially not when you are so clearly in love with Prince Cambrian."

She inhaled sharply. They had made no effort to conceal their feelings since their return from Cambrian's last mission. It was just that hearing those words so shortly after facing Cambrian and telling him of her contract with Arnold was like having storm clouds part to let the sunshine through to warm her. Together, she and Arnold tore their marriage contract in half.

"Thank you." Her words were barely a whisper, completely overshadowed by the hubbub around them, but he smiled anyway, having seen her lips moving and guessed her message. "Have you discussed this with Michelle?" she asked, reaching up to remove the necklace chain from around her neck. Holding his heavy signet ring between her finger and thumb, she coiled the chain into his palm, pressed the ring on top, and closed his fingers over it.

Arnold blinked, completely baffled at the question. "Michelle? The waitress at Do'tore?" he asked, not certain that he had heard her correctly. When she nodded, he shook his head. "No, of course not."

"Really?" Constance hugged him hard, relieved that they were back on a friendly basis. Michelle had more than beauty to offer; she was also savvy, spunky, and had shown that she could hold her own against Arnold. Constance thought they would make a fine match. "Perhaps you should." She was turning away when she got the unmistakable sensation that she was being stared at. Looking around, she saw Cambrian watching her from across the street.

Arnold stifled a sigh. It was bad enough to have given Constance up of his own free will without seeing her light up the instant she saw Cambrian.

Cambrian, once spotted, descended from the rooftop where he had paused in his search for Arnold to join them on the far side of the street. His feelings flipped from near-rage to elation when he got close enough to see the torn paper that Constance was holding. He would not begrudge them a goodbye hug!

"Arnold," he clapped the man-fairy on one shoulder. "I have been looking for you everywhere. We have an urgent need of the *Seeker's Wind.*" With his free hand, he beckoned for Jennings, whom he had noticed following him several stops ago, to fly over. "If you will go with Jennings, he will take you to my father."

"Urgent you say?" Arnold hid his confused emotions behind a broad smile. "Best be off, then." He gave Constance a polite nod, clapped his hat firmly on his head, and flew away with Jennings.

Cambrian watched them go for a moment, then turned to face Constance. Except she was not where she had been. He followed her a few wingbeats to where she had retreated to stand between the buildings, well out of sight of the majority of the crowd. Gently, he took the paper from her, opened it and read it to confirm his assumption. Separation was a rarely invoked custom of their tribe, a way out of a dreadful mistake, and an option that expired after the first twenty-four hours of marriage. In short, it dissolved a marriage contract, leaving both parties as free and single as if it had never occurred.

"Your idea or his?" he asked, holding the paper out to her.

"Ours," she answered simply, taking the paper and buttoning it safely in an inside pocket.

"Oh." He took a step towards her. "Good." Cupping her face in his hands, he searched her eyes for permission. Finding it, he pressed his lips to hers.

Constance slipped her arms around his neck and came up slightly on her toes, grateful to be in his arms again. As his thumb rubbed the base of her left topwing, she curled her fingers in his hair, not caring if she ever breathed again.

At last, Cambrian came to his senses and drew ever so slightly back. Her mouth was made to be kissed, but not on a public street. He should have known better.

For her part, Constance was still ignoring the rest of Fairydom. Instead of stepping away, she rested her head against his shoulder. She needed a moment to collect her wits after a kiss like that.

"The next time you marry someone," Cambrian murmured into her hair, "it had better be me."

She giggled softly. "Is that a proposal?"

"It will be," he kissed her forehead and straightened away from her, "as soon as I have had a chance to talk to your brother."

"My…do you mean Todd?" Puzzled, Constance rested her hands against his chest. "My *younger* brother?"

Cambrian took her hands and kissed her palms lightly. "I do mean Todd, your *younger* brother," he agreed, echoing her emphasis with a smile. Not wanting to remind her that he could not ask her father, who had died centuries ago during a training exercise, for permission to marry her, he instead explained, "Todd is the only member of your family that I know. I would at least like his opinion on the matter."

"Of course." Constance agreed quietly. Cambrian's humble words very much reminded her of when he had declared his intentions towards her. They were barely acquainted at the time, but even then his sincerity had reached deep into her heart. Reluctantly, she tugged her fingers free.

"You have to get back to work," he noted, taking a long step back.

"I do." She blushed slightly at her choice of words. "You better get going. There is no telling where Todd is, what with half of the city shut down for winter."

"Captain!" Watts, Constance's first officer on the *Nadauld*, stopped suddenly when he came around the corner and saw them. After a noticeable pause, he nodded at the prince. "Your Highness." Without waiting for a response, Watts' attention returned to Constance. "The first load of lightning machines has arrived."

"Wonderful." Setting her personal feelings aside, she began flying briskly away from Cambrian. "Do we have enough mast-tables installed to begin securing the machines in place?"

"The craftsfairies finished installing the tables nearly an hour ago." Watts easily kept pace with her as they flew back towards the center of the dock. "And the," he lowered his voice, "ammunition has not even left the, um, warehouse."

She waved one hand dismissively. "Probably some confusion over paperwork." The ammunition he spoke of was hundreds of silver ingots, which was actually just arriving via the ant carts she had rerouted. There had been a short, but heated, debate on the merits of waiting until after the craftsmen and cart drivers had mostly been cleared from the area before transferring the precious metal from the bank to the chasers; however, having to wait to begin loading when a chaser was otherwise ready for departure could delay the entire mission by precious hours. So, they compromised. The ingots were transferred to various-sized boxes, marked "flares," "powder," etc., and then loaded onto the ant carts—which had just arrived. But only six fairies knew that, and Watts was not one of them.

She was beginning to think that they were going to pull this off. The preparations, at least. Kuntza's idea of turning the snowstorm into a *thunder*snow storm was initially met with horror. One of many reasons that they almost never wrangled regular snowstorms, was the enormous amount of danger involved—ship-crushing snowflakes and fatally cold temperatures, for starters. They avoided thundersnow at all costs. It was not until after Kuntza demonstrated his lightning machine and explained that the lightning could be easily stored in silver that the king and the admirals began to listen, even grudgingly. Entering a thundersnow cloud was out of the question. If the graupel, or soft hail, did not kill them, the lightning would. However, using Kuntza's method, they should be able to trigger thundersnow from a distance, forcing the storm to drop the bulk of its snow where they wanted it to and well before it got within range of any outlying towns or villages.

Working the machines took training, of course, and there was the small matter of refitting the windships—exchanging the metal cannons for the wooden ballistae—so that the treated ingots could be launched into the top of the snowstorm, but somehow it was all coming together. She grinned wearily at the memory of ordering the incredulous craftsmen to add a silk lining to the ballistae beds and pushers; even though Kuntza had explained to her that doing so would help keep the lightning in the silver, it had been a strange order to give. Ballistae looked like what they were, weapons. From the spring frame where the torsion bundles were housed all the way down the grooved ammunition bed to the windlass that they used to cock the enormous, crossbow-like weapon, it was business-like and deadly looking. But, if she wanted silk added, then so be it! She was still chuckling to herself when she spotted what she was looking for.

"Look alive there," she shouted to the windfairies that were loitering near the pile of ballistae parts. Beckoning for them to follow her, she landed near the royal carriage that stood out on the docks like a white handkerchief in a coal mine.

Taking one of the hastily constructed lightning machines from the driver, she turned to face the windfairies who had obediently gathered around.

"Fill your hands with these and be careful about it!" She gave the machine she held to the windfairy nearest her. "Three per chaser," she ordered, loudly enough to be heard over the din and holding up three fingers just in case. "That is one per mast." She pulled out a second machine, handed it to the next windfairy. "Leave them at the base of the mast, then help unload the ant carts." She moved back a wingbeat to give the windfairies room, simultaneously pointing at where the first ant cart was moving onto the docks from the side road.

There were more than enough windfairies to empty the coach without any of them making return trips and several of the lads broke towards the ant carts as soon as they realized that. Constance's main regret was that there was not more work for them to do. Their captains had been briefed by the admirals, and were now rotating through briefing their crews as ordered— this was a mission for volunteers only, with a select few receiving training on how to use the lightning machines. Unfortunately, the arrangement left a lot of time for the rest of the windfairies to gather at the rumor mill, so to speak, producing any number of wild theories.

"Look," Watts nodded towards the ant carts. "Smart fellow," he mused aloud as a watchful dockworker backed the first few ant carts up to the loading cranes nearest the chasers that were currently between major refitting steps.

A quick scan of the docks revealing that everything else was under control, her thoughts slipped away to chase after Cambrian. *Has he found Todd yet?* she wondered.

"Captain!"

Surprised, she turned to find Jennings approaching from the direction of the port master's office. They automatically exchanged salutes before either of them remembered that he was officially retired from the royal fleet.

"Captain," Jennings shrugged past the awkwardness to get to the point. "Do you know where I can find Prince Cambrian?"

"He just left. Why?" Her heart constricted when Jennings' gaze shifted before he answered. *Another mission.*

"The king sent me to find him." Jennings dodged the underlying question and tried to ignore the fear in his captain's eyes. "Do you know where he went?"

"I think so. Watts." She looked over her shoulder at her first officer. "Take command." She hesitated, wrestling briefly with whether or not she should tell him about the ingots, then turned back to Jennings. "Follow me."

Jennings opened his mouth to protest, but she was already moving away from him. Inwardly muttering to himself about stubborn women-fairies, he hurried to follow.

Since Cambrian's first stop would probably have been at Uniquely Yours, a perfume shop her family owned in Regalis, that was where she headed. Oddly enough, Constance was the only one to follow her father into the military. Her mother ran Kimberlite Perfumeries from the family home, while her brothers and sisters worked at gathering, preparing, transporting, or selling the perfumes. Ordinarily satellite shops, like the one in Regalis, were closed for the winter months and the family gathered at home. This year, however, Todd had made the unfortunate decision to keep the shop open all winter in an effort to turn a profit while the competition was closed. As the youngest brother, he felt keenly the need to prove that he was a valuable part of the family business.

"There," she pointed at the shop as they cleared the final row of rooftops. The curtain on the main display window was down, indicating that Uniquely Yours was closed. "Come on, we can try the back door." They had no sooner landed than she had flung the back door open and led the way into the kitchen.

"About time you got here," Todd greeted her cheerfully from where he stood, pouring punch into drinking glasses. "Nice of you to warn me that the prince was coming over."

Constance flew towards him, rested her fists on the counter between them. "Is he still here?" Something about the glasses bothered her, but she could not put her finger on it.

"Who?" Todd grinned to let her know he was teasing. Noticing the tension in her shoulders, he decided it would be a bad idea to pursue that course further. "Upstairs." He almost poured punch along the counter and floor as he hastily turned, following her flight path. "Constance, wait!"

Three glasses. That was it! Why would two fairies need three glasses? Without even pausing to see if Jennings was behind her, Constance flew up and around the privacy double-back wall, right into her brother's parlor.

"Mother!"

"Constance!" A lovely woman-fairy, her deep blue eyes sparkling with joy, sprang up from where she had been sitting by Cambrian and hurried over to hug her.

Constance inhaled deeply, savoring the familiar scents that clung to her mother's hair and clothes. Poet's Jasmine grew thick on the low mountain peak that they called home, and its sweet odor permeated every corner of their house from late spring through fall. Their specially-made daffodil shampoo brought back memories of late night talk fests with her sisters as they did each other's hair before bed. A hint of sugar and cinnamon, no doubt from recently baking Todd's favorite pie, trailed along after her mother's fingers as the woman-fairy pulled from the hug to take Constance's face in her hands.

"I have said it before and I will say it again," Norah Kimberlite smiled. "You have the loveliest complexion of any captain in the royal fleet."

Constance managed a small smile at the old joke, which had started with her parents teasing each other about the aging effects of weeks on the wind.

"I suppose you would like to know why I am here." Norah knew her daughter too well to beat around the bush. Glancing over Constance's shoulder at the privacy wall, then back into her daughter's eyes, she was relieved to see understanding there. "Todd told you why he chose to keep Uniquely Yours open over the winter?" At Constance's nod, Norah smiled faintly. "I worried when he volunteered to take over here after your sister's wedding, but when I got his letter saying he was going to spend the winter here instead of at home, I knew I had to do something. So I came to visit." The idea of Todd spending a winter with nothing but empty perfume bottles and ledger books to keep him company made her heart ache for him. It was her hope that spending time with him this winter would convince him that she did not measure him against his siblings based on his profit and loss margins.

From where he sat, mesmerized by the incredible similarities between two of the most beautiful women-fairies he ever hoped to meet, Cambrian also had the better vantage point of the privacy wall. Realizing that Todd was about to rejoin them, Cambrian coughed discreetly.

"And what do I find when I arrive? Not one, but two of my children." Norah switched gears breezily. "May I just say that your surprise at finding me here pales in comparison to my surprise at meeting your fiancé?"

Constance met Cambrian's eyes, aware that she was blushing furiously. It was easier than looking at Todd, however, who had entered the room with five filled glasses on a tray and Jennings on his heels.

Chapter 4

"Your Highness," Jennings pounced as soon as he saw Cambrian seated on the worn couch. "Your father requests your presence at the port master's office at once."

Cambrian blinked up at Jennings, taken aback by the stuffiness of the message. Jennings was a former able-bodied windfairy, usually a bit rough around the edges. In fact, Cambrian had narrowly escaped a fistfight with him early on in their relationship. That was part of his charm, especially after Roberts, Cambrian's previous valet, a smooth-talking man-fairy who had nearly gotten them all killed.

"It must be important," Cambrian surmised aloud, coming slowly to his feet. He was surprised to see Constance there instead of at the docks, a sure sign that something had happened; however, he had not expected to be called away. Especially after locating Arnold, he had assumed he would have a solid block of time to devote to what he hoped would be his new family.

"Mother." Constance squeezed her mother's hands tightly, "I should go with him. And, I may not have time to return before it is time for me to launch." She had not as yet been given an assignment aboard a chaser, but there was no way she was going to be left out of this. Neither was there time to explain to her mother the intricacies of her involvement in the original investigation, the recent developments, and so on.

"Then we will come with you." There was no hesitation in Norah's response. The short trip to the port master's office would not add much time to their visit, but she would take all the time with her daughter that she could get. "Todd," she looked apologetically at the drinks he had just carried in, "I think you should come, too."

"I will get your coat." Todd, while not unfazed by the turn things were taking, knew there was no point in protesting.

The flight to the port master's office should have been a short jaunt, but as the news of the monster snowstorm spread, fairies were gathering around the docks to watch and make predictions.

"We could go up and over," Cambrian mused, eyeing the crowd.

"If they spot you," Constance began, then almost laughed as he scanned her up and down, making a point of the fact that she was in uniform. "Right. If they spot either of *us*, we could get tied up answering questions until dusk." At times like this she wondered if it would not be simpler to assign someone to answer the civilians' questions so that the rumors could be kept to a minimum.

"I have an idea." Norah, who watched their easy interaction with keen interest, began dropping towards the street. She had noticed that while the rooftops around the edge of the docks were crowded, and the streetways, especially right around the docks, were all but jammed, the area just below the edge of the roofs was deserted. The widow of a career windfairy, she had no trouble leading a winding path to the port master's office without once going up to take her bearings.

"Well done." Cambrian smiled broadly at her. "I doubt even Dixon could have done that so easily!"

Norah, being well acquainted with her daughter's navigation officer, took his words as the compliment he intended.

"Perhaps," Todd spoke for the first time since leaving his shop, "we should wait here." Civilians, he knew, were not always welcome at military planning meetings.

Cambrian hesitated, relieved and embarrassed at the same time. Todd was probably right, but he hated to ask them to wait outside.

"We will be out as soon as we can," Constance promised, hugging her mother tightly. "If it looks like it will take a while, I will try to let you know." She hugged Todd next.

That appeared to be that. Cambrian nodded quickly to them both, then followed Constance into the office, the guard passing them and Jennings through as soon as he recognized them.

"Where exactly would you like me to take you?" Arnold's voice came to them clearly as the door shut behind them.

"He-rio."

Constance caught her breath, recognizing the stilted pronunciation almost more quickly than Kuntza's voice.

"Arnold knows about Kuntza?" she nearly squeaked the question.

"They all know more than they should about," Cambrian glanced at the guard posted on the inside of the door. By now they could see Kuntza, who was still hiding inside his cloak and hood. "About things than they should." He had not as yet explained to her about the map of Water Fairy portals, but what had been thought a secret kept by kings had spread almost too far to be contained.

Constance, following his gaze from the guard to Kuntza, nodded slowly. Things had gotten a lot worse.

"Even at full speed," Arnold leaned over the map they had spread out, "it will take the *Wind* a good four days to reach Port Herio."

Jasper, who stood on the far side of the table from Arnold, was relieved that he did not detect any unusual interest in the map. Granted, Arnold had given them an identical map earlier that morning, but now that they were aware of what Harold had hidden on that copy, it would not have taken much of a misstep on Arnold's part for Jasper to have thrown him into a deep, dark cell. With that in mind, Jasper had wisely hidden the map with the secret message and substituted the identical map Cambrian had found aboard the pirate Bane's flagship before meeting their with Arnold.

"That is at least a day sooner than anything else in port," Constance said, flying forward.

"True."   Arnold tried not to smile too broadly, uncharacteristically aware that he merely owned the windship, as opposed to having designed or built it.   "And it would be my pleasure to serve the crown."   He bowed slightly in Jasper's direction.

"Then please have your captain make haste to prepare the *Wind*," Jasper requested after nodding acknowledgement of Arnold's gracious words.

Arnold nodded once, half-bowed to the others, and took his leave.

Jasper caught Jennings' eye when the man-fairy made as if to follow Arnold and shook his head. There was a strong possibility that Jennings was going along on this journey, and he deserved to hear it all from the beginning.

"Please withdraw and take up your posts on the outside of the building," Jasper commanded the marines who were stationed near the windows and door. As the number of fairies in the room dwindled, a lone figure, leaning in a shadow against the far wall, became increasingly obvious.

Once the door had closed behind the last of them, Kuntza removed his hood and beckoned for the figure to join them.

Constance and Cambrian both blinked in surprise when Rolf got close enough for them to recognize him. He had spent a short time aboard Constance's previous windship, the *Falcon*, during the recent pirate offensive. Oh, he was a little taller, a bit broader in the shoulders, but he had the same steady gaze that caught Constance's attention the first time they met. It was almost disconcerting coming from one so young.

"Constance," Jasper decided to begin by updating her, and Rolf for that matter, on what they had missed earlier. "The map that Arnold gave us is more than just an accurate depiction of the world around us. It also contained a hidden treasure trove of names and information on the back, and the precise location of several portals that lead to the Water Fairy Tribe." He half-smiled when Constance shot a look in Rolf's direction. "He already knows most of what we know. In fact, our ambassador to the Silver Fairy Tribe had entrusted him with a letter of introduction to the Water Fairy Tribe."

Constance was beginning to wish that she was sitting down. She was tired from not sleeping well, exhausted from keeping secrets, and still susceptible to being shocked by the new secrets she was learning.

"Ambassador Julene, as you may have guessed, is a recent descendant of a full-blooded Water Fairy." Jasper could see from the faint loss of color in Constance's face that she had jumped to no such conclusion. "Perhaps we should sit down," he suggested. "This has been a long day already."

Constance gratefully sank into the chair Cambrian pulled out for her and almost smiled when, as soon as he was seated, he reached under the table to take her hand in his. She found it quite comforting.

Rolf, at the king's nod, took up the story from there. "The rest of Fairydom has been experiencing the same fickle water variations that the Sky Fairy Tribe has, but it was not until the yearly histories came in from the other tribes that the historians realized it and brought it to the attention of the Silver Fairy king and queen. Shortly after that, Ambassador Julene approached them and discreetly revealed what she knew on the subject. At her request, I was tasked with delivering this year's histories, as well as determining what the Sky Fairy Tribe knew of the situation." He looked around the table at the tired faces and tried to smile. "Apparently, I got here just in time."

Cambrian frowned. "Do you mean to tell us," he stopped to inhale and assess his word choice carefully, "that Julene knew in advance that we could get you to the Water Fairy Tribe?" He had no desire to hurt the young historian's feelings, for he, like Constance, liked Rolf quite a bit, but he seemed an odd choice to be sending into what was relatively unknown territory.

Rolf nodded. Understandably misinterpreting the lingering doubt in Cambrian's face, he added, "She also told us that, if there was no other way for me to obtain your assistance, I should ask for Kuntza." They all inhaled sharply at that.

"Per-haps I should vis-it this Ju-lene, not go home," Kuntza scowled.

"Oh no," Rolf hurried to intervene. "She stressed the importance of us both going to Cachora at once."

Cambrian caught his father looking at him thoughtfully just then and wondered why.

Kuntza's face softened at Rolf's words. "You are too young," he said simply. "Our council will not listen to you." To Kuntza, youth was not something to be embarrassed about. After all, what could any of them do about their age? Unfortunately, the council followed a different line of thinking when deciding what audiences to grant.

"In her letter, she specifies," Rolf began to explain, but Kuntza was already shaking his head. Nonplussed, Rolf stopped speaking. How had he not anticipated this? Even at the Silver Fairy court, where he was known by sight, there were many who saw just a boy-fairy. The embroidered historian's emblem that he wore on the left shoulder of his jacket was routinely overlooked.

"Well, Rolf," Cambrian spoke gently, "I guess we will both have to go." He managed to look Rolf in the eye and observe his father at the same time. The slight slump in the king's shoulders when he volunteered more than explained the looks his father had been giving him since his arrival. But what else could Cambrian have done?

Jennings snorted softly. "Better tell Mosley to make room for me, too, then."

Constance sat silently, not sure what she would say even if she somehow felt that she had a right to speak. Looking at the king, she was troubled at how much he had changed in the short time since they first met.

"Your Majesty." She leaned towards him, slipped her fingers free of Cambrian's, and asked quietly, "Permission to accompany them?"

Jasper's thoughts drifted back to a time before he had been taught to fly. He had been on a camping excursion with some of his cousins, who added rocks to his backpack while they walked from the castle to the camp site. Today his burden seemed again to be growing heavier by the step, and he was powerless to stop it.

"Granted." The word was barely more than a whisper, but they all heard it.

Cambrian caught her hand in his once more and gave it a squeeze.

"Before we leave, Father, there is someone you need to meet."

Moments later, Norah Kimberlite, looking perfectly at ease in a worn jacket and her regular travelling clothes, was introduced to her king.

"I am most pleased to meet you," King Jasper, sensing the strength in her grip, compromised with a smile and a half-bow instead of actually kissing her hand. "Your daughter is a rare gem."

Norah flushed with pride at the old compliment.

In Sky Fairy thinking, one precious stone looked pretty much like the next in one's purse or even in a jewelry setting. It was a 'rare gem' indeed that captured the attention of a tribe known for mining the best gems in Fairydom.

"Thank you."

"Mother," Constance stepped forward, her face also a becoming shade of pink, "there is something I have to tell you." They had agreed, before sending Jennings out to summon her family (and start packing), on what she could reveal. "I have to spend the winter somewhere else, and…I wanted to say goodbye before I left."

Norah had spotted the young historian and the mysteriously cloaked fairy as soon as she entered the office. Now, she hesitated. Taking her daughter's hands, she led her away from the others.

"Will they be going?" she asked, motioning toward the corner where Rolf and Kuntza were talking quietly.

Constance nodded.

"Will he be going?" Norah stressed the word 'he' ever so slightly.

Constance blushed, but nodded again.

"Constance," Norah took a deep breath. "You know I love you. Because I love you, and because I am your mother, I have to tell you that I do not like the idea of you spending the winter with him."

Constance felt her face go from pink to bright red. "You…what? Mother," she lowered her voice when the others began shifting uncomfortably, "I routinely spend months at a time on the wind with a crew that is well over half male."

Norah held up both her hands in self-defense. "Have you ever been in love with that half of your crew?" She smiled, trying to lighten the mood. "All I meant to say was, if you love him as much as I think you do, you should marry him before you go."

"Which boils down to now," Constance responded shortly. "We are packing, and we are leaving. That is how quickly this has to happen." She gestured vaguely with one hand. "I am not even sure I can marry him. At least, not so soon after," she swallowed hard, "my separation."

Norah stared at her daughter in complete shock. "Your…" her voice refused to finish the sentence.

"My separation," Constance repeated. "Yes, well," she shrugged, "it has been a busy day."

Norah felt a distinct need to sit down.

"If I may?" Cambrian appeared beside them and guided Norah to a chair. "Forgive me, but this is a small room."

"You heard." Constance clung to her training and succeeded in remaining standing there despite an overwhelming urge to fly very, very far away.

"We heard," Cambrian agreed. As he expected, she shook her head when he offered her a chair, so he took it himself, turning it so that he was facing her mother. Todd had already taken one of the other available chairs and was staring up at Constance like he had never seen her before. It would never do to let him continue staring, so Cambrian began to speak, hoping to draw their attention to him instead. "Not very long ago, we began investigating some strange occurrences. Constance was gracious enough to assist us with that investigation, and as a result, became good friends with someone in Regalis."

Constance, sensing that he was about to gloss over Arnold's story, put one hand lightly on his shoulder to stop him. "That…someone was Arnold Mosley, a fellow that Dad would have shut the window on if he had dared come visiting me at home. In point of fact, he was in league with the traitors responsible for the snowstorm we told you about."

Norah watched her daughter closely, wondering at the odd smile on her face when she spoke of this Mosley character.

"He was hardly the roughest rogue I have ever matched wits with," Constance's smile hardened. "It was much worse than that. He was suave, debonair," she shrugged, "wealthy. And a smooth talker. I went to see him on business this morning and signed a marriage contract while I was there."

"He convinced her that it was necessary for the safety of Regalis," Cambrian continued when she ran out of words. "I was," he looked down at the table, "upset when I learned what had happened." He waited a beat and was grateful when Constance decided not to elaborate on his statement. As a rule he did not throw things, and even now regretted ruining his favorite chair. "Even so, I must admit that Constance makes a good point. There may be some law requiring her to wait a set period after her separation."

"An easy matter to research," Jasper interjected into the silence that fell over the room. At last, some welcome news. Catching Constance's eye he added quietly, "That is, if you wish to marry my son?"

Cambrian rose abruptly, facing his father. "Excellent. You and the others return to the castle, research to your hearts' content, and we shall join you shortly."

Jasper's eyes were twinkling as he offered his arm to Norah. "I suppose her intentions are a moot point until we have more information on this practice of separation."

Todd and the others discreetly joined them as they left the room, securing the door behind them.

Cambrian looked over at Constance, who looked back at him. Her wingtips were twitching erratically, a sign that she was under great stress. Pushing a chair back into its place at the table, he shook his head ruefully.

"This has been a very long day indeed," he smiled. "Of course, it is not over yet." Switching gears, he began talking about other things. "I noticed the crews were making good progress in mounting the ballistae." Clasping his hands behind his back, he waited anxiously for her to respond.

Constance inhaled slowly, wishing that she felt as calm as he looked. It was one thing to be openly in love with someone; it was quite another to have parents from both families suggest that they marry.

"Yes, they were." Strangely enough, the painful tension in her neck began to ease as she refocused her thoughts on the business of the day. "I estimate another hour before the installation is complete. Then, once the lightning machines are secured and the ammunition loaded, they can depart."

"You wanted to go with them?" Cambrian could not help the slight hesitation in his words as he spoke of her flying once more into danger.

"I did." There was no reason to conceal the truth—no reason at all. "Until I learned that you would be taking on another assignment."

Cambrian, all of his senses honed in on her, instantly caught the shift in her tone of voice. Taking a short step towards her, he smiled tentatively.

"It seems to be one thing after another in my life of late." Pausing to reassess her signals, he slipped his hands into his pockets, something else he never did. "Constance Kimberlite, you are far and away the best thing that has ever happened to me." Taking a final step towards her, he dropped to one knee, in the process producing the ivory box he had been carrying with him for the last few days. "I believe I mentioned," he lifted the lid from the box, "that the next time you married, I hoped it would be me." Slowly tilting the box towards her, he exposed an exquisitely cut fire opal, mounted in a rare palladium band, to view.

Constance watched the opal's fire dance in the flickering candlelight, unable to speak through the tears constricting her throat. He might have waited for her to answer his father's blunt question. Or, he might have dismissed the proposal as a formality. Instead, he had deliberately carved a moment out of their tight schedule just for them, a moment she would never forget.

"Cambrian Bijou," she reached past the ring to clasp his wrist, drawing him to a standing position, "I will never willingly marry anybody else. But you."

His fingers shook slightly as he slipped the ring on her left index finger. Humbly, he lifted her hand to his lips. By mutual consent, they hugged.

"Darling?" he said after a long moment.

"Yes?"

"I like calling you that."

She laughed softly and gave him a final squeeze before drawing back. It was time to go.

"I like being called that."

Chapter 5

Edgar Twain, master metal smith, waved a lazy acknowledgment of the palace guards' challenge as he approached the gate. "You know well enough who I am," he reminded them.

The guards exchanged glances. Until just recently, their orders had been not to allow him to leave the palace grounds without an escort; even the princesses had taken their turns at accompanying him. That being said, they *did* know who he was. The senior guard relaxed his stance and waved him through.

Edgar thought he heard the guards muttering something as he passed, but he only caught enough to assume that they were still making assumptions about him. It was almost enough to make him go back and satisfy their curiosity about the apparently ordinary man-fairy who was the king's guest—and had been for well over a month now. His arrival there was far less mysterious than most of the gossip he had overheard thus far. His friend, Port Captain Braxton of Herio, had asked him to deliver confidential papers to the king. It was not Braxton's fault that the king decided to keep Edgar at the palace indefinitely. It would be some time, nevertheless, before Edgar did another favor for anybody.

Shifting the bundle under his arm into a more comfortable position, Edgar forced himself to mosey along the path that led to the palace gardens. It was difficult, at this time of day and in his current mode of dress, to not feel completely out of place amongst the pressed and polished gentry that dotted the way, especially dressed in his own clothes instead of the loaners Prince Oliver had graciously supplied. A group of young nobles were playing airball on one side of the lawn, while a group of equally young ladies occupied the other side, pretending to read and whispering behind their fans every time there was a development in the game. Edgar almost missed using the hole in the palace walls that had been his semi-private entrance and exit, but the king's quietly delivered admonition on the dangers of such a security breach had sunk deep. A practical man-fairy himself, Edgar had been chilled to his core by the thought of what might have happened if Arnold Mosley had shown the hole to the vermin who were trying to take over Fairydom.

Anyway, he reminded himself, now that things were much more in the open, his freedom of movement had been extended to the city of Regalis. Unfortunately, it looked like he would be spending the winter season there. The bundle under his arm slipped again, and he switched arms with a sigh. With his luck, it would take him that long just to find Captain Kimberlite. The soldier who pointed him towards the docks earlier had been confident that she was there. Mister Watts, her first officer, had been equally confident that she was with the king. Somewhere.

"Ready?" asked a woman-fairy's voice from almost dead ahead.

Edgar stopped moving forward to hover in place. He had come further than he meant to, almost as far as Princess Gemma's little herb garden. But he recognized that voice…it belonged to one of the triplets, or the king's private guards, as he called them. Lesley, the eldest, spoke with polish and precision, and behaved in general as though constantly under inspection by the female half of the tribe. Lila, the youngest, was much friendlier; if she just had a little gumption, she would make a fine companion. Her voice was soft, soothing, almost petal-like.

"Sure you are ready? Huh?"

It was Laura. He was certain of it. Easygoing, alternately teasing and tender, she seemed to have gotten Lila's spunk and most of Lesley's sparkle, in addition to her own. Silently, Edgar dropped almost to the ground and began making his way towards the row of statues and tall hedges that screened the far section of the lawn off from the rest.

His lips twitched as he remembered his first visit to this spot. He had successfully drifted away from a guided tour only to run smack-dab into the triplets. Now, here he was again, half-hidden behind, half-leaning against a statue in the palace gardens, Captain Kimberlite's surprise tucked securely under one arm. Hearing a fair bit of giggling, he peered around the statue and grinned, thoroughly enchanted by what he saw.

"No, no," Laura admonished her young niece, catching Selice's hands a fraction of a second too late. Selice pouted briefly as her fingers were removed from Laura's ringlets, but she was chuckling and babbling again in a moment. Sunshine had that effect on them both. "Oh really? Tell me all about it." Laura giggled softly as her niece looked up at her, her little face screwed up in adorable concentration. "Never mind." She scooped Selice up and flipped her front to back so that Selice's back was pressed firmly to her chest. "Ready?" Selice started to shiver in eager anticipation. "Set…go!"

Edgar watched in delight as the typically-disciplined young princess whirled around and around, laughing giddily along with her niece. He had been of the opinion, nearly from the get go, that Laura had the most common sense of the three girl-fairies, but it was positively endearing to see her so lighthearted. Forgetting that he was hiding, he reached up to push his hat further back on his head. The evening sun promptly reflected off one of the several hundred metal mesh pieces that crisscrossed the open sky above the castle, protecting them from bird and fairy foes, and caught him squarely in the eyes.

"Blast," he muttered, taking a quick step back and rubbing away the pain. That was how he happened to miss noticing that the giggling stopped. When he did notice, he went perfectly still, listening. Once before, in that very garden, Lesley had managed to slip up behind him. He frowned as heartbeats passed in silence. Had she slipped and fallen? No, probably not. Selice would be sure to kick up a fuss at being unceremoniously dumped on the ground. His mind continued to work through the few remaining possibilities as he flew upwards to get a better look.

"Laura!" He almost dropped the bundle when he spotted her, leaning limply against a tree. Diving towards her, he was at her side in moments. Selice was also at her side, her face hidden in Laura's shirt and probably still spinning a little on the inside. "Laura." Dumping the bundle onto the grass, he scooped her up, Selice and all. Not until she buried her face in his shoulder did he stop to think about what he was doing. *Too late now*, he grumbled to himself.

Easing himself into a seated position, his back against the trunk of the same tree she had been leaning against, he carefully settled her on the ground beside him. It was no improvement for her at all, he admitted. But he was able to keep an arm about her, and he found he liked that very much. She was pressed so close that he could feel her heartbeat, still leaping wildly from her spate of spinning.

"Easy there," he advised, patting her shoulders and smiling down at Selice, who seemed to be feeling more herself already. "I guess you spun a little too hard." His own heart did a little leaping when she moved closer. "Deep breaths, now." He was talking as much to himself as to her. "Deep, steady breaths until your head stops spinning, too."

Laura shyly turned her face so that her cheek was resting against his shoulder. "I doubt it ever will stop," she smiled hazily. She indulged in one of the deep breaths he had suggested. The scents of charcoal and smoke were fresh, as if he had just come from the castle smithy. But there was something else, something that reminded her of when her brothers came in for lunch after a practice match or a race. Strength exuded from Edwin now, just as it had when they first met. She smiled, remembering how he faced her and her sisters with that charming air of anxiety that— she eventually came to realize—plagued him around all women-fairies. She had started falling for him that very day. Still a little dizzy, she reached over to trace the edge of a neatly sewn patch on his sleeve. "In fact, I hope it does not."

Edgar watched her hand slide slowly up his arm to touch his cheek. He had shaved that morning, as he had every morning since arriving at Regalis, and had never been so keenly aware of his evening stubble as he was when she ran her fingertips over it.

"Your Highness," he protested softly, capturing her hand in his. "We had best be careful." Her hand felt so small in his; her face, which was too close to his own, was so young and open. Even her perfume was young, fruity and fresh. "You see, I easily could fall in love with you."

Puzzled, Laura frowned up at him. "Would that be a bad thing?"

Edgar indulged in a deep breath of his own before answering. "Depends how you look at it. Here." Releasing her hand, he reached down and drew his belt knife, holding it up for her to see. As a master smith, he loved all metals, but understood their personalities, their strengths and weaknesses; why this metal was better for that task, and so forth. "This knife is made of hardened steel. Back home, in Feo'lyn, I use it to lever open boxes, carve meat, and for beating the," he stopped himself from saying 'pants off' and substituted, "other lads at throwing. A thing of beauty, to my way of seeing things." Restoring the knife to its sheath, he pointed at the family ring on her hand, careful not to touch her.

"There is another thing of beauty." Their eyes met and he had to clear his throat of all the poetic thoughts that jammed in there before he could continue with his analogy. "Fine gold, mined at the peak of the season so that it would never lose its natural glow." He decided to overlook the appropriately high price that went with such quality; gold mined later in the year was cheaper, but of a much lower quality. "Daintily crafted, with your father's crest carved in remarkable detail, marking you as a member of the royal family."

"So you look at me," she whispered through the tears crowding her throat, "and see someone who would be out of place in your world."

As it was not a question, Edgar found he could do nothing but hold his peace. He would not change a word, for her own sake, but oh how it hurt him to hurt someone who had been nothing but kind to him. Well, once they had started getting to know each other, anyway.

"Thank you for," she swallowed painfully, "being honest with me."

Edgar nodded and bent to retrieve his bundle. Together they watched Selice happily pulling handfuls of grass and throwing them up over her head so that they fell down on her.

"Must be nice," Edgar remarked quietly, "to be so carefree." He was about to leave when Laura wrapped her arms around his waist, hugging him fiercely.

"Take care of yourself, Edgar Twain," she ordered him.

"You do the same," he returned soberly. When there was a safe distance between them, he paused to say, "To be perfectly honest, Princess, there is not a man-fairy in court this season that would be half good enough for you." Without even an inkling of how bewildering a statement like that could be after what he had just explained to her—which she had taken to mean that he thought she fell short of his standards for what a woman-fairy ought to be—he lifted off and flew away.

"Well." Laura plopped back to the ground beside her niece. "Do you understand him?" As she expected, Selice answered her question with a steady stream of disjointed words. "Neither do I."

Edgar, meanwhile, had reached the castle and resumed his search for Constance. He checked her rooms first. As she was not there, he asked the guards on his way out if they thought Constance was in the castle at all. They had no idea.

"Regular pebble in an avalanche today," he muttered to himself as he hesitated between two hallways, trying to decide what to do next.

"Edgar, there you are!" Cambrian hailed the man-fairy cheerfully. "I was just about to send a swarm of pageboys to find you!"

Baffled, Edgar just stared at Cambrian and Constance as they swooped down the hallway towards him.

"Figures," he snorted when they landed. "I hunt her from one side of Regalis to another while the two of you are out looking for me."

"Well," Constance chuckled, "we had not begun looking for you quite yet."

"Almost, though," Cambrian was quick to say. Finding that they were both looking at him with some amusement, he decided to get to the point. "We have good news for you. There is a windship leaving for Port Herio today and you are going to be on it!"

Edgar's grin suddenly drooped on one side. His brief visit to Regalis had been extended by days, then weeks, while King Jasper and Prince Oliver investigated the information Edgar delivered to them for his friend, Port Captain Braxton. Frustration, compounded by inactivity, had accompanied him everywhere at first. Until Laura… He swallowed hard. He never expected the opportunity to return to Feo'lyn to feel like he was leaving home to do it. Unwilling to risk even well-meaning questions into his lack of enthusiasm, Edgar reworked his grin.

"Just in time," he informed them. "If winter had set in, I might'a gotten stuck here for good!" That was when he noticed the ring on Constance's left hand. "I told you it would fit!" Edgar slapped Cambrian lightly on the shoulder.

"You…" Constance stared at Edgar in amazement. "You made this ring?"

"Naturally." Edgar kept grinning. "The queen's ring passes from queen to queen, so," he lifted her hand so he could watch the fire dancing on the opal, "this was the perfect opportunity to make something unique to you." The thought of Cambrian asking Queen Marta to surrender her ring for Constance added an extra gleam of humor to his expression.

Constance stepped forward to embrace him. "Thank you!" She laughed as his return bear hug forced air out of her lungs and inhaled deeply to add, "It is a work of art." Her heels were back on the ground before she grasped the import of the perfume she detected on him. Her eyes narrowing, she inspected his face carefully. Lesley, the oldest triplet, wore a variety of perfumes in no particular order, all of them floral and most of them a little too old for a woman-fairy her age. Lila, the youngest of the triplets, wore one scent almost exclusively, a scent Constance designed for her at Todd's shop. Which left Laura.

Edgar, feeling uncomfortably as though he had been caught in the act of, well, what he did not know, flushed.

"Constance?" Cambrian was puzzled. She had gone from elated to guarded in the blink of an eye.

"Here," Edgar thrust the bundle towards her. "And congratulations."

Constance watched him closely for another few heartbeats before accepting the bundle. It was surprisingly solid for being so narrow, and yet not heavy at all. Her breath caught when Edgar pulled off the cover to reveal…

"A sword?" Cambrian asked, surprised.

"My father's sword?" Her voice broke and she had to blink back tears.

"No, not exactly," Edgar answered soberly. Her father's sword had been stolen from her by the pirates when they took over her windship, the

Nadauld. "I found an old bo'sun who knew him well, and he described the sword for me. The smithy knew your family crest, so from there it was easy." He felt more than a little pride when he saw how happy his gift made her.

Gripping the leather-bound hilt, Constance drew the sword and extended it before her. The light glanced off the highly polished blue steel as if she had parried it.

"I hope I balanced it alright," Edgar said anxiously. The folks at Feo'lyn were interesting and the work was diverse, everything from cart wheels to silver service sets, but it had been at least fifty years since he had crafted such a fine sword.

Constance managed to smile through the tears that had escaped. An experimental coupe confirmed that the balance, like the length of the sword, was flawless for someone of her slightly smaller build. Returning the sword to its sheath, she caressed the hilt lovingly.

"This is chamois leather," she admired it aloud. An exceptionally soft leather, chamois was usually reserved for ladies' slippers or gloves, that sort of thing. Only the most expensive swords used such fine materials for such a small area. The wrought work on the basket above the crossguards was exquisite as well. It appeared almost delicate, so much so that she was a little amused that she had at first mistaken it for her father's sword, but Edgar was a fine smith. She estimated that it would take a brute twice her size, swinging with his full weight behind the blow, to even dent the protective basket.

"Should give you a good grip." Edgar was back to grinning. "Oh, you will probably want the belt." From a final fold in the cover cloth, he produced a fancy leather belt. Black, like the scabbard, it met military regulations. Finding it a bit drab for his tastes, however, Edgar had swapped with a leather craftsmaster—materials and a new set of fine steel tools—for the intricate carving and silver doodads evenly spaced around the waist of the belt. His own supply of cash nearly exhausted, he traded his time and services to the palace smith in exchange for the steel leather-working tools. It was almost like being back in Feo'lyn!

"Oh my." Constance accepted the belt for examination. The leather was more than beautifully worked, it was soft and supple. She smiled wryly at the memory of her first military issue sword belt, a stiff three inches of roughly tanned leather that dug into her sides and stomach at every opportunity. "How can I thank you?" She smiled when Edgar ducked his head and lifted his arms out to his sides.

Cambrian sternly dismissed the jealousy that pricked him when Constance hugged Edgar again. A sword might be an unusual wedding gift, but Constance was an unusual bride. And Edgar did beautiful work. Understandably, while they were busy wrapping the sword and belt carefully up again, Cambrian's mind strayed to the ring he had commissioned from Edgar. Despite his best efforts, Edgar had refused to accept payment. He made a mental note to have Jennings present the next time he brought it up. The former windfairy had more in common with Edgar, fundamentally speaking, than Cambrian did, and might be able to worm a straight answer out of him.

"Here," Cambrian slipped one hand under Constance's arm and one under Edgar's arm. "You had better come along with us."

"Why?" Edgar stopped asking questions when the triplets, Princess Gemma, and Queen Marta appeared in the hallway beside them. Laura was still holding a slightly grass-stained Selice.

"We will tell you in a minute," Cambrian promised, too caught up in his own concerns to detect the nearly palpable tension between his sister and his friend. While he was glad to finally have his ring on Constance's finger, thanks to Mosley there might still be a legal barrier to find a way around. As they made their way down the hall, he continued racking his brain for any memory of a similar situation. He could recall exactly one instance of separation in his lifetime, and that had been between a young couple whose parents had caught them in the act of running away together. Following a violent quarrel, they ended up going their separate ways for the rest of their lives. Cambrian sighed. No help there.

Constance, assuming correctly what Cambrian's mind was on, transferred her sword to her right hand, and moved her arm so that she could tuck her left hand into his right hand. Most fairies that she knew of were engaged at least long enough to gather their families about them, so she was philosophically trying to decide which of her cousins to invite. On her father's side, the family tended to be a bit rough and ready, which might interfere with the clockwork precision of a military wedding. And then, there was the little matter of her retirement. She was worrying about remembering to discuss that with Cambrian when they reached their destination.

Cambrian felt a mental shadow as his feet sank into the plush carpet in front of the library door, as if something was…missing. He immediately eliminated the ring and his family as being present. *What was it?* He smiled at Edgar, who jumped ahead of them all to open the door. The shadow darkened significantly when he looked down at the carpet. But why would two smallish indentations set the hairs on the back of his neck on end? It was not until he flew through the door, Constance on his arm, and saw the guard from the hall in a heap on the library floor that he finally made the connection. His head snapped up from looking at the guard, his muscles bunched for action while his eyes swept the room.

"No." Constance spoke softly. Casually, she lowered the sword bundle to her side, where she thought it might go overlooked by the two thugs holding the king between them. Her mother and brother were in one corner of the room, with a ruffian of their very own to keep an eye on them. There was another one guarding Oliver, two beside the chair where the king sat, and two more just generally watching all of them. Six, all told.

"Come in and shut the door behind you," ordered an unfamiliar man-fairy from where he sat across from Jasper at one of the library tables.

Edgar stiffly obeyed the low command, careful to keep his hands where they could be easily seen. That done, he continued moving forward until he was between the women-folk and the enemy.

"Well, now that we are all here," the man-fairy's silver hair, styled in an unusual nape-knot, brushed the collar of his dark, bark-cloth suit as he gestured airily at the new arrivals. "You cannot deny that signing this paper," he spoke to Jasper, tapping the document that lay on the table between them, "is really a very small concession."

Jasper forced himself to breathe evenly. The unthinkable had happened, so it was imperative that he keep thinking rationally. Someone should. Count Bullierd, for that was his name, was obviously obsessed with his scheme to take over Fairydom. Jasper had read the report of Bullierd's attempt at usurping the Silver Fairy throne and assumed Bullierd's banishment was only temporary, a matter of convenience until he could be located and tried in person. Pity Bullierd had not been possessed of the courage to appear at his lackey's trials earlier that year; he might have been dealt with long ago. Never had Jasper been more grateful that he had chosen to marry Marta instead of Bullierd's daughter, Amber.

"I will admit this much," Jasper smiled coldly. "Your arguments grow more persuasive by the moment." Just then Selice, sensing something was wrong, began whimpering. His reflexive attempt to go to her was futile, for Bullierd's thugs held him fast. "But as I have already stated, I will not sign the crown over to you, Bullierd."

"Here," Gemma, Oliver's wife, held her arms out for her daughter. "Shush, my love," she bounced Selice gently. "Shh, shh, shhhh."

"It would be best for everyone," Bullierd announced icily, "if you keep her quiet." Despite his best efforts, he found himself counting the royal family. Marta he knew. Then there were the five girls, the child-fairy, Cambrian, and Oliver. He took no notice of the roughly-dressed young man-fairy with a stubborn look about him. The thought that those should have been his grandchildren—the realization of all the setbacks he had endured over the last few centuries because Jasper had spurned Amber—all combined to fuel his insane anger.

Gemma's blood temperature soared, but she wisely held her peace. *No one threatened her daughter.*

Oliver, seated at a table across the room from them, was likewise fuming. Bullierd wanted the crown? Fine. But the second anybody thought about harming his sweet little girl, he was going to lose his temper.

"Is it permitted to ask a question?" Cambrian asked, offering a half bow as he moved forward an inch. All of the silver-haired strangers in the room glared at him. All six of them. Which meant that, for a few heartbeats, the thug guarding Norah and Todd was distracted.

"No," Bullierd answered curtly. He jerked his chin in Jasper's direction. "He knows what I want."

Chapter 6

Rolf waited tensely in the passageway for Ian, King Jasper's bodyguard, to do something. Almost anything would have seemed more acceptable to the youth than waiting in darkness while his tribesfairy threatened the entire Sky Fairy Royal Family. Not to mention the larger threat to Fairydom. Rolf fingered the dagger on his belt, grateful that his historian's kit called for more than a penknife. When Bullierd's Rebellion failed in the Silver Fairy Kingdom, he was sentenced to life imprisonment. His escape, months later, had triggered a flurry of communication between the tribes. Rolf himself had spent days copying reports from sundry parties that all amounted to the same thing—Bullierd had given them the slip. His thoughts continued round and round while he waited for Ian's instruction.

Ian, meanwhile, had one eye glued to the peephole in the library wall. There were other peepholes, but Ian refrained from mentioning them to the anxious historian at his side for fear that he would somehow give them away. The only glimmer of hope Ian had seen as yet was when Prince Cambrian had spoken up. Three separate thugs had been distracted from their posts—one at the windows, one at the library door, and the one that was guarding Todd and his mother. That left Oliver and Jasper still too closely guarded for comfort, but if Cambrian could get close enough to his father, and if the others were on their toes, there was a chance.

On the other side of the wall, Cambrian was going through roughly the same mental computations, except that he saw no help for their situation. Instead, he saw primarily the risks in choosing to act. His entire immediate family, for one. Taking a deep breath, he plunged forward. Literally.

"Well, no need to be churlish, friend." Cambrian was in the act of pulling a chair out from the table where his father and Bullierd sat before one of the thugs holding his father could react. "I just had this shirt pressed," Cambrian said indignantly as a spot of blood appeared around the sword tip promptly held against his chest. "Do you have any idea how hard it is to keep shirts clean enough to get by around here?" Brushing the sword aside, he finished pulling the chair out and seated himself. If the enemy was counting threats as well, they would probably count him out now, for what could a seated opponent do but serve as a target? Most importantly, they probably had not counted Constance at all.

"Sit, sit." Cambrian employed his best presumptuous air as he waved for Bullierd, who had come halfway out of his chair, to reseat himself. "After all, the kingdom will soon be yours, and you must accustom yourself to behaving as a king." While outwardly absorbed in mocking Bullierd, Cambrian moved his right hand towards one of the many brass candlesticks that littered the tables. He must have unwittingly given his plan of attack away, for Bullierd's sword all but materialized in his hand. From Cambrian's seated position it seemed as though the sword's tip it would surely catch on the ceiling as Bullierd swung it up over his head, then brought it down with all of his force.

Cambrian took the brunt of the swing on the brass candlestick, but was sitting so loosely that he was jolted out of his chair and onto the floor. The rest of the room erupted in chaos while he rolled under the table, popping up in time to bash one of his father's thugs on the back of his head with the candlestick.

Constance, as soon as she saw Bullierd begin to twitch, had begun unrolling her sword. Seizing it by the hilt, she whipped the sheath off in the direction of the guard at the door, and lunged for Bullierd. Too late to protect Cambrian, only her finely-tuned reflexes saved her life as Bullierd, alerted perhaps by his peripheral vision, swung his double-bladed rapier towards her. Bending her knees, she slid under the blow, her wings beating rapidly to keep her from falling flat on her back. Her left hip struck the table, jostling it and bringing her to an abrupt halt at the same time.

Catching sight of Bullierd attacking again, she threw herself to her right and up, just in time to avoid being skewered. Bullierd's lunge so badly overextended him that he fell half across the table, subjecting one of his own to the very fate Constance had just escaped. In the instant before he recovered, Constance looked to her family's safety. Their guard was rapidly succumbing to the battering of three fairies, while Ian was just finishing off the guard at the window.

Settling to the ground with a thump, Constance faced Bullierd. She knew of him, professionally speaking. He had been the champion of the Silver Fairy Tribe under King Nathaniel. She ignored two obvious feints before deftly parrying Bullierd's true attack. It was said that he was an expert in every weapon made in Fairydom. Her sword rang with his blows as she fended him off. And now she could say from personal experience that he was just as good as his reputation.

Ian caught Cambrian's arm, forcibly preventing him from interfering in the duel that continued after the thugs had been subdued.

"You fought your fight," Ian nodded at Jasper and Oliver, safe and sound with their wives and children. "This is hers." Constance had never spoken to him about the injuries Cambrian sustained during their last mission. But he would have been a poor bodyguard indeed not to understand that she needed to fill her role as a protector of the crown this time. That this might, perhaps, in some small way, make up for her inability to protect Cambrian last time.

Cambrian tried once more to pull away from Ian's iron grip, then surrendered to watching his worst nightmare play out before him. After his investigation into Major Layton had stranded them near a pirate stronghold, he had dueled Layton—well, Bane—with rapiers. One enormous reason he had taken the risk, and the kicks and jeers of their pirate audience, had been to protect. To protect the windfairies they had just rescued from the pirates' brig. To protect Constance.

Backhand, forehand, reverse cut, thrust…Bullierd's blade flicked through the air like silver lightning, here then there, then back again. Constance, comfortable in her uniform, matched his speed and agility, blocking, parrying, returning his attack whenever she could. When he stumbled on the cloth Edgar had used to wrap her sword, Bullierd lifted off and flipped it at her from his sword's point.

Constance shot straight up into the air, the cloth striking her on the legs and sliding down off her polished boots. Grinning, she saluted Bullierd with her sword. Up here she had the advantage, for Bullierd was easily five times her age. She lunged at him, spiraling easily out of the way of his wild slash. Reversing mid-maneuver, she reached out and used the tip of her sword to slice open one of his sleeves. Darting out of his reach again, she shot straight up to the ceiling, nearly hitting her head on it. Enraged, he followed her like a blood-thirsty mosquito.

Folding her wings, she dropped like a rock to the floor, extending her wings at the last second. Timing was critical here, for Bullierd could certainly fall as rapidly as she had! Slamming her wings forward, she blew herself back out of his way, then leaned forward and sliced the buttons off of his vest. For the next few seconds she was able to evade him entirely, but then they were hard at it.

Cambrian watched in amazement as Constance neatly parried one of Bullierd's increasingly erratic lunges, sending him lurching past her and hastening him on his way with an elbow in his back. He almost broke from Ian's hold, though, when Bullierd bellowed like a stuck dragonfly. Brute force had decided more than one fight! But Ian held him fast.

Constance watched coolly as Bullierd pivoted less than a sword's length from the wall she had intended him to bash himself on. Very well. The time had come. She flexed her knees and assumed an en garde position while Bullierd carved up the air threateningly. A small shadow of fear stole out from the depths of her mind and slid down her throat to her stomach, leaving a chill in its path. With great effort, she controlled her breathing. And waited.

Bullierd was in an insane fury. He had plotted for centuries to control Fairydom, only to be beaten at every turn. His daughter, Amber, had been rejected by not one, but two kings. His son had lost the Silver Fairy throne to a half-breed raised by travelling entertainers. The four tribes defeated his pirates with almost contemptuous ease. And now, in less than an hour, he had slipped from almost four-to-one odds to facing a lone woman-fairy who was a devil with a sword.

Constance held her place as he erupted in her direction. The rage emanating from him was enough to make her break out in a sweat, and she wished she had a moment to wipe her sword hand on her trousers. At the last second, she moved nimbly to her right. Pain sliced through her left arm up to the hilt of his sword. She locked eyes with him, waiting for him to comprehend that he had just run himself through on her sword. But when his legs began to buckle out from under him, she released her sword to help him, taking no pleasure in the outcome of their duel. And there was no longer any question in her mind as to his fate, for she had seen death before.

Edgar hurriedly shooed the royal family out the door before they could see anymore, closing himself outside with them as the situation in the library was well in hand. Jasper and Oliver, being on the other side of the room, remained where they were, watching grimly as Bullierd's life faded from him.

Constance dropped to her knees beside him, wishing silently that there had been some other way to be absolutely sure he would never harm anyone else ever again.

"Amber?" Bullierd spoke weakly. "Amber…beat me…they…" He swallowed hard and tried to breath around the sword lodged in his chest. Blood soaked the carpet beneath him as he coughed, a harsh, racking sound. "Win…you win for us…"

Cambrian, freed at last to come to Constance's side, frowned as Bullierd's dying words registered.

"Constance." Taking her carefully by her uninjured arm, he pulled her to her feet. "Constance," he repeated. "Look at me. *At me.*" He spoke more urgently when he saw her reluctance to look away from Bullierd's still form. "We have to tend your arm."

"Here." Norah appeared beside him. "Sit down, Constance."

Constance allowed herself to be led away and seated in a chair that faced away from Bullierd's body.

Ian was beside them at once. "May I?" Even in his concern for Constance, he noticed that the woman-fairy at her side bore a charming resemblance.

Norah happily turned the matter over to him, reasoning that a bodyguard of his experience would have at least as much training as a field medic. Besides, her aid kit was still packed away in her bags at Todd's.

Lifting her arm onto the table, Ian inspected the wound carefully.

"Sorry," he murmured when she flinched.

She nodded, grateful to be alive to feel anything.

"Water and a glass, please." Ian took two vials from his aid kit. "Fill the glass," he instructed Todd, who had leapt anxiously at Ian's previous command and brought the entire silver serving tray from where it usually sat on the table by the door. That done, Ian began preparing a medicinal soak by combining the water remaining in the pitcher with a few liberal shakes of powder from a vial he carried in his kit. A fresh quill was close by and he used that to stir the concoction just until the top layer of powder mixed in.

"With your permission?" Producing a handkerchief from some hidden pocket, Ian wrapped it around Bullierd's sword hilt.

"Granted." Constance hooked her feet around the legs of the chair she was sitting on and deliberately relaxed. Ian was good. The exquisite pain of him removing the sword lasted only seconds.

The sword clattered onto the table as Ian resumed tending her wound. "Missed the bone," he murmured as he probed the wound with his fingers and found no bone shards. "Did you mean for him to catch you on the outside?" he asked when she went pale. Her nod became a forward list, and Ian was grateful when her older sister-mother-aunt-whoever-she-was moved quickly to grasp Constance by the shoulders. "Stir that."

Ian tied his handkerchief around her upper arm without looking to make sure his command had been obeyed.

"Goldenrod?" Norah asked, watching closely as Todd obeyed Ian.

Ian nodded. "If the solution stops the bleeding, then we can avoid packing the wound."

"Do it." Constance had regained herself. She hated deep wounds, and the process of packing especially.

"Jackets, please." Ian laid his own out on the floor, then used the other jackets to form a double-thick bed for her to lie on. "Here."

Constance allowed Ian to help her move from the chair to the floor, grateful when her mother took her head in her lap.

Oliver, left standing with his jacket in his hand, hesitated, then draped it over Bullierd's head and shoulders.

"Hold her," Ian commanded as he reached for the glass Todd was still stirring.

"No." Todd stepped forward. His head still ached from the blow he had taken during the scuffle, but he ignored it. Handing the glass off to Ian, he spoke to his sister. "Constance." He knelt beside her, offering her his hands. "Ready?" he asked when her good hand was clasped around his.

At her nod, Ian proceeded. On the edges of his awareness, he heard guards enter the room and begin taking custody of the prisoners while he was reaching for her. Focusing on the need at hand, he sloshed a liberal amount of the antiseptic solution into her wound. Her arm's convulsive muscular contractions forced most of it right back out of the wound, soaking that side of her shirt and the jackets beneath her, but each time she relaxed before he could admonish her. Anxiously, he continued his ministrations.

"There. That is better." Satisfied that the bleeding was under control, Ian set the nearly-empty glass aside. Delving into his kit again, he was producing bandages and ointment when Norah spoke up.

"I have a fair amount of experience with this sort of thing," she offered. Craig, her oldest son, was always coming home after his expeditions with one injury or another. "If we can just get her to her rooms, I can bandage her there."

Ian looked into the woman-fairy's white face and smiled, confident that his first guess had been correct. She was definitely Constance's mother.

"I will have the necessary items sent there at once."

Nodding back to him, Norah motioned for Todd to help her lift Constance to her feet. Todd, positioned on Constance's left, folded the clean shop towel that he found in his pocket and wrapped it firmly around her arm.

Constance smiled wanly at the concerned faces between her and the door. They wavered briefly, but she resisted the temptation to pass out.

"Nothing to it," she lied as cheerfully as she could.

"Balderdash," Norah huffed. "Even Craig hates having his wounds dressed." Craig was Constance's twin brother.

"Before you go."

Constance eyed the clean glass in Ian's hand warily. Even from that distance she could smell the potion.

"Something to help with the pain?" Norah asked. When he nodded, she promptly reached out to pinch Constance's nose shut. "Drink it," she ordered.

Defeated, Constance inhaled deeply through her mouth, then downed the bitter brew. Once she pried her eyes back open, she caught site of a pale Cambrian trying to smile, no doubt remembering his own recent pains after taking a beating at Bane's hands. She pretended to glare at him, but was actually glad he was taking it all so well. The emotional trauma he suffered during that same time period was not nearly as easily overcome as cuts and bruises.

"Must be pretty bad stuff," Todd observed, grinning as well.

Constance kicked him lightly in the shin.

"Your Majesty." She addressed the pensive-looking King Jasper. "I am fit enough to go on this mission."

Jasper frowned at her. "I dare say you are," he agreed after a moment's consideration. The simple fact that she was thinking of it instead of her pain certainly showed her determination to go.

"Thank you." Content, she nodded instead of saluting.

"Alright, enough," Norah reproved her gently. "Time to get you taken care of."

Constance leaned on Todd all the way to her rooms, where they had yet another surprise. Natalie, Gemma's personal maid, was there, dutifully arranging Constance's things for her departure.

"Oh my!" Natalie turned an unbecoming shade of green. "What h-h-happened?"

"Nothing, nothing," Constance soothed her. "I am fine."

"But we do need some old sheets. Quickly!" Norah's added emphasis on the last word snapped Natalie out of her daze.

"Old sheets? Why, I am not sure…wait." She stopped shaking her head and cocked it to one side. "The very thing!" She zipped out the door behind them.

Norah was about to settle Constance on the chaise lounge *without* covering it first when Natalie buzzed back past them, her arms loaded with what turned out to be sheets.

"They are not worn out, of course," she explained, dropping the stack onto the nearest table. Expertly, she shook out the top sheet and snap-flipped it over the chaise lounge, the only proper place in the room for an injured fairy as far as she could tell. "But they were used for almost two whole seasons before they were rotated to the servants' wing." She snapped two more into place in rapid succession for good measure.

Constance chuckled at Natalie's self-satisfied air.

"Shall I begin cutting one up for bandages?" Natalie asked, looking up at Norah instead of down at Constance's wound, where blood had begun seeping through the edges of Todd's towel.

"No need." Cambrian opened the slightly-ajar hallway door the rest of the way with one foot, his arms being full, and carefully eased himself and his burdens through it. As Todd and Natalie began relieving him of the bags and bundles, Cambrian observed, "I think there is enough here to take a small town through harvest time."

Constance managed a small chuckle at his quip. They were both glad when Norah shooed him away from the table where she was working and he was able to come sit beside her.

Pulling up a footstool, he seated himself to her right. "Hello, beautiful." Taking her right hand in his, he leaned forward to kiss her lightly on the forehead. "How can I help?"

Constance, feeling the blush in her cheeks, squeezed his hand. "Keep talking."

"Watts and the others have launched." Producing his razor-sharp belt knife, he slit the left shoulder seam of her jacket, moving carefully so as not to jar her. That done, he slit the sleeve down to just above her wound and eased her arm out of the sleeve. "I know you would have liked to speak with him first, but there was no time."

She sighed softly. "His first command." She grimaced a little when he went on to remove her shirt sleeve, for the shirt and jacket had both been brand new that morning.

"He captains the *Wind Sorter*," Cambrian continued as Norah came over with some supplies. Restoring his belt knife to its sheath, he recaptured Constance's right hand. "Admiral Taylor commands the fleet."

Chapter 7

Eyes closed, Constance leaned against the wall of the port captain's office, listening to the water clock drip off the seconds while she and Kuntza waited for the others to join them. Her new uniform, part of the expensive wardrobe the king had commissioned to replace what Bane had tossed overboard, fit perfectly. So much so that she and her mother had a little difficulty getting her jacket on over the bandages. She unbuttoned the cuff now to ease her movements.

Funny how things worked out. When she first went to the quartermaster's office to get her wardrobe, she had been disappointed to learn that it would be some time before it would be ready for her. Now here she was, getting ready to leave town for the winter, and the wardrobe arrived at the palace just in time for them to turn the delivery cart around and send it to be loaded on the *Seeker*. She kept back the tricorn and a uniform to wear in place of her ruined one. The tricorn had been the first warning of her promotion. From captain to admiral in a single leap was a bit preposterous, but the king's note, which a page boy delivered along with the appropriate insignia, left no room for discussion. She was due a promotion, the note informed her sternly, and as Kuntza was confident nothing less than an admiral would impress his tribe, she was just going to have to live with skipping two ranks.

Idly she tapped one pocket, listening to the sound of the papers crackling in there. After hugging—carefully—Gemma and the others goodbye, she had slipped off to arrange her resignation from the fleet with Admiral Waban. The signed, sealed papers in her pocket were hard won, indeed.

The choice is yours, naturally, Waban acknowledged. *But decisions made in haste can be mourned for centuries.*

Without explaining her very personal reasons, Constance had quietly convinced the admiral that her decision to resign was well thought out and quite deliberate on her part. They discussed the trip briefly, which the admiral was already aware of, of course, and decided that it was possible, albeit on the boundaries of legality, for them to arrange her resignation today for an undetermined date in the future. Should they complete their mission before it was safe to return to the surface, she would still be at liberty to resign and concentrate on her newest adventure—wife and hopefully, someday, mother. All that now remained to make her resignation official was for Constance to present her papers to a member of the royal family, and Cambrian fit that description nicely.

A lump formed in her throat as a dismal thought struck her. It would be months, perhaps a full year, before she saw her mother, or her brother, again. Even now they were off somewhere preparing a going away present for her. If it had been a routine tour, she would have tried to dissuade them, as that sort of behavior made leaving on tours a special hardship to her. Her father had felt the same way. But this…this trip was very different. For one thing, she still had no idea what the king had determined regarding her marriage to Cambrian. She might leave single and return married. Or, they might have to wait a year or even a decade to satisfy some obscure law regarding the practice of separation.

"Alright." Cambrian slammed the door behind him and stomped his cold feet on the entryway rug of the port master's office. "Our luggage is aboard. Another half an hour or so, and we can launch."

Constance looked up, frowning as she watched Cambrian make a beeline for the stove. The temperature had been dropping slowly all day, but now that the sun was beginning to set, it was uncomfortably cold.

"We should leave as soon as possible," she warned him. "Before the season finishes changing."

"Yes." Cambrian's thoughts lingered briefly on the wish that there was time for him to hug her until he was warm. "The *Seeker*'s captain is beyond anxious to depart."

"Then what are we waiting for?" She colored adorably when her tone of voice registered in her consciousness. "I…sorry, I…"

Cambrian took her right hand and drew her near. "Take a deep breath," he suggested. "Then try again," he finished gently. That was his mother's favorite remedy for frayed tempers. It was better to respond gently, to offer another chance, than to go around getting upset with everyone. It worked, too, for they all used it eventually, and that set them on an even ground.

Her eyes half-closed as his scent filled her senses. "I trust we have a good reason for delaying our launch?" Her voice, as well as her words, had softened considerably.

"We await letters of introduction from my father for myself, you, and Rolf," Cambrian explained, reluctantly drawing back to arm's length. The official paperwork and reference materials that they might need had already been gathered by Oliver, assisted by several scribes, and stowed in locked trunks aboard the *Seeker*. "As well as his decree regarding our…situation." He let that sink in a little before he leaned slightly closer. "Also, they have only just begun the application of an anti-ice compound to the wing fabric."

Sighing, Constance rested her head against his chest. She relaxed a little when he slipped his arms about her waist. "Well, then." She took another deep breath. "I suppose we shall just have to wait." Her inner-captain rolled her eyes. "Though we really must leave as soon as possible."

Cambrian chuckled at that.

"Indeed you must." Jasper held the door open for Norah and Todd, waving the latter through when he hesitated. "Here are your letters of introduction," he set a packet of papers on the desk, well away from the potion glass he found there, "and where is Rolf?"

Cambrian blinked in surprise as his father switched subjects. "Aboard the *Seeker*," he answered promptly. "Writing furiously to try to catch up with all that he has experienced since arriving." He chuckled. "I suppose by now he has wheedled a crew list from the bo'sun, even."

"I should not be surprised," Jasper nodded, mentally exhausted just by the thought of dealing with the persistent young man-fairy. "This," he held up another packet of papers, "is to be opened when you reach our border. Not before then, but certainly **not after** you descend into the Water Tribe's territory. Understood?" He smiled encouragingly at them, for the papers held the answer they both desired.

Constance accepted the packet anxiously, wondering at the three separate seals on the packet's seam. The king's seal of crossed sword and quill she recognized instantly; she had seen it often enough in the course of her duties. Oliver's seal, as the heir apparent, was nearly identical to their king's, except that it bore only the figure of a quill, he not having authority to command the military yet. But the third seal, consisting of a backwards question mark and what looked like a lightning flash, striking from right to left—the two sharing a single period point—was completely unfamiliar to her.

Jasper took her free hand in his, his smile a little sad now. "I will miss you while you are gone." He pressed a light kiss to her forehead. "Daughter."

A few of the tears Constance had been holding back breached her defenses, slipping swiftly down her cheeks and making her collar damp.

"I wish you could come with us," she blurted out. "All of you." Her gaze moved to where her brother and mother were standing.

Cambrian, hearing the beginnings of homesickness in her voice, took no offense at her words. He was away from Regalis enough that he barely recognized his own niece when he returned, a regrettable circumstance. In short, he found the prospect of visiting another tribe for an undetermined length of time as disheartening as Constance did.

Norah smiled and gently confiscated her daughter from the king. When they were safely ensconced in a corner of their own, she pressed a small book into Constance's hand.

"Here. It will not be the same as being there to talk to you," she smiled and brushed a tear away, "but I hope it will help."

Constance tucked the papers from King Jasper under her right arm and took the book in both of her hands. 'Norah Izar Niyol Kimberlite' was written in her mother's neat handwriting across the top of the journal's cover. She found she could not read aloud the years listed just beneath her mother's full name. In fact, she could not speak at all.

"I started this journal the year you and Craig were born," Norah confirmed, brushing away another tear. "I was so happy, so full of advice as I planned out all of our futures." She laughed a little at that, shaking her head. "You each chose your own way, of course. But I also found that writing things down helped me think them through. Even things about being married."

Constance hugged her mother as hard as her wounded arm would permit.

"We were both so young, your father and I. You two came along so quickly…" Norah's voice gave out, and she just held her daughter.

"Thank you." Constance searched for words to express her feelings, but it was too much to put into words. "Thank you *so much*."

"Be happy, my darling." Norah straightened away and wiped the tears from Constance's face, ignoring the dampness of her own cheeks. "Not every day will be perfect. You two will even disagree once in a while. Just remember that whatever is wrong between you two will have to be solved between you two."

Constance did her best to smile.

"Tell Wyanet that I am sorry she did not get to plan my wedding like I promised." Her younger sister, who had planned Constance's future wedding at least three times already, would be crushed to miss out on the actual event.

Jasper, watching their emotional interaction, cleared his throat. "I hope you checked your luggage thoroughly," he told Cambrian, who lifted one eyebrow questioningly.

"To make sure your mother and sisters have not tucked themselves into one of your trunks," Jasper explained, only half-joking. Marta had privately bemoaned the fact that they would not be present when Cambrian and Constance were joined, then resumed her duties, allowing them to consume her energy to the point that she begged off coming to the dock and hugged them all at the castle. Jasper predicted that later on that evening he would have great need of the spare handkerchief he always carried. Why, even Laura had expressed a strange and extremely determined interest in going along. When he pointed out that she could not go with them to Cachora, she had meekly agreed, then astounded him by countering that she could winter at Feo'lyn. It was not until she mentioned that she was sure *Edgar* would know of a place where she could stay that he began to get an inkling of what was really going on.

Cambrian groaned at what he thought was the worst joke he had heard in a long time. "I suppose that coming along with us never crossed your mind," he quipped, deciding to go along with the joke anyway.

Jasper's lips twitched slightly. "I suppose it has." He was, he assured himself, quite young enough to make the trip. Unfortunately, any attempt on his part to leave Regalis would most likely be seen as abandonment by the citizens. "I suppose," the smile left his face completely, "that I have also thought about packing your mother and sisters along with you whether they like it or not." Risking the lives of those he loved most for the sake of public opinion was tantamount to torture. Unfortunately, that did not change the fact that Regalis' civilian population would misinterpret any attempt to remove the royal family in the face of such danger. They would either all survive together or…not.

When Cambrian realized how serious his father was, Cambrian found himself unable to look his father in the face. The more he thought about it, the more tongue-tied he became. If he allowed himself to agree with his father, they would go through with rescuing their women-folk, much to the horror of the citizens; and frankly, of the women-folk themselves. Even assuming the storm was tempered by the chasers so that it merely dusted Regalis with snow, the stories would circulate all winter and be shared in the spring when tourists and businessfairies commenced visiting Regalis again. Whether the stories would more than vaguely resemble the truth or not by then was anybody's guess. Likewise, if he disagreed with his father…in all honesty, he could not disagree with him, not on something he felt so deeply. Neither would he lie and try to cajole his father into feeling better. Which left him awkwardly silent.

"Smile, Jas-per." Kuntza flitted over to squeeze his new friend's shoulder lightly. "The lightning machines will work. You and yours will be safe."

Jasper exhaled the breath he had not realized he was holding to keep from speaking the rest of his thoughts on the subject. His tongue was sore from being bitten to keep from suggesting to Marta that she not risk remaining with him.

"Thank you, Kuntza." Jasper appreciated the reassurance. It even made him feel a little better.

"Hey! You plan to winter here?" Edgar scowled at them all from him position in the doorway, not particularly concerned with the cold air swirling past him into the warm room. "Captain says he is ready." The roomful of surprised, disappointed, and in Jasper's case, intrigued, expressions left him feeling sheepish. Closing the door behind him, Edgar stuffed his hands in his pockets and headed back to the *Seeker*. It was not their fault he felt like he was leaving his heart behind.

Constance gave her mother a final squeeze and kissed Todd on the cheek.

"Sorry," she whispered as she pressed her forehead to his for a moment afterwards. "On special occasions, there is always a chance your big sister will kiss you."

"I have heard that somewhere before," Todd grinned at her. Still hiding his concern for her and the others behind his smile, he held out both of his fists, palms down. "Pick one."

Constance examined them carefully without touching them. Both fists were loose enough that she knew he was trying to disguise which was holding something and which was empty. However, he was right handed. Watching his face closely, she reached for his right hand. At the last second, when his eyes narrowed fractionally in anticipation, she switched.

"As usual." Todd grinned, wondering how she always knew. Turning his left hand palm up, he opened it. "Promise me that you will only wear this on special occasions." Holding it up just in front of his nose, he whistled softly. "Very potent."

Accepting it from him, Constance waved it in front of her own nose. Both eyebrows shot up as the scent hit her.

"Special occasions only," she agreed. Special, private, *romantic* occasions, to be specific. Grinning mischievously, she kissed his other cheek. "Take care of yourself…and Lila." She winked at him. He and the younger princess were seeing each other every day, for one reason or another.

Todd blushed from his collar to his roots and fervently wished he had not. There was no way under the sun or moon that his mother would rest until she had wheedled the reason from him. Sure, she had her back to him while she hugged Cambrian goodbye. But somehow, she would know he blushed. And she would want to know why.

"I do love her," Cambrian said softly to his future mother-in-law.

"I know." Norah smiled at him. Constance had been her main focus for the last few hours, with her wound and all. But she would have had to be blind to miss the way the two of them interacted. "This will be a difficult time for you both," she warned him. "When you are tempted to seek advice, I trust you will remember that she is *your* wife and speak kindly of her."

Cambrian paused to absorb her words before responding. His first real argument with Constance had taken place earlier that same day. While he was confident that they would never encounter that precise situation again—he had just learned of her marriage and *attraction* to Arnold Mosley—it was only logical that there would be instances where they were both under stress again, short-tempered even. And how easy it was to see only the worst points of someone else when angry, regardless of the true source of irritation.

"Thank you," he told Norah sincerely. "That is excellent advice." Glancing around the room, he knew it was time to leave. It would get dangerously cold over the next few days, he knew, but that was why the tunnels beneath the city were being opened. Everyone here would be fine.

"Are we ready?" Taking the letters of introduction from the table, Cambrian buttoned them inside his jacket.

Kuntza pulled his hood into place so that it covered his unruly pink hair and cast a shadow on his hazel eyes. Wrapping his thick, ankle length robe tightly about him, he tried to smile. There was almost more danger in his returning home with these cocheta, or stra-n-gers, than he had anticipated when he agreed to visit them as a truth seeker.

Constance likewise allowed her brother to assist her into her overcoat, left arm first.

"May you always find the right wind."

They all smiled when they realized that Jasper, who was hugging Cambrian goodbye, and Norah had spoken the same words at the same time.

Chapter 8

Dawn, the next morning

It was eerily quiet aboard the *Wind Sorter*, so much so that Watts wished he could order the wind whistles unstopped. But the risk of alerting the enemy cloud chasers was too great. Thus they, and the entire fleet, had gone silent on the third watch change, twelve hours into their journey to the snowstorm. More than the noise, though, he missed Captain Kimberlite's company. He was perfectly confident in his role as the commanding officer on the *Sorter*; however, just having her there would make things seem more normal. He smiled faintly when Dixon, the navigator, spoke up. They had served together aboard the *Nadauld* for years.

"Come two degrees to starboard," Dixon advised the helmsman calmly. Of all the officers and windfairies aboard, he was the least affected by the change. The sun and stars were where they always were, naturally. Removing the sun guard from his sextant, Dixon secured them both in their case and snapped it shut. "Winds from the northeast during the night, Captain," he reported to Watts, enjoying using his friend's new title. "The sun might be over the high peak before we reach them, but I doubt it." He had never wrangled such a large storm cloud, but the process was the same for every cloud, making it easy for him to deduce where they should encounter the enemy chasers.

Watts frowned. Ideally, they would have arrived with the rising sun behind them, its rays blinding the enemy lookouts. He laughed a little at himself. Ideally, they would all be snugly inside, getting ready to ride out another winter in port somewhere, playing Stratagem and running drills. Well, beggars could not be choosers. This storm was not his doing, but he was only too happy to contribute to its undoing.

"Signal from the admiral," the first mate, Miss Dunn, called. Squinting through the morning haze, she read them aloud even as Watts came to join her. "Ghost ships break off. Rendezvous two bells."

Watts clasped his hands behind his back to conceal his eagerness. This cryptic order was what he had been waiting for. The *Wind Sorter* and the *Sanuye* each carried two squads of ghost jumpers, elite marines assigned to attack and capture the enemy chasers nearest the storm assault point. Their best chance lay in approaching from the north and the south instead of due east, where the enemy would be expecting an attack to come from. Most important to him, however, was that the waiting was almost over.

"Acknowledge the order," he instructed Miss Dunn. Making his way to the helm, he waved the man-fairy on duty aside. "Starboard flaps half down." Dixon hurried to relay his order to the main deck. They banked to the north, as per his earlier orders. "And give me all the sail she will carry!" During the night it had been important to stay with the fleet. Now, if they were going to reach and incapacitate the near enemy chasers before the admiral arrived with the other friendlies, speed was of the essence.

"Aye, aye!" Dixon passed the order on to the bo'sun, then went below to alert the ghost jumpers. They had been napping off and on since the *Sorter* left Regalis, but the first thing he noticed was that none of them seemed the least bit foggy.

Major Pakuna, a woman-fairy of indeterminate years, took the news calmly.

"Listen up." Her command stilled the soft chatter that Dixon's arrival had excited. "Half an hour, maybe less. On your feet for a weapons check."

Dixon watched with genuine interest as the two squads leapt nimbly to their feet. It was a widely accepted truth that a ghost jumper's most important weapon was surprise. Accordingly, the suits they wore for this mission were mottled sky blue, gray, and white. It was quite unlike the jauntily-colored gear the rich young nobles wore for sporting about the recreational jumping areas.

As they stretched, he noticed that their jumpsuits were not that different from windfairy workwear—they covered them from wrist to neck to ankle, with enough ease of material to allow full range of motion and sturdy boots to protect their feet. That was where all but basic similarity ended, however. Protection for their wings from the weather and low temperatures was provided by a thick pad down their backs, which also served to foil attacks from the rear. A hard but flexible material formed a ridge down their shoulders and along what would be the fronts of their sleeves while they were in flight between windships, designed to function almost like a windship's rounded-edge wings, creating a slight upward lift.

Small, barely visible slits in the backs of the jumpsuits' shoulders allowed air to stream into compartmented sections of fabric, inflating portions of the suit and reducing the strain on jumpers' muscles. That allowed them to maintain a fully-extended position, both arms and legs, for longer than they could on their own, thus increasing their maximum flight time. And of course, the extra material extending out from their sides and down from their wrists to their ankles, as well as between their legs, helped to hold them aloft by increasing their surface area in the same way that a bird's outstretched wings did.

When their attention moved from stretching to checking their weapons, so did his. Some started at their belts, confirming that the fist-sized envelopes of gunpowder were held firmly in place. Others patted themselves down, checking for the meticulously weighted cords on their wrists, which could be used either as weapons or to secure subdued enemies; the three slender daggers strapped to each thigh; and the thin, telescoping metal rods that rode vertically on their calves. Wherever they started, they all finished at approximately the same time.

"Have they sighted our targets?" Pakuna asked Dixon, amused at his keen interest in their routine procedure. Ghost jumpers trained constantly, but were rarely given the chance to live up to the stories folks told about them.

"Not yet." Dixon smiled back, aware that he was the source of her amusement. Wisely, he kept his misgivings about sending a ten-fairy squad to capture a fully-crewed chaser to himself, and focused on the situation at hand. "The storm should be in sight at any time now, so I recommend coming on deck to complete your final preparations." Saluting her and bowing slightly to them all, he winged his way back above decks. They had already corrected from due north to northwest, and he felt a twinge of anticipation at the flurry of activity about him.

On both sides of the main deck, windfairies were focused on watching the ballistae crews prepare them for use.

Amidships, a ballista captain thumped a torsion bundle experimentally. Sisal twine was the best material for the job, but it could be tricky to work with in damp weather like this.

"Give me another quarter turn on those pegs." He threw up one hand as the throwing arms snugged firmly against the spring frame. "That should do it," he announced. "Place the holding pins." With the ballista set for maximum extension of the throwing arms, he examined the machine from the bowstring back to the ammunition launcher. Finding all in order there, he tugged on the windlass, watching as the launcher eased towards him, the bowstring pulling the throwing arms back along the grooved ammunition bed, which ran from the windlass in the back to where it exited at the bottom of the spring frame in front. He scowled a little at the silk lining, but obeyed his orders to leave it be.

Harrumphing his way past the oddity, he snuck a glance at the unguarded boxes of ammunition that were stacked around and secured to the masts. He had only seen one piece and it looked like silver. Silver ingots, to be precise. It could not actually *be* silver. But it most definitely resembled silver!

Just then a lookout's signal, a small square of colored cloth tied at deck level to the mast, began waving frantically.

"Take the helm!" Watts passed the wheel back and fumbled for his scope. It was in the same place that he had always carried it since his academy days, but he still nearly dropped it when he finally got his hands on it. The flag was sky blue, indicating the highest lookout post. Glancing at the lookout, he saw an arm pointing urgently due east. The storm was easy to see. A rough estimate of distance and the time it took him to look from one side of it to the other left his mouth dry. "Monster indeed," he muttered. Adjusting his scope further, he managed to spot some of the mercenary chasers patrolling the storm's outer edges. They were keeping to the top third of the cloud, relying on their weaponry and weather charges to bully the snowstorm into staying put. They were probably half-frozen, too.

"Time!" Watts barked the half-order, half-question to nobody in particular.

"A few minutes more, Captain," Dixon answered, having already examined the hour glass.

Watts collapsed his scope. "Get those jumpers on deck now," he ordered Dixon. "Dunn!" He made eye contact with her. "Get the weapons crews to one side, then drop all flaps full!" Accepting the helm from the expectant fairy, Watts glanced at the colorful windtells streaming from the trailing edges of the wings and waited. The instant that he felt the *Sorter*'s nose begin to rise, indicating that the flaps were down and locked, he brought her about to her best point before the wind. They climbed higher and higher into the morning sky until they were well above the altitude of the enemy chasers. They could not remain there long, he knew.

"Now!" Dixon braced himself for the inevitable bucking-twist of the *Sorter* heeling to the west.

"Flaps up and locked!" Watts pointed at the enemy chasers and returned the wheel to the helmsman. "Strike those sails!" The deck under his feet slowly leveled out as the flaps locked back into their neutral positions. Cloud wrangling was a challenging process, requiring incredible versatility in a windship. Like right now, when they were transitioning from climbing at full speed to simply maintaining their altitude and relative speed. "Glider wings."

"Glider wings, aye!" Dunn signaled the windfairy that was waiting in the bow.

Several of the ballistae crew members stared in surprise as some of the wing crew zipped below decks while the rest produced handles and attached them to winch shafts that were built into the chaser's gunn'ls. Working the winches rapidly, they extended the glider attachments, sections of strong wood the length of a wing and wide enough to all but close the gaps between the three standard wings. As the attachments creaked out from where they were stored at the base of the main deck, they each drug a brace out with them, unfolding it like an elbow from the chaser's hull. When all four attachments were fully extended, the crew below decks locked the braces down.

"Glider wings in position!" bellowed Miss Dunn.

At almost the same time, the bo'sun shouted that the sails were struck.

"Very well!" Watts acknowledged them both.

Turning to the woman-fairy who had appeared silently at his elbow, he informed her, "The *Wind Sorter* is at your disposal, Major."

Pakuna nodded her thanks. Tugging her helmet down over her short blue hair, she signaled her crew to do the same. Producing her own glass, she studied the enemy chaser, looking for any vulnerabilities peculiar to that particular windship. Chasers were all made alike, theoretically. But there was always the chance of poor maintenance or faulty craftsfairyship.

"Once we are away," she commanded mildly, "drop to their altitude before manning the lightning machines. That way they will be focused on you when we strike."

"As you say." Watts accepted the command pragmatically. They had depended upon him to deliver them safely to their drop zone and now he was depending on them to clear his path to the storm. And to pepper it with every load of canister shot they could get their hands on. "Will this be your first mission?"

She shook her head. Collapsing her glass and returning it to the safety of its button-down pocket, she expounded, "I was at Altsoba." The Wood Fairy Tribe had tried to forget that time, when they had nearly been overrun by rabid animals, but she still had nightmares about it.

Watts discreetly kept his surprise to himself. Still, he felt certain that she must have been very young at the time. "Time to go?" he asked, noticing the ghost jumpers lining the gunn'ls. He offered her his hand. "Confusion to our enemies."

She smiled faintly. "Make sure you point those lightning bricks in the right direction." She stored his answering grin in her memory for the dark nights that often followed active assignments and made her way down to the main deck.

Her second-in-command, Patamon Pakuna, met her amidships.

"Strike first," she offered her hand to her son.

"Strike last," Pat finished the ancient ghost jumper motto, her hand warm in his. A hard lump formed in his throat as he watched her flit over to join her squad. Somehow, having his own command was not so exciting anymore. Fortunately, hand commands were built-in to their ghost jumper training, and he fell back on that now, signaling for his squad to form up at the gunn'ls. When his mother mounted the port mizzenwing, he mounted the starboard mizzenwing. They leapt together, their squads streaming after them like a swarm of hornets.

"Pity the enemy," Dixon muttered under his breath as they disappeared from view, lost in the half-mists common at this altitude.

"Retract the glider wings! Flaps up full!" Watts barked the orders. "Helmsman, come about." He pointed at the nearest enemy chaser by way of instruction. As they approached their targets, he shouted, "Bo'sun! Unstop those wind whistles." He imagined it seemed to the enemy chasers as if the *Wind Sorter* had magically popped into existence almost exactly between them, announcing her presence with the wild, screaming whistles of a chaser travelling at top speed. Chaos erupted on both enemy chasers as the crews began scrambling in all directions, some windfairies literally flying into each other in their confusion. Perfect conditions for the ghost jumpers.

"Lightning machines, at the ready." Watts knew the second the first ghost jumper landed on the chaser on his port side. The captain of that vessel, who had erupted out of his cabin and begun vainly striving to sort out what was wrong, suddenly hit the deck. The *Sanuye* screamed into the area seconds later, with precisely two enemy chasers between them. Watts' gut clenched with fear as he and his fellows plunged into what could have been a death trap, but the enemy cannon remained silent. Outnumbered roughly twenty to one, the ghost jumpers were moving swiftly down the enemy decks, as evidenced by the piles of incapacitated enemy crew members they left behind them like so many uneven rows of freshly cut hay.

On Watts' own deck, things were proceeding more slowly than he would have liked, but it was really quite forgivable. Even the master craftsfairies who had volunteered to be taught to use these machines did not understand them, and were more than a little afraid of them.

The craftsfairy nearest the quarterdeck checked her machine carefully, beginning with the sterilized nectar bottle suspended by brass fittings extending from either end of the bottle, and fitted into two wooden pillars that held it steady above the table. Satisfied that the trip had not jarred anything loose, she removed a tin box from one pocket and smeared some of its strange contents on the face of the leather cushion. That done, she reached for a tool in her belt and tightened the screw that held the leather cushion in place on the left side of the bottle until the cushion was pressed lightly but evenly against the side of the bottle.

The cushion and the fine-toothed, silver comb on the opposite side of the bottle were each seated atop glass cylinders, which she and others had protested as foolhardy in such a rough climate as a chaser deck during a battle, until someone explained that it was necessary to keep the lightning from escaping. That reminded her of something else she had to do. From the buttoned pocket on her belt she drew out an oilskin pouch. Carefully, she lifted an oiled silk cloth from the pouch and fastened it to the back of the cushion, then draped it up, over the top of the bottle. That was also to keep the lightning from escaping.

While she worked, a nervous windfairy came up beside her, his attention only slightly diverted from the fearsome lightning machine by the stack of boxes at the base of the mast labeled

'MISCELLANEOUS' and stuffed with silver ingots.

"Where are your gloves?" she asked, noticing that he was bare-handed.

"D'nae need no gloves," he announced huffily.

Her frown deepened into an expression of displeasure that had set many a new apprentice to quaking in their boots. "Go get those gloves right now!" she ordered sharply. "Or else the lightning will jump from the ingot into you!"

While the suddenly sick-looking windfairy scurried away to find his thick leather gloves, she made one last adjustment, taking a delicate, silver chain from about her own neck, and fastening it to the back of the silver comb. When an ingot was in the silk-lined box on her right, ready to be processed, she would drape the chain over it so the lightning could travel off the bottle, down the chain, and into the ingot. The chains, combs, and even the hair that stuffed the leather cushions, had all been donated by the women-fairies of the royal family.

"Strange lookin' gadget." The windfairy, who had returned already wearing his elbow-length gloves, muttered under his breath as he eyed the lightning machine.

She certainly agreed. In fact, she would have laughed at the whole thing if she had not witnessed for herself that the machine was capable of producing lightning. If all went as planned, the storm would expend its fury here instead of further down the mountains, where the small villages and towns were waiting, defenseless.

"Ballistae, at the ready!" The ballistae crews leapt into action at the bo'sun's bellow, the windlasses creaking slightly as they drew bowstrings back until the throwing arms were fully extended. As the crews understood their mission, it was absolutely impossible to miss their target; however, getting the ingots as high above or as far into the cloud as possible was vitally important.

"Quickly, put an ingot in the box," she snapped. When he had done so, she draped the free end of the silver chain over the ingot. "Stand back now," she ordered. Slowly at first, she began turning the handle that rotated the bottle. Her confidence grew as she saw that this machine operated exactly like the demonstration model she had seen at the palace. Silently, she began to count, increasing the speed of her cranking at the same time. Stopping suddenly, she looked at the windfairy. "Put the ingot in the ballistae and do not drop it!" She used her severest tone, having no time to repeat the command.

The windfairy seemed quite glad of the heavy gloves as he reached for the ingot. They concealed how badly his hands were shaking. Crossing the deck, his safety line trailing behind him, had never taken as long as it did now, with the ballistae crew and everybody who was not completely occupied with something else all staring at him. His shoulders sagged with relief when, finally, he set the ingot into the silk-lined ballistae bed.

"Right!" Shouted the ballistae crew leader. "Snug that ingot up…"

"No!" Yelped the windfairy as one of the crew members automatically reached for the ingot. "Tell me what you need done, but do not touch it yerselves! Not without these gloves or some like 'em." Twisting his face into the expression he usually saved for telling scary stories to raw recruits, he warned, "The lightning will jump from that," he pointed at the ingot, "into you otherwise." His dire message delivered, he 'snugged' the ingot up to the face of the ballistae's pusher, a small block of wood attached to the throwing arms by the bowstrings. "Good enough?" he asked the crew. When their leader nodded, he smiled and sauntered away, wiping his nose on his shirt sleeve with a knowing sniff as he went.

"Took your time," the craftsfairy stated bluntly. She was no weakling, but one of the reasons they had decided on assigning a windfairy to each lightning machine station was so that the machine operators could focus on what they were doing, instead of continually having to mess about with the silver ingots. "I could have prepared at least two ingots in that amount of time," she went on, cutting off his excuse before he got it started.

"When the firing starts, we will both have to do our jobs." She set the ingot in her hand carefully into the box. "Understood?"

"Understood." Suitably chastened, the windfairy dipped into the box and came up with a spare ingot, ready to trade it out on her order.

"Good idea," she nodded, understanding his action. "Please be careful that the ingot for the ballista does not touch the next one, alright? Or else I will have to start all over."

He scratched his chest with his free hand. "Right slippery stuff, ain't it?" he observed. "Jumps about jest like," his face brightened and he finished, "jest like lightning!"

She almost laughed at his quip, it took her so by surprise.

Meanwhile, Watts and Dixon were on the quarterdeck, each of them studying a different enemy chaser, waiting for the signal. Once the ghost jumpers had triumphed, they were to move to the outsides of their small fleet in the hopes of hiding their actions from the rest of the enemy chasers.

"Green flag here!" Dixon announced.

"Admiral sighted!" The call was echoed down from the lookouts as far as the quarterdeck.

"Nothi…" Watts broke off mid-mutter, his voice changing to a roar. "Helmsman, come about! Prepare for a broadside into the cloud!" The helmsman, his knuckles white from waiting, spun the wheel sharply.

Watts, thrown forward despite being aware of what was about to happen, grabbed hold of the forward railing with one hand and held his precious glass to his chest with the other.

"Flaps down and locked!   Hang on every scrap of sail we have!"

Chapter 9

Dixon stared, mesmerized, as he watched a goodly portion of the Sky Fairy Tribe's riches shoot out over the gunn'ls and into the top of the monster cloud. He had been watching for at least twenty minutes and grew only more intrigued. The ingots should have faded into the obscurity of mist and sky rather quickly, but the closer they got to the cloud, the more easily they were spotted thanks to the strange pink haze that formed around them.

"Lightning!" screamed a ballista crew member. Hysterical jabbering broke out among the rest of the ballistae crews, most of them pointing at the jagged bolt instead of readying their next barrage.

"Hold your course!" Watts ordered the helmsman tersely. Chasers avoided lightning when they could, naturally. "Get those crews back in order!" He shouted to anyone on the main deck who could hear him. That lightning bolt was just the beginning and he did *not* want to have a treated ingot aboard when the next bolt began to build.

On the main deck, the bo'sun and Miss Dunn shoved their way into the crews, equally anxious to have the ingots off the *Sorter*. A couple of ballistae crew leaders, shaken somewhat to their senses by the thunder, brought their crews around with frightful roars and threats. The last ingot was barely away before Watts ordered a change in course.

"Take us clear of the storm," he ordered the helmsman. "Dixon! Watch for more lightning." Every hair on his body rose as the lightning bolt crackled to an explosive finish. The subsequent thunderclap nearly rattled the *Sorter* out of the sky.

"Aye!" Dixon, busy patting his short hair back into place, needed no urging. A forward spotter, in the bow, was performing the same job. If the first bolt triggered a rush of sympathetic bolts, their job might well be done. Short of guiding the storm as best they could along a predetermined 'safe' route.

"Snow!" The cry was repeated back to the quarterdeck from the bow, the sound of cheers nearly overwhelming it before it could reach Watts.

"Snow," he repeated the word softly. That was only half of the battle, though. Once released from her captors, it had been a foregone conclusion that the storm cloud *would* snow. On top of that, Major Pakuna and her chasers had each peppered the cloud with canister shot, the cylinders stuffed with volcanic ash and finely ground sea salt. He waited, hoping. Unfortunately, the lightning did not continue.

"Run us out for a count of twenty," Watts instructed the helmsman. Then, gathering his fear and anger into a potent rage, he faced an unpleasant task.

"Attention on deck!" he roared. He did his best to frighten the ballistae crews with his glare. "No more of those ragged broadsides from now on. You ballistae crews will load together and fire together." He deliberately insulted their pride, hoping it would spur them to greater courage. "I do not want to take another thunderclap like that because we are waiting on sloppy crews."

Miss Dunn and the bo'sun slipped out of the ballistae nests where they had also been anxiously watching for lightning. Miss Dunn was particularly careful to hide her dismay at Watts' underlying message. They were not done with the lightning machines.

"Prepare, load, and wait for my command." Watts heard the sneer in his own voice, the implication that even that might be too much for them to reasonably accomplish. Sullen faces turned to their jobs as the crew leads called them to order again.

"Twenty, Captain!" the helmsman reported.

"Bring her about," Watts ordered. The temperature at this altitude was dangerous enough; above the cloud it was fatally cold. The admirals had gravely proposed a last resort and now that they were down to their final few broadsides, Watts saw no alternative. "I will take her," he informed the helmsman. "Send Miss Dunn to me and go below." Risking all of their lives was part of the mission. Doing all that he could to protect as many as he could, that was part of who he was.

"Reporting as ordered." Miss Dunn, having served her time aboard a chaser, the same as every fleet windfairy, knew the dangers inherent to their position relative to the storm. Anvil clouds reached high into the sky, well above a fairy's temperature tolerance, even in their best protective gear.

"Hoods and goggles," he ordered. "Get the flaps in neutral and locked, then clear the deck of everyone but those handling the ingots. Ballistae at the ready."

"Are we going in, sir?" she asked, white lipped.

"We are." He saw two other chasers beginning what looked like the same maneuver. The *Kiwidinok*, the admiral's windship, was one of them. "Prepare the final ingots now. It will take too long to reload while we are in the cloud. They will have to be dumped overboard as we fly through." Watts smiled thinly. The idea that they could just 'fly through' the cloud was humorous. They would have to fly in, toss the remaining ingots, and come about on the slim chance that they could exit the cloud before a round of lightning obliterated them.

"Aye!"

"Miss Dunn!" He called, stopping her in her tracks. "We will enter on your signal." Bringing their heading about so that they were travelling alongside the storm instead of towards it, Watts tied the wheel in place. Reaching back, he flipped his hood up and over his face, smoothing it in front and buttoning the neckline catch to hold it firmly. Detaching the goggles from his utility belt, he tugged the hood down so that the too-large eyeholes were in place and lashed his goggles on, pulling them almost too tight. He could recover from a headache, providing he lived through the storm. A little more shifting put his nose squarely above the double-layered vent that allowed him to breathe no matter what the storm cloud kicked in his face. For a while, anyway.

"Dixon. Go below and make sure things are battened down tight." Watts waited a heartbeat before adding, "And stay there."

Dixon turned to face him, ready to argue. Except what could he say? With Watts at the wheel and Dunn on the main deck, Dixon was just one more potential casualty.

"Report to the steering pit." Watts held Dixon's gaze steadily. The steering pit was a small, sheltered area on a lower deck that accessed the rudder via tiller. The bar currently hung from braces on the wall near where the rudder post made its way through that deck and up to the quarterdeck. "Watch the compass for when we come about after delivering the ingots. I will try to steer a safe course clear of the storm," he left off there, knowing Dixon could fill in the rest.

Resigned, Dixon took a half-step back and saluted. Accepting Watts' curt nod, as well as the responsibility he had been given, Dixon went dutifully below.

Watts smiled thinly when he saw Dunn take the initiative and set a few windfairies to easing the sails. If they went into the cloud with all sails set and taut, they could easily lose a mast to the strain of the tempestuous winds.

Amidst the scurrying of windfairies adjusting lines and ballistae crews preparing to fire, the lightning machine operators were cranking away furiously. The silver chains were much too short to reach the boxes of ingots on the deck, prompting Dunn to order the assisting windfairies, still protected by their long, leather gloves, to hold the nearly-empty boxes at waist height. Their fears dulled by exhaustion, they complied with minimal protest.

Dunn stopped to assess their situation. The deck was nearly empty now. The sails eased, the remaining windfairies were already taking cover below. The half-frozen ballistae crews likewise were being dismissed by their crew captains; it only took one fairy to pull a release lever. Even the cranks were falling silent as the machine operators finished their count, having multiplied it according to the number of ingots they were treating.

With the storm cloud on their starboard side and stretching as far as they could see, they were flying in an easterly direction, exactly as predicted. That meant their destination city, Takoda, was roughly half a day's flight to the west. No windship accommodations at Takoda. The *Sorter* would be lucky to survive the landing and might easily be cut up for fuel before the winter was over. She frowned, upset at the thought.

"Set those boxes by the gunn'ls and get below," she ordered.

"Belay that!" Watts' voice rang out clearly over the hubbub. "Stack those boxes here on the quarterdeck." Confused, the lads all stopped to look at each other, so he prodded them verbally. "Get a move on, you lazy lumps!" he roared, startling them into obedience. "Dunn! Fire when ready."

"Ballistae at the ready!" she bellowed, ignoring the fear she felt for her captain. It was almost certain that he intended to remain above decks alone while they were in the storm. Having the boxes closer to him would make even the impossible job of dumping the rest of the treated ingots overboard a little bit easier. "Count three, two, one, fire!" Several sets of throwing arms slammed against their spring frames, ingots away. "Get below, all of you!" she ordered.

"But the other ingots," the nearest crew captain began to object.

"You have done your jobs," she shouted. "Get below now, before we enter the storm." The bow of the *Sorter* was already swinging to starboard. Slipping long, leather gloves over what she was already wearing, she raced towards the quarterdeck. Too late, she realized that she had overlooked one simple fact—her safety line.

Like every other windfairy in all of Fairydom, Miss Dunn wore a uniform that had a harness built into it. She could hook a safety line either to the ring located at the center of her waist or to one on either hip, as she chose. The safety line's other end was attached to one of dozens of places strategically arranged around the main deck. The most basic intent of this system was to preserve lives, for there was little hope otherwise of rescuing a windfairy gone overboard. At this precise point in time, however, as she plotted a course from amidships to the quarterdeck, the safety line tangled with a line carelessly dropped by a ballista crew member.

"Dunn!" Watts watched in horror as she reached the end of the fouled line and was jerked off her feet to land on her back. Hard, by the looks of it.

The *Sorter*, pivoting as swiftly as a sturdily-built chaser could, began to tilt so that her port wings were higher. It might still have been alright, if either of them had been in peak condition, instead of in their exhausted and half-frozen state. Miss Dunn, trying to rescue herself, caught hold of the wrong line and gave a mighty tug, sending herself sliding directly into the base of a ballista, where she struck her head.

Muttering something unintelligible, Watts began turning the wheel fractionally from side to side, hoping to get Dixon's attention via the compass below. They had almost reached the cloud now, but Watts found he could only pursue one line of thought at a time, and right now he was thinking about Miss Dunn.

"Captain!" Dixon shouted to be heard over the roar of the wind as the *Sorter* nosed her way into the cloud.

Watts swung his head towards the sound of the voice. "Take the wheel!" Releasing the wheel before Dixon could reach him, his mind still focused on rescuing his crewmate, Watts was flung to one side by the suddenly bucking chaser. He thought he felt something break as he struck the charthouse. He was too numb from the cold to be sure.

Dixon, refreshed from his time below decks and a pot of steaming broth, sprang forward to catch the wheel. Wrestling the chaser back into submission, he checked the compass, returning them to the final single heading he had seen before realizing something was wrong and zipping above decks. While he fumbled with the wheel lashings, he thought he saw something strange amidships. The *Sorter*'s forward mast was enveloped by the cloud by now, and he feared for the life of any fairy left topside for very long. Including Watts. Dixon could see at a glance that the man-fairy was in a bad way. Dixon shivered as the cold began nipping at his gloved fingers.

"Bo'sun!" The bo'sun had been on Dixon's wingtips when he left the steering pit and now Dixon nearly sagged with relief when the manfairy leaned out the aft companionway in answer to his call. "Get Captain Watts to the surgery, then come take the wheel!" Waiting just long enough to be sure that he had been heard, Dixon ran to the edge of the quarterdeck and traded safety lines so that he could access the main deck. His heart sank when he got close enough to see who it was. "Dunn." He shook her shoulder gently, but with no result. He had to hurry.

Whipping his hood up and fastening the neck pieces, he hunkered down by her, his eyes shut against the first bits of frost whipping about him while he clawed at his belt for his goggles. The *Sorter* was belly deep in the cloud, and picking up speed. It was not all forward speed, to be sure, and Dixon had to grab hold of the ballista to keep from being pitched across the deck. If he lost track of Miss Dunn now, he might not find her again in time. At last his goggles were in place and he dared to open his eyes. She must have rolled a little away from him in the midst of it all, and his hands were barely visible to him as he patted the deck, searching frantically for her.

Finally laying hold of one of her arms, he reached up with his free hand and jerked his hood around until his nose gap was in the right place. Taking deep, measured breaths, he reached for his belt knife and cut her free of not one, but *two* lines. Rather than puzzling over that, he forced his thoughts back to the situation at hand. After buttoning his knife back in place, he tugged an emergency safety line from the side of his harness and clipped it to her harness, linking them together. Then, hand over hand, he began pulling them both to safety.

They could not have been halfway to the quarterdeck when he felt an answering tug on the line. Abruptly, he and Miss Dunn slid several twig-lengths forward. The slack in the line was taken up by an unseen force and they slid forward again.

"There they are!"

Hands reached for them, lifting them and carrying them to the shelter of the companionway.

"D'ye feel that?"

All activity ceased at the question. All but Miss Dunn's, who had begun to stir. The individual hairs on their bodies were beginning to stand on end, despite all the gear they were wearing.

"Look!" The voice was nearly a scream of terror. There was no need to see the pointing hand, though. As they looked around for anything at all, their gazes seemed drawn to the far side of the quarterdeck, where a strange pinkish glow hovered.

"I think it is gettin' bigger," one of them observed in what passed for a dramatically hushed voice under the circumstances.

Dixon, his senses recovered enough that he had reached down to undo his emergency line from Miss Dunn's harness, suddenly grasped the import of the gloves she was wearing. The ingots were glowing in sympathy with the lightning buildup!

"Get below." He snatched the gloves off her hands. "Do it now! Immediately! At once!" He continued shouting similar commands as he tugged the gloves onto his own hands and raced up the stairs to the quarterdeck. Unable to switch safety lines because of the clumsy leather gloves, he wrapped the quarterdeck line around a bit of his harness, pulled it tight, and cut his other line free. Reaching the boxes, he grabbed the first one and heaved the whole thing over the side. He was reaching for the next box when his fingers curled into his hands. All the metal pieces on his harness were glowing. Wrapping his forearms around the second box, he used his back muscles to lift it as high as the railing and shoved it overboard as well.

"Dixon!" It was the bo'sun.

"Glad to see you," Dixon grunted. "Bring her about!" he shouted. "Four points to port and dive!" They needed to get out of there as quickly as possible, and diving was a guaranteed method of acceleration. As he stooped after the third box, his arms cramped so badly that he could not move them away from his chest. His legs were stiffening as well, so he chose to fall while he still had some control. As he landed, he aimed his body so that he knocked the box over, spilling some ingots out through the gaps in the railing. As they streamed away, he felt his muscles begin to loosen. Weakly, he scrabbled the last few ingots out of the box and off of the chaser. He supposed that if a giant ever came along and ran him through their clothes wringer, this was pretty much how he would feel if he lived to tell about it.

Curling up on the deck, he noticed that it was beginning to tilt forward. Apparently the bo'sun had found and engaged the rear flaps, which, peculiar to chasers, added to the overall versatility of the windship design. Right then, it was Dixon's favorite feature.

"Help me get him to the surgery!" ordered the bo'sun's voice from an arm's length away. "Lash that wheel and get a helmsman down to the steering well." Huffing under the burden of Dixon's limp frame, the bo'sun grumbled, "Not as light as he looks."

The trip to the surgery was awkward, as one might expect from cramming three windfairies and Dixon, whom they were carrying between them, into a passageway designed to permit two at a time, assuming they both turned aside as they passed.

"Another patient?" The surgeon waved them over to his last remaining bed. "Put him there and get his hood off." Recognizing Watts' distress, the surgeon patted him lightly on the shoulder. "Nothing a potion cannot cure." That said, he handed Watts a beaker of bone-healing potion. "Drink that down," he ordered. A cracked collarbone was a nasty bit of business. Without the proper potion, that was.

Checking on Dunn as he passed her, the surgeon smiled. "The broth will warm you best from the inside," he admonished her, nodding at the mug she was idly holding.

"Now." He rinsed his hands in antiseptic and dried them on the clean towel hanging from the rod beside the bed. "You know, this bed here is really my surgery table. So if you are just playing possum," he grinned at the old Wood Fairy expression, "we have no time for that." His grin faded when Dixon failed to respond. His words and his touch elicited the same lack of response. Like Miss Dunn when she first arrived in the surgery, Dixon's body temperature was dangerously low. "Blankets," he ordered. "Wrap a hot stone in one of them and set it near his chest." Knowing they were headed into cold weather, the surgeon had asked the cook to add a few stones to the cook fire, in case of just such a situation.

"Hmm." Tilting Dixon's head back, he hunted for a pulse. When he finally found it, it was so faint and thready that the surgeon had to check twice to be sure, even though he was examining the major pulse points in Dixon's neck.

Removing both the heavy leather glove and the gauntlet from Dixon's near hand, the surgeon's own pulse quickened as Dixon's fingers promptly curled back in towards his palm. He had volunteered for this assignment specifically on the chance that something like this might happen. Assuming, of course, this injury was what he thought it was, and it resembled nothing else he had ever seen. "Fetch me that case!" he ordered abruptly, jerking his head towards the desk where his personal case lay. He had not studied the effects of lightning shock on living organisms for three hundred years without coming up with a few hypothesis. And, sad to say, that was as close to a treatment as he could come for this lad.

"Clear!" A windfairy shot past the doorway to the surgery, en route to points deeper in the chaser. "We have cleared the storm!"

"Hold fast! What of our commandeered chasers?" Watts snapped, bringing the windfairy to an abrupt halt.

"Cut their colors and ran," announced the windfairy.

Watts waved him away, satisfied that the ghost jumpers—and their prisoners—were successfully off to the city of Aterpe where they would winter. They could only hope that, between the city's stores and the supplies on the chaser, there would be enough food to sustain them until spring when the trade routes opened again.

"Bo'sun." Before his thoughts could shift to their own, equally bleak winter plans, Watts turned back to where the surgeon was still working on Dixon. "Get us to a safe range, then keep watch for lighting and our other chasers. I want a report every twenty minutes for the next hour."

"Aye, sir." The bo'sun obeyed promptly, but not without a final, worried look over his shoulder at Dixon's limp figure.

Chapter 10

Port Herio, Midday

Four days after they left Regalis, a cold breeze chased Constance, Cambrian, and Kuntza all the way from the dock at Port Herio to the port captain's office.

"Well!" Michael Braxton, in the outer office discussing the duty roster with his aide, Lieutenant Foster, looked up in surprise. "Late season travelers, eh?"

Constance took off the tricorn she had been struggling to keep on her head and smiled at him.

"Exactly." Cambrian's response was less an agreement than a basic acknowledgement of the fact that Braxton had spoken. "You just never know who the wind will blow in, do you?"

Braxton watched Prince Cambrian's hood settle on his shoulders and slip down his back. The two of them he knew, Constance better than Cambrian. Who was the third arrival? The one whose hood remained firmly in place?

"Welcome back." Braxton started to salute, then accepted Cambrian's proffered hand. Constance, he hugged. There might, a long time ago, have been something between Constance and himself. He officially dismissed any future hopes, however, when Cambrian merely smiled at the affectionate gesture. "Would you care to join me in my office?" he invited, looking just over

Cambrian's shoulder at the still-silent visitor to be sure whomever it was knew they were included.

"Yes, thank you." Cambrian captured Constance's right hand and tucked it under his arm while he nodded for Braxton to lead the way.

Constance, amused and flattered by Cambrian's attention, made a mental note to apologize to Jennings later for all of the fuss she had made when he insisted she take her potions—*all* of them. In just four days she had gone from an open wound to hugging Braxton back with both arms!

"Just like old times," Braxton beamed as he shut the door behind them. He trusted Lieutenant Foster, but doubted the others would accept her on his recommendation alone.

"More or less," Cambrian agreed, escorting Constance to the seat that faced the window between the two offices. His casual nod indicated that Kuntza should sit in the center chair, and Cambrian took the one nearest the door.

Cambrian grinned a little at Braxton, who quickly seated himself behind his desk. During Cambrian's last visit to Port Herio, Braxton had quietly passed him some classified reports on water levels in the area. Much like Rolf's report of water levels in the Silver Fairy Kingdom, there had been no explanation for the day-to-day variations. Until they accidentally met Kuntza while escaping from Bane's pirate stronghold, that was. Braxton, having recently come to

Regalis to testify at the military board of inquiry, knew all that was publicly available.

"Port Captain Braxton," Cambrian leaned forward slightly in his chair, "permit me to introduce Kuntza." When Kuntza had moved his hood enough for his face to be seen, while still protecting it from the window side of the room, he continued, "Truth seeker for the Water Fairy Tribe."

Braxton calmly reached over and pinched his own left hand. The pain confirmed that he was, in fact, not dreaming.

"Welcome to Port Herio." Braxton somehow managed to bow while seated.

"Thank you." Kuntza slipped his hood back into place and folded his hands in his lap. He was not yet convinced that this was the wisest decision, probably the result of millennia of living solely with his own tribe about him, and hoped that folding his hands would help him to not fidget while he waited.

"How can I help?" Braxton got right to the point.

Cambrian smiled, grateful now that Constance had suggested they try here first.

"We are on a highly classified diplomatic mission to visit the Water Fairies. However, during our flight from Regalis to Herio, we learned that we need a few things."

"The port is at your disposal." Braxton ran the port smoothly, but not unreasonably. And at times like this, it worked to his advantage. Every merchant, craftsman, and transporter in the area owed him at least one consideration.

"First, we need transportation to the Sumendi. Ant carts or an ant train if necessary." Early on, the colonists in the area had enjoyed searching the lava tubes of the dormant volcano; fortunately, they never discovered the portal to the Water Fairy territory. "There will be the three of us, plus two more, and our luggage." Rolf had declined to come with them to Braxton's office, choosing to visit Edgar's smithy instead. An odd choice for a historian, perhaps, but perfectly logical for someone who made friends quickly. Cambrian added, "Including several, very heavy boxes. At least a dozen." He was privately astonished that the Silver Fairy Historians had been able to condense several generations of history into so few volumes. "Also, we require a one hundredweight chest of sugar." Kuntza had let it slip that sugar was nearly priceless in his underwater world.

Braxton finished scribbling and set the quill aside. "Your pardon." Rising, he flew to the door, shutting it behind him.

"Do you really believe he can gather this so quick-ly?" Kuntza asked, his tone of voice frowning slightly.

"I assure you he can." Constance smiled in Kuntza's direction. "He is not only resourceful, he is efficient."

Cambrian watched as Braxton reentered the room.

"Foster is making the arrangements now," Braxton informed them, resuming his chair. It was more exciting than that, to him at least. Another few days and he would have had to fine one of the port's original merchants, an honorable lady who could not afford the fees for next year's trading licenses. And the request for an ant train served as the side door he had been hunting for in his dilemma over having to punish someone else for trying to keep a bad situation from getting worse.

"Excellent." Cambrian brought up a point that Braxton seemed to have overlooked. "Of course, we will pay the going rate for these things."

"That is already taken care of." Braxton smiled. "The price of the sugar will cover new licenses and permits for a local merchant. And the ant train owner is thrilled to be able to pay his debt for disturbing the peace with a single job." Noting the slight lift to Cambrian's eyebrow, Braxton explained, "He is a good sort, really. Just got caught in a misunderstanding between two enemies." Naturally, Braxton had warned the lad to leave breaking up fights to the professionals in the future.

"Oh." Cambrian, for once, was speechless.

"We really should leave as soon as possible." Constance strictly avoided looking at Cambrian, who had been teasing her the whole way from

Regalis that she would no sooner arrive than insist they leave.

"Of course." Braxton rose, a little disappointed they were leaving so soon. "I will personally ask the ant train captain to meet you at the docks."

"Outstanding." Cambrian offered Braxton his hand again.

Kuntza, following suit, shook hands with Braxton as well. Constance elected to lag behind a little, even going so far as to rest one hand on the office door and partially close it between herself and the others.

"We brought Edgar back," she told Michael. Then she asked the question that had been bothering her ever since she had met Edgar. "Why did you pick him to go to Regalis?"

Michael Braxton frowned thoughtfully. "Because he was available, I suppose."

"Hmm." Constance glanced at Cambrian, who was pretending to inspect the duty roster that Foster had left behind. Granted, the reports and documents Braxton had entrusted to Edgar were vitally important. But that he had endured weeks of time at Regalis as an unwilling guest because he was *available* seemed highly unsatisfactory. Especially since his heart had clearly become entangled. "Will he be very busy this winter?" She hoped aloud.

"Hard to say." Michael shook his head. "Ordinarily he would spend it catching up on his backlog of work, or playing darts with the lads at the Wandering Tattler."

"And now?" Constance prompted. She felt partially responsible for Edgar's glum disposition, even knowing intuitively that it related back to Laura more than to his concerns about being supplanted as Feo'lyn's resident metalsmith. They had bonded quickly over mutual feelings being out of place at Regalis and affection for members of the royal family. "He has been gone for months."

"Shall I keep an eye on him?" Michael volunteered, experiencing a faint twinge of guilt. Truth be told, a wandering metalsmith had semi-settled in at the lodging house. Small towns like Feo'lyn needed a metalsmith too badly to leave the job open long. He frowned at himself. How could he have known they would hold Edgar at Regalis?

"I would appreciate it," she nodded. "Discreetly?"

Michael smiled. Taking her gently by the elbow, he accompanied her over to where Cambrian was waiting. The clues he had been absorbing since they entered his office solidified in his mind when he finally took a good look at Constance's left hand.

"Congratulations," he murmured when he hugged her goodbye. It did not seem like enough, but this was no time for a speech.

"Thank you."

Cambrian slipped his arm around Constance, gave Braxton a friendly nod, and escorted her out the door, Kuntza on their wingtips.

Braxton would have gone right then to check on Edgar, but he first had to make sure the ant train captain knew it was urgent that they report to the docks. His side-trip proved more fruitful than he had hoped, though, when the captain volunteered to pick up the sugar on his way to the dock. It was a short detour and they arrived at the dock mere minutes later than they would have otherwise.

Mosley greeted the proceedings with a black scowl. He had tried to finagle an invitation to join the mission as they were docking and had not yet forgiven them for turning him down. Again. Constance ignored him completely, opting instead to address his captain.

"Captain Gazia," she smiled sweetly at the salty old Wood Fairy, "thank you again for as smooth a flight as I can ever recall enjoying." Indicating the ant train, she added, "If only the rest of our journey could be so comfortable." Ants were fabulously strong, reasonably swift, and rode like a rocking chair with a severe case of the hiccups. When moving at a slow pace, the lurching eased to swaying and usually made Constance nauseous. She could only imagine how spending over an hour aboard one loping along would impact her spine.

Gazia smiled back. He accepted the compliment for what it was, having learned that she was the honest type, but he found her flattery delightfully subtle and unselfish. He knew they were in a hurry and she, a captain in her own right, knew that everything on a windship moved faster when the captain wanted it to. And knowing that Mosley liked her despite his irascible behavior, Gazia figured it was alright that he had set more lads to offloading the party's gear than he had assigned to preparing the *Seeker* for the long, cold winter.

"More the *Seeker*'s doing than mine," he answered in his most polite, indoor voice. It was guaranteed not to knock the hats off his audience. Usually. "But we thank ye." He had refused to leave the *Seeker* when her original owner foolishly lost her to Mosley, and his fondness for the yacht softened his voice further still. Finding a bit of a tear in one eye, he promptly blamed it on the female captain and flicked one hand in the general direction of the luggage pile his lads were making as they offloaded the group's gear. "Get along wid ye," he admonished, back to his gruff self. "And d'nae go fallin' off them things." He eyed the nearest ant, a skittish younger male, with a considerable amount of distrust.

"I promise," Constance murmured to herself. Gazia was already flitting away, keen eyes searching every inch of the *Seeker* for lollygaggers or sloppy work.

"Goodbye, Mosley." Cambrian, in the supreme triumph of willpower over his baser instincts, extended his hand. He had not quite given up hope of one day decking Mosley, but today was not that day.

Mosley, for his part, was as reluctant to take his hand as Cambrian was to offer it. Their dislike of each other went beyond their rivalry for Constance, beyond even Mosley's short-lived treason. In Mosley's case, it was a reflex built over cumulative centuries; the need to be the best, to come out on top of every situation. Fantastically spoiled as a child-fairy, he now lived for the thrill of competition.

Constance felt a wave of relief wash over her when she saw Mosley take Cambrian's hand. Friendship was still a long ways off for them, but at least they would not have another negative moment wedging them apart.

"Hi." Rolf spoke from where he was helping an ant wrangler keep one of the younger ants calm. While he had not intended to spy on anybody, he had the distinct feeling that he had just witnessed history. The kind that would never be recorded or referenced as a great achievement.

"There you are." Constance smiled at him, glad he was along. "I have been meaning to ask you," she paused to size him up. "Have you grown since the last time I saw you?" The last time had also been the first time, aboard the *Falcon* during the pirate offensive. Being a Silver Fairy, he did not really look that different now, despite the fact that his hair and face had been covered with volcanic ash at the time of their first meeting.

"Oh yes," Rolf nodded, not the least bit perturbed by the question. He had two aunts and three younger sisters, plus the added—and completely unofficial—designation of *nephew* to nearly all of the Silver Fairy court. "I am nearly a twig taller now than I was then."

Constance's smile widened at his frank answer. She had thrown various questions his way during their trip, wanting to make sure he could handle himself in an unpredictable climate. If anything, he seemed even more mature than he had aboard the *Falcon*, where it had been he who had convinced her that he and his party were not pirates by showing her his history book. Still, she was glad that Jennings was around to act as a sort of rough-and-ready uncle for the lad. Kuntza made it an odd threesome, and while they clearly enjoyed each other's company, all too soon Kuntza would be busy keeping them all out of trouble at Cachora.

"Hi-oh!" called the ant wrangler at the far end of the line. A few others chorused it back, but not all.

"Nearly ready," Cambrian observed, having flown over to where Constance and Rolf were standing.

Constance allowed herself a final thought about Edgar, a wish that he would be able to settle back into his life at Feo'lyn, then looked around

for Kuntza. Predictably, he had found an out of
the way spot to wait in while he observed the
goings on.

"Rolf," Cambrian had followed her gaze. "Do
you think you could keep track of Kuntza for us?"
Deciding that sounded insulting, he quickly
clarified, "Ride with him, help him keep from
being discovered or confused, that sort of thing?"
Technically, Jennings had that assignment, but he
thought it might serve to keep Rolf occupied for
the next little while.

Rolf was already grinning at the idea. "We
claim the first passenger ant!" he nearly whooped
and zipped over to where Kuntza was standing.

Cambrian stared after him blankly. An old
friend of the Silver Fairy royal family, he had
known Rolf off and on for years without ever
observing such behavior from the lad.

"What in Fairydom," he began to ask, only to
find that Constance was chuckling. "Oh, I
suppose you know exactly what that was all
about."

"Of course," she agreed. Winking at him
from under her tricorn, which was still trying to
escape on every passing breeze, she put her left
hand on his right arm. "And so do you, if you
have not forgotten that his aunt, Queen Rebecca,
is a newlywed."

At first, Cambrian saw absolutely no
correlation between her statement and Rolf's
exuberant behavior. Then, he groaned aloud.

"Oh, the poor fella!" Wrapping his right arm unabashedly around her shoulders, he gave her a quick squeeze. "From one set of newlyweds to another!" He hesitated momentarily. "Are you sorry? I mean," he explained hastily, "that it is such a short engagement?"

Constance laughed a little and decided not to point out that her 'engagement' to Mosely had lasted about a minute and a half.

"No," she shook her head. "I am just glad that the law permits us to marry so soon after my marriage contract with Mosely was dissolved." The prospect of marrying Cambrian in an all-but-empty clearing on the border between two tribes was not especially attractive, but she understood why it was happening that way. Time was a huge factor, naturally; the less time one has, the more important it becomes. And then there was the small matter of making sure their marriage would be legal in the Water Fairy territory. Yes, overall, this was the best way available to them.

Her eyes fluttered closed as Cambrian's breath fanned her face. The *Seeker* was even smaller than the *Nadauld*, and the last four days had been bereft of even public-private moments like these.

Seeing her eyes close, Cambrian swallowed hard. Muttering something about going over the cargo list with the bo'sun, he tenderly set her away from him and flew off before he embarrassed them both by bursting into poetry or something.

Rolf, cheerfully answering Kuntza's terse questions with garrulous replies, congratulated himself on his new assignment. What a narrow escape. Still, it was enlightening. Apparently couples all around Fairydom, when matched correctly, enjoyed each other's company with equal fervor. His thoughts strayed to a rather pretty young woman-fairy who would be wintering at Castlemain, then snapped back to the present when Kuntza posed another question. It was just as well, anyway. Rolf was only sixty-eight and much too young to be thinking seriously about romance.

"Hi-oh!" This time it was the wrangler at the tail of the train that sang out and all of the others replied.

"Here," Rolf took Kuntza by the hand as naturally as if he were one of Rolf's younger siblings. He had already explained in detail how riding an ant worked, so he stuck to the basics. "This ant is used to being ridden," he led Kuntza over to an older ant, whose wrangler was holding her for them. "We sit on these benches," he directed Kuntza to sit on one side while he sat on the other. "And the wrangler rides up front." He waited while Kuntza observed the wrangler getting comfortable. "If this was a longer trip, we might fly alongside for a while. Since it is just over an hour," he shrugged, "it will be faster to stay put."

Kuntza nodded. He definitely understood that part. The *Seeker* had done her best, yet still he felt compelled to go faster. Thoughts of his young companion slipped to the back of his mind as he once more reviewed his plan to get them all to Cachora with as little trouble as possible.

Rolf, recognizing that Kuntza was distracted, sat back to enjoy the experience. His family did not travel often, so this was an adventure for him.

A few ants back, Cambrian cleared his throat. "I suppose," Cambrian took Constance's left hand in his, "that this is the wrong time for poetry."

Constance smiled and slid a little closer, so that he wrapped his right arm around her. It was good timing, too, as the ant lurched into motion a mere heartbeat later. Once the animal had reached a smooth-ish traveling speed, Constance's mind returned to Cambrian's question.

"Poetry," she informed him with mock severity, "is inherently impractical."

"Oh." He pressed his lips to her forehead, right in the middle of her furrowed brows. "Our marriage is going to be terribly awkward at times, I see ." He continued kissing the frown lines on her forehead until they were all smoothed out. "You did know that I am a poet, right?"

Constance smiled into his shoulder. "I recall hearing something about that…I think." While stranded in a lava tube, waiting for the sun to rise and hoping they would not be interrupted by the other survivors, he had recited a poem written especially for her. When his first love, Princess Joanna, of the Silver Fairy Tribe, died in a tragic flying accident, he mourned her for decades, not writing a single line. Now Constance was doing her best to accept his poetry as a sign of the strength of his love for her—that it at least ran parallel with his love for Joanna.

"Do you really not like poetry?" Cambrian asked, deciding he would rather find out now than a few centuries into their marriage. "Because if not, I could …" His words trailed off when she kissed him.

"Shhh," she whispered against his lips. Pressing her cold cheek to his, her back already protesting at the awkward position, she tried to think how to answer. "I like poetry," she began, leaning back against the bench. "In time, I may even become accustomed to having the most romantic husband in all of Fairydom." She blushed and giggled when he wriggled his eyebrows at her. "Just do not be dismayed if, for a while, it catches me by surprise."

They were nearly at the edge of town, having had to travel more slowly while they skirted a few back streets to reach their trail, and the pace would soon increase exponentially.

"I see." He smiled reassuringly at her when she frowned questioningly up at him. "You think poetry is romantic," he snugged her a little closer to him. "And I think I had better get a blank poetry book so that I do not drown you in the poems you inspire in me."

Still blushing prettily, Constance looked at the trail ahead of them. Things were definitely about to speed up.

Chapter 11

Kuntza pretended to be absorbed in watching Jennings supervise the process of unloading the ant trains at the border while, from the corner of his eye, he watched Constance inspect the still-sealed papers King Jasper had given her before they left Regalis. The affection between herself and Prince Cambrian was obvious even to an old widower like Kuntza, so he had readily agreed to add his seal, and later his signature, to the papers, an act that would make their union legal both above and beneath the West Sea, as they called it.

Rolf, his usual observant self, was also looking in the general direction of the ant train, with the majority of his attention focused on Kuntza. He had never anticipated that his first official mission—well, his first mission since entering the Scribe's Academy—would take him into a culture he had never before heard of. Kuntza had been patiently advising them of the protocol, customs, and peculiarities of life in Cachora, but Rolf still felt woefully unprepared.

Following Kuntz's gaze over to where Constance had begun flitting back and forth, Rolf studied her unhappily. Kuntza had taken Rolf into his confidence about the content of the papers, so Rolf's sigh was heartfelt. His aunt and uncle, queen and king of the Silver Fairy Tribe, respectively, were usually paragons of discretion. Even so, he had accidentally encountered them in an embrace a time or two since their recent wedding. He fervently hoped that Cachora was as large as Kuntza said it was, because he wanted to give Prince Cambrian and Admiral Kimberlite an extra-wide berth until some of the novelty of their marriage had worn off.

Kuntza, hearing Rolf's sigh, chuckled and wrapped his arm around the boy-fairy's shoulders. "Do not be so down-hearted," he chastened the youth. "Marr-iage will come for you soon enough."

Rolf, knowing a tease when he heard one, smiled tolerantly.

Cambrian, meanwhile, was busy assisting Jennings in the interest of dismissing the ant train as quickly and as nonchalantly as possible. Kuntza had stressed the importance of there being absolutely no one else about when he signaled for his tribesfairies to come for them.

"Here," Cambrian offered a diamond carat to the lead driver. It was not much of a tip after calling them out on such short notice, but it should be enough to get them all a hot meal when they arrived back at Herio.

The driver looked at the diamond sliver for a moment, then up at him. "No, thank you, sir." He touched two fingers to his hat deferentially. "This job pays my fine, and that is enough."

In the time that it took for Cambrian to register his words, the driver had flown up to land lightly on his ant's back. Easing himself into place on the front of her pronotum, the driver used his goad to scratch as far under his ant's chin as he could. Speaking softly, he urged the ant into a distance-eating trot, the other ants falling obediently in line behind them.

Impressed, Cambrian now wished he had been able to persuade the young driver to take the carat. Clearly he had a healthy respect for his animals. Reluctantly replacing the carat in his waistcoat pocket, Cambrian flew over to where Jennings had joined the others.

"Wait, a moment more," Kuntza interrupted when Constance seemed about to break the seal on her papers. "We need wit-ness from my tribe, too."

Constance managed a small smile and tucked the papers away again so she would not be tempted to do anything foolish—such as peer in through one of the open ends of the folded packet in an attempt to read what they said.

"I will be right back," Kuntza promised, correctly diagnosing her impatience. Anticipation could make even the slightest delay painful, he knew. Fortunately, he had already identified the largest and smallest lava tubes, which simplified things.

Approaching the smallest tube, he drew a thin piece of copper wire from an inner pocket. The wire had a simple, insulated handle in the middle and served, to him, a very basic purpose. Kneeling down by the tube, he examined the walls carefully.

Slight inconsistencies between two lumps and the lumps around them, coupled with the fact that the distance between those two lumps was just about right, satisfied him that he had found what he was looking for. Two quick flicks of his fingers lifted the camouflaged covers from the lightning terminals. Inserting an end of his wire into one terminal, he tightened the attendant screw enough to ensure a stable connection while he tapped the other end of his wire against the other terminal. The lightning sparked a little at first, the power source having gone too long unused, then settled down and allowed him to transmit his request for transportation to be sent to their current location.

"What do you suppose he is doing?" Rolf asked, his youth and curiosity getting the better of his training.

"Perhaps we can ask him to explain it to us when he is done." Constance did her best to smile and act as if the delay was not making her own curiosity itch like a new rash. All the way from Regalis she had been able to ignore the papers. Now that they were at the border, every passing moment would seem a waste until the papers were opened and she learned her official relationship with Cambrian.

At last, Kuntza straightened away from the tube, one hand on his back.

"I am getting too old for this," he sighed. Raising his shoulders towards his ears and hunching his back, he produced a back pop that they all heard. "Better." Grinning a little morosely, he began hobbling back over to where they stood. "If only my knees were so easily relieved." Clapping Rolf on the shoulder, Kuntza asked, "Have you quill and ink, my friend?"

"Why," Rolf stifled his reflexive indignation. Kuntza was no sixth-year scribe, sneering at a 'wet-ears,' as some of the bullies called the first-year students. "Yes, of course." He produced them without even having to search inside his shoulder bag. "A historian who lacks recording materials may as well have nothing to record," he parroted a first-year maxim. Rolf, and every other first-year he knew, was perfectly capable of drying behind their own ears, but he loved the simple maxims he was learning.

"Very wise," Kuntza nodded appreciatively. "Very true, also." He was glad that the king of the Silver Fairy Tribe had thought to send this boy-fairy along, despite his youth. Rolf might prove more useful in persuading the council at Cachora than all of the history books they had packed along. Kuntza stifled a sigh. Of course, he would have to first persuade the council to listen to him.

"Zorion." The voice was soft, feminine, and came from behind where they were all standing, looking in the general direction of the smallest lava tube. The word, while unfamiliar to surface dwellers, was a traditional Water Fairy greeting.

Kuntza very pointedly held his hands slightly away from his body, palms forward in a gesture of peace, and made eye contact with first Cambrian, then Constance. It was considered an important part of a first meeting to take cochetas by surprise. He could coach them, but their actions and reactions would be related in detail when the committee reported to the council.

Cambrian slipped on a fake smile and glanced casually over at Rolf. They were all wearing swords, except Kuntza, and Cambrian was hoping that no one would be foolish enough to overreact. Especially not Constance. While Jennings was Cambrian's valet, he had spent centuries on the wind and years under Constance's command. If she felt unduly threatened by the newcomers, Jennings would back her without a moment's hesitation, including following her into battle.

Constance was busy talking herself out of combat mode. Kuntza's behavior was more than a little strange, to her way of thinking. If he had been taken by surprise, like the rest of them, why was he so calm? If he was *not* surprised, why had he not warned them? As the seconds ticked safely by, she did her best to relax. Taking her cue from Cambrian, whom she supposed had taken his from Kuntza, she turned her palms forward.

Rolf was the only one to physically turn to face them. He still had his hands full of fresh quills and a specially made ink bottle for travelling, so he could not show them his palms like the others were. But he did give in to a natural reaction. He smiled.

Kuntza, trying to watch all of them at once, smiled also. Things were going very well. With a barely perceptible nod at Cambrian—Kuntza sensed that Constance was displeased with him, but trusted she and Jennings would follow Cambrian's lead—he also turned to face the committee of five Water Fairies. Palms still up, he took a step towards them.

"I am Kuntza, truth seeker of the Mugan region." He did not address any of them in particular, knowing they considered themselves a single unit of observation, but he spoke in the language of the surface so that his guests could understand.

The woman-fairy who had greeted them frowned in disapproval of his choice. "And what have you learned," she asked in the language of the Water Fairies, "that made you think to bring strangers here?"

"I have learned," Kuntza switched to seahorse Margua, the delightful, fluid language of his own tribe, "that there is a stranger among us who would wantonly sacrifice hundreds of lives to further their own goals. A woman-fairy with silver hair and a black heart."

The mood of the whole committee changed when they grasped his meaning.

"What do they know of this?" demanded one of the younger fairies, his tone neutral.

"Assuming that by 'they,' you mean my guests," Kuntza placed a faint emphasis on the word *guests*, "they have come voluntarily to speak with our tribe on this and other matters."

Cambrian did his best to maintain the same neutrality that the Water Fairies were exhibiting, but when all five of the newcomers extended both hands, palms forward of course, towards Kuntza and lowered their eyes, he was highly intrigued. Clearly they recognized Kuntza as having authority, which made Cambrian realize how little he knew about Kuntza.

Constance held perfectly still. This latest development had her thoroughly perplexed. Who exactly was Kuntza? Why were they bowing to him? It was frustrating not to be able to understand them when they spoke, though she did recognize a word or two from the old wind chanties her grandfather used to sing.

"As a court-esy to my guests," Kuntza resumed the language of the surface, immediately feeling the stiffness of its words, "we will speak their lang-uage for now."

"As a cour-tes-y," the others intoned, bowing their heads again.

"Come for-ward," Kuntza commanded, "and wit-ness a con-tract of marr-iage."

Constance stopped breathing. Her anticipation took a sharp left turn and she found herself emotionally nose to nose with her fears.

Concerned at the symptoms of near-panic that Constance was giving off, Cambrian held out one of his hands towards her. Winking, he waited for her to respond.

Sheer willpower, fueled by love and trust, enabled her to take his hand.

"I love you," he mouthed.

Kuntza, who had begun to be alarmed when Constance turned white, stepped forward now.

"You have the pa-pers?" he prompted her gently.

Deciding that knowing was better than wondering, Constance took the papers from her pocket and offered them to him.

Kuntza held them up, seals turned away from him, until each member of the committee had come forward and viewed them.

"The pa-pers I hold," he had been thinking about what to say ever since he had been informed of the situation, "give per-miss-ion from King Jasper of the Sky Fairy Tribe for his son, Prince Cambrian," Kuntza put his free hand on Cambrian's shoulder, "to wed Admiral Constance Kimberlite." He paused to allow himself a moment of relief that he had pronounced her name correctly. "You wit-ness the seals, whole and intact?"

"We wit-ness," agreed the committee.

"You wit-ness my seal, whole and intact?" Kuntza, who had allowed himself to assume a slightly less intimidating posture, drew himself up to his full height again.

"We wit-ness the seal of Kuntza, of the Botere clan," they intoned.

Satisfied, Kuntza offered the papers to Constance again.

Thrown more than a little off balance by the unusual behavior of the group, Constance accepted the papers. Finding that Cambrian was still smiling at her, she took a deep breath and broke the seals. She also nearly flung the papers into the air when the Water Fairies suddenly began humming loudly.

"Here." Cambrian rescued her by catching hold of her wrist with one hand, and the edge of the papers with the other. "I want to see, too." He had the bizarre feeling that this was all some sort of test. Too many years of working investigations, no doubt. However, assuming that Kuntza was still on their side, Cambrian wanted to keep things as friendly as possible. Not that this was how he had imagined his wedding would go, any more than Constance probably had…

Constance smiled back at him, grateful that he was there. She even blushed a little as he released her wrist to slip his arm about her waist.

The explanation was quite straightforward, thankfully. The law, as it turned out, was usefully vague on the subject of separations. In fact, the only stipulation they found was that both parties had to be unmarried for the space of forty-eight hours prior to the (duly witnessed) signing of the enclosed marriage contract. No cake or flowers, or fancy dresses here, not that either of them cared.

"Rolf." Cambrian looked up from the papers. "Can we borrow a quill?" Not only did the enclosed marriage contract require their signatures, they were going to have to fill them out in triplicate. When Rolf gladly obliged them, Cambrian dipped the quill, tapped the excess ink back into the bottle, and offered the quill to Constance.

"My lady first," he smiled.

Constance was glad she had herself back under control by then, or she would have pinked from collar to hairline, and that was not something she wanted to do in front of strangers. Signing her name on the line that read 'bride' on all three copies, she handed the quill back to Cambrian.

Cambrian signed each copy with a flourish he had practiced during his youth, when he had great dreams of becoming a widely-acclaimed poet. Grinning a little, he held the quill out to Rolf. It was odd, having such a young witness, but thanks to his grandfather, Prince Nathaniel of the Silver Fairy Tribe, Rolf held the full authority of his title Historian, and could sign as tribal witness on any legal document. The laws of Fairydom having been observed, all that remained was for Kuntza, as an adult Water Fairy, to witness per their laws.

Kuntza motioned for the committee to cease humming. Taking the quill from Rolf, he signed his name on the second 'witness' line, adding the mark of his clan each time so that all of the copies would be free from challenge.

"A copy for their kaga." Kuntza held one paper up and handed it to Rolf, grateful that he had thought to explain to them that a kaga was a Water Fairy historian. In turn, it was Rolf who had taken the time to help Kuntza practice saying *Kimberlite* until it had rolled off Kuntza's tongue instead of tying it in knots. "A copy for our kagas." He held up a second copy and handed it to the nearest committee member, who stowed it without examination in the pouch at his waist. The marriage now duly legalized and recorded by the laws of the surface and of the water, he took Constance's hand and placed it over Cambrian's signature on the third copy. Then he placed Cambrian's hand over her signature, their wrists and their lives touching. This was a critical part of the Water Fairy wedding ceremony, and he had a moment of nostalgia, remembering his own wedding.

"The marr-iage contract is signed," Kuntza announced for the benefit of the rocks on the far side of the clearing. "Let the two lives become one of part-nership and unity." While Rolf and Jennings had both assured him that most surface weddings were not so bare and formal, Kuntza still felt a pang of regret that there were no choirs of children to serenade them or flowered wreaths to drape about their necks.

The committee resumed humming, a single, sustained note that ended on some imperceptible signal.

"We go now." Kuntza spoke kindly, but with urgency. The longer they remained here, in the open, the greater the chance that they would be discovered.

Constance watched Cambrian blink, then very properly collect their marriage contract. As a child-fairy, she had always found something else to do when her sisters and cousins gathered to plan their future weddings. Until she found someone she wanted to marry, Constance had figured that sort of thing was a waste of time. Now she felt a tinge of sadness that not even one member of her family had been present to share her joy.

"Darling?"

Constance looked up at Cambrian, then down at his proffered hand. "Come with me?" Cambrian asked, feeling a need to personally extend the invitation.

Those three words took Constance's partly cloudy and redid it in clear blue skies. Why fuss over a little thing like normal when wonderful was within reach?

"Always." Slipping her fingers through his, she smiled up at him.

Rolf, busily engaged in collecting information, had his back to the two of them and was watching the Water Fairies lower their luggage into the largest lava tube. Since they were working with no sign of hesitation, he decided to assume they knew what they were doing.

Jennings was more skeptical. "Thought they lived underwater," he muttered to himself, "not in a volcano." Later he would learn, much to his surprise, that they did both.

Chapter 12

"It is not a long flight," Kuntza reassured his guests as they entered the lava tube.

"After you," Cambrian smiled. He noticed that Kuntza complied without consulting the other Water Fairies, which implied a basic knowledge of the area.

"He has come a long way in a short time," Constance murmured to Cambrian, nodding towards Rolf, who was already at Kuntza's elbow. "His aunt, Rebecca, told me that he could not yet fly at the time of pirate offensive."

"His mother, Arabella, is overly cautious," Cambrian explained, "due in large part to the tragedy that befell her sister, Joanna."

Constance searched her heart for jealousy or pain when he mentioned his first love, and was glad when she found nothing but sorrow for Arabella's loss. Joanna had died young, much too young.

"What is this?" Rolf's voice echoed around them. He and Kuntza paused briefly, then flew into the lava tube wall. Jennings, who was right behind them as usual, disappeared as well.

Cambrian and Constance hurried to catch up, mildly alarmed. To their mutual surprise, they found a hole in the tube wall that lead into a cavern that stretched out far enough that they could not see its other walls from where they hovered in the lava tube. Still hand in hand, they flew in as well. It did not even occur to them that the area should be dark due to a lack of the sun's rays.

Cambrian immediately noticed the cavern was not tall enough for a fairy to fly safely over his fellows' heads. Given that the Water Fairies dotting the cavern were all walking, he came to the surprising conclusion that the Water Fairy Tribe must walk considerably more than the surface tribes did.

Rolf was busily counting the boxes his precious history books were travelling in, to be sure that they had all made it safely from the *Seeker's Wind* down the lava tube, and onto the open-sided cart that their luggage was being transferred to. He also automatically accounted for the boxes of surface medicines, the chest of sugar, six trunks, two satchels, and one bag that Constance had added to the ant train without explanation. He did all of this without conscious effort, a natural extension of the memory training he began in place of his handwriting courses at the academy, since he already wrote a neat hand. That came in handy now, as well, when he checked his list against Jennings' to convince him that everything was there.

Constance, instinctively tuning in to the rhythm of movement within the cavern, traced it back to a single man-fairy at a slightly elevated station near another hole in the far wall. Without leaving his post, the man-fairy directed the activity, from ordering the false wall placed over the hole they entered through, to mysteriously removing the open-sided cart that contained their things from the room with no visible means of locomotion. No ants, no ropes or pulleys. The cart simply wheeled itself along its track and out the far door.

"Amazing." Rolf looked at Kuntza. "How do these work?" he asked, pointing at the glowing glass balls that adorned the cavern walls, providing light where the sun could not reach.

"They are lightn-ing globes," Kuntza told him. "Ma-chines much lar-ger than the ones on your cha-sers make the light-ning."

"And you store it in these?" Jennings asked incredulously. He knew enough about lightning to want no part of it.

"No." Kuntza worked hard not to laugh. "Not ex-actly. Ask me a-gain later, my friend. We have much farther to go today." He indicated the new vehicle just pulling up on the tracks.

Rolf brightened considerably when he realized that they were going to take the same track as their luggage. The carriage was not as sleek as the ones he was accustomed to, more of a windowless box on wheels, but it was still better than flying. Despite his hours of practice, his wing muscles were still underdeveloped for a boy-fairy of his age, and he would have been humiliated to be the first to call for a rest.

Constance reluctantly boarded the carriage and seated herself on one of the rows of benches inside. It was roomier than the royal carriage she and Cambrian—and King Jasper—had ridden in at Regalis. The benches were not wooden, either. They were made of some sort of bone and covered with a strange fabric, similar to leather but different. The carriage floor was made of obsidian and seemed to soak in the light from the globes, adding to the dreariness of the bare interior.

Cambrian, still trying to politely ignore the five Water Fairies accompanying them, sat beside Constance. He was already missing the sun. Not seeing the sun was one of the worst parts of the bitter winter months for him. Of more immediate concern was the fact that the carriage they were riding in stank of fish. Resigning himself to his fate, he tried to distract himself by pondering the council they were going to see. Kuntza tried to explain it during their flight from Regalis, with the one point of emphasis being the need for diplomacy at this first meeting. But as they whirred along, the only sound being that of the wheels turning, it began to feel like his head was too small for his brain.

"Rest stop." Kuntza rose, swaying slightly with the carriage as it slowed to a halt. "We are un-der the sea now. We must rest, breathe, and ad-just to the press-ure." He had been so long above the sea that the change was affecting him, also. Sliding the carriage door open, Kuntza stepped down and looked up. It was good to be home.

"How…" Rolf stopped himself before he could finish asking how they had created the glass bowl they were standing in. A glass bowl with walls he could look through and out into the sea. Flocks of fish darted in every direction while meadows of underwater grass swayed gracefully in a silent wind. Further out still, Rolf could see what looked like a rocky outcropping, except these rocks were a vivid pink and pocked with tiny, regularly-spaced holes.

Constance leaned against Cambrian, overcome with the beauty of the scene surrounding them. Her headache forgotten, she watched with delight. For the first time, she had a glimmer of an idea as to why the Water Fairies were content to remain earthbound instead of sailing the skies as she had chosen to do.

Curious, Jennings flew over to the glass and—very carefully—touched it. It felt cold to him. Strange. The carriage and the air inside the bowl were a little cool, but not cold. How could that be? A glance in either direction confirmed that the track they were using ran mostly through dark tunnels, and as far as he could see. He kept that fabulous bit of news to himself. How would they live without the sun?

However long the rest, it would have seemed too short, so Constance and the others stifled their protests when Kuntza announced that they must resume their journey. At least by now the odor inside the carriage was less noticeable, their noses having adjusted somewhat. Their headaches had eased, as well, allowing them to travel more comfortably. So much so that Kuntza had to gently shake them awake when they reached their destination.

"Rolf." Kuntza shook the lad's shoulder. "Come now, we will be late."

Rolf snapped awake, straightening from his slumped position so quickly that he nearly knocked Jennings, who had stretched out comfortably beside him, onto the floor.

"What? Where…" Jennings' vision cleared quickly, and he knew what had happened.

Sheepishly, Rolf grinned up at Kuntza. "Did I snore very loudly?"

"Perhaps," Kuntza shrugged. "But I had trouble hearing anyone else over Jennings." He looked at the retired windfairy-valet, who pretended to glower back, the natural extension of their banter aboard the *Seeker's Wind*. She had been fast, but small, so when the cabins got doled out, they wound up sharing.

Rolf chuckled and went to wake the others.

"Your Highness." He bumped Cambrian's knee with his own. "Prince Cambrian?"

Cambrian blinked up at him, wondering why the carriage was on its side. Then the crick in his neck began registering urgent protests and he grimaced in understanding. Carefully, he began to ease his head into an upright position from where it had flopped over towards his shoulder whilst he slept.

"We have arrived, Your Highness." Rolf had quickly come to feel quite comfortable with Cambrian, but decided that observing formalities lent some badly-needed dignity to the situation.

"Thank you, Historian." Even half asleep, Cambrian followed Rolf's reasoning without difficulty. However, he found he could not move his left arm at all. Turning to look, he found himself with a face-full of Constance's hair. An attempt at wriggling his fingers confirmed that his left arm was completely asleep. "Constance?" Cambrian happily noted that the others had left the carriage already. "Darling?" Using his right hand, he located her chin and raised it so that he could see her face.

"Hmm?"

She was adorable asleep, he decided. Steeling himself against the temptation to kiss her awake, Cambrian tried something else.

"Admiral?" The effect was instantaneous.

"Aye?" Constance was awake, alert, and somehow sitting at attention.

"Ah." Cambrian leaned away from her enough to finish freeing his arm, which then lay useless at his side. "We seem to be here." Coming to his feet, he turned so that he could offer her his fully-functioning right arm. "Shall we?"

They exited the carriage together, Cambrian's crown properly straightened and Constance's tricorn tucked safely under one arm since they were indoors. She would figure out the protocol involved with always being indoors later.

"The council waits for us," Kuntza announced, slipping his hands a short ways into the sleeves of the opposite arm to grasp the wrist. It was a habit from the public speaking class he took in his youth: a simple, practical way of preventing himself from talking with his hands.

"Jennings." Cambrian turned to his friend and valet. "Would you mind?" Cambrian nodded over at where the cart with their luggage was being offloaded just a few twigs away, their things neatly stacked but with complete ignorance as to ownership. The relief on Jennings' face was so obvious that it was comical, and Cambrian almost laughed out loud as he watched him zip away from the impending formalities.

The walls of the tunnel they took were lined with lightning globes, which gave off enough light for Cambrian to see the chisel marks in the stone clearly. It was all remarkably similar to the network of tunnels beneath Regalis that they used during the winter, when it was too dangerous to go outside. Except that their tunnels lacked lightning globes. How he wished he could send a few to his family! Lesley pretended not to be affected by the dark tunnels, or the weird shadows that the lanterns could throw, but Lila and Laura unabashedly held hands whenever circumstances forced them into the tunnels. He smiled faintly, remembering the first time he had been brave for his mother, offering her his arm and a confident smile when she hesitated in the doorway to a particularly cramped tunnel.

Constance, acutely aware of her lack of control under the circumstances, was carefully studying her surroundings. The tunnel was wide enough for four fairies to walk shoulder to shoulder, but only just tall enough to fly through. She flexed her wing muscles, let them droop, then re-tucked them into her dress jacket. If the rest of Cachora was this cramped, she was going to have to invent some sort of exercise system to keep herself in flying trim.

Rolf simply absorbed it all like a dried-out sponge. Accustomed to home-bound winters on the small estate where he had grown up, he found the tunnel system fascinating. The two or three false doors they passed between the carriage platform and wherever they were going fanned his already burning curiosity. They were probably nothing more than supply closets, but not *knowing* for sure was what made it so interesting. They might at least have hidden them better, or spaced the lightning globes far enough away from them that a casual glance did not reveal the obviously mismatched colors. The doors were slightly darker than the walls around them, as if they had been cut from a different source, fitted, and subjected to a few chisel strokes around the edges to make it look as if they were part of the original wall. Sloppy. Even the nook where he found his

Aunt Rebecca's top secret map before the pirate offensive was more subtly disguised than that.

A cool breeze patted Cambrian's cheek, drawing him from his reflections in time to see that the walls were widening out before they entered a subaqueous cavern that was quite a bit larger than the one where they got off the carriage. A semi-circle of seven chairs faced away from them, while seating for approximately a hundred fairies faced towards them, the rows rising in tiers as far as the back of the cavern would permit. Only the near seven chairs were occupied at the moment. And while he could see that lightning globes extended back into the cavern, only the front area was lit.

As they progressed into the cavern, Constance squeezed Cambrian's hand lightly, then released it. The group of seven Water Fairies waiting for them had to be the council Kuntza briefed her on. Newlyweds or not, right now they needed to be viewed as separate individuals, a prince and an admiral, chosen and empowered to speak for their tribe. By the time they were all arranged behind Kuntza, facing the council now, she had almost convinced herself that this was a routine military encounter.

Rolf, who had slipped to the back of the procession before they quite reached the bilera, as Kuntza referred to their council hall last night over dinner, gave himself a quick mental shake. It was fine to be the inquisitive youth in front of his friends. This was business, and none of the council members looked friendly. If his history book had been a private journal, he might have described them as looking like bored frogs or dried-out reeds; but since it was not, he supposed he would have to find something more dignified to say.

Kuntza nodded slightly in approval as his guests formed up behind him and slightly to his right as previously instructed. The committee, of course, formed up to the council's right, they being agents of the council and justly taking the honored place. Here, in the bilera, he could not hope to exercise his own will, so he could only hope that Cambrian, Constance, and Rolf would be patient while they were discussed in a language they had never learned.

As the committee droned on, however, recounting the tiniest of details, Kuntza found his own patience stretching thin. Most of what they mentioned seemed inconsequential to him. The sky was blue when they arrived at the surface. The visitors had never seen lightning globes before. They all wore swords. Was the council truly going to be swayed by the way Constance's hand rested so naturally on her sword hilt? As if the habit of a single woman-fairy could be construed to represent the intent of four entire tribes! At long last, the final committee member bowed her head and stepped back into line with the others.

"We will adjourn for a rest period." The council's speaker, an elderly man-fairy, watched the visitors closely while his colleagues rose as if to leave.

Kuntza felt his irritation at the delay drain away when he realized that this, too, was part of the test. Science could not be rushed. Neither could the council. "Smile." Kuntza demonstrated to his friends. "They will leave to con-si-der what the comm-ittee has said. We must smile." He repeated the admonition when Rolf opened his mouth to ask a question. "For now, they know only what they hear and see."

Cambrian, his calf muscle beginning to cramp from standing in one place for so long, smiled. "Might one ask how time is kept here?" Upon recognizing that the committee's report was going to be a lengthy one, he had resorted to mentally quizzing himself on what he knew of the Water Fairy culture. They valued knowledge above gems or metals, so he deduced that this council represented their intellectual elite.

"We have clocks, as you do," Kuntza answered, his tone low and faintly puzzled.

"I see." Cambrian narrowed his eyes pensively. "Are there any in the bilera?"

"Clocks?" Kuntza's smile grew, for he thought he understood the question behind the question. "No, time does not rule here."

Cambrian blinked. What an odd perception of time. And yet, the more he thought about it, the more sense it made. How many years of his life had he spent rushing about, unwittingly subservient to time's exacting, relentless pace? Appointments, assignments, etc. Hmm. He promised himself that, once they had settled things peacefully with the Water Fairy Tribe, he would give this notion a more careful examination.

"You may go." The council's speaker, flanked by his colleagues, dismissed the committee. Reseating himself, he looked over at Kuntza. Personally, the speaker was pleased with the way the visitors had tolerated the committee's detailed report. The ancient histories he reviewed when the pirates first began to sally into their underwater sanctuary, added to Kuntza's reports of the pirates' frequently petulant and short-tempered behavior, had not led him to view Kuntza's decision to visit the surface favorably. Not that Kuntza had given them a choice in the matter.

"Kuntza, step forward."

Constance hastily shut her mouth, which had dropped open in shock when the speaker addressed them flawlessly in the common tongue. She had supposed that they, like Kuntza and the committee, would have a barely passable knowledge of it. Her eyes narrowed as she also realized that the 'adjournment' had been a simple feint, designed to make them relax, perhaps get them to say something in the common tongue that they would regret later. Were the tests here never-ending?

"When it was reported that surface fairies were beginning to visit our realm, you were instructed to learn what you could about them. You were appointed a truth seeker for our tribe." The speaker frowned. "Yet the last report we had was that you had vanished. Where did you go?"

Kuntza bit back the flood of information that leapt to mind. A simple question deserved a simple answer. "I went to Regalis, capital city of the Sky Fairy Tribe." To say that the council was stunned was an understatement. One of them even found himself with his mouth open exactly as Constance's had been.

The speaker's frown deepened, evidence enough that he was rattled by the news. "Why did you go?"

"To seek the truth."

The council exchanged troubled glances. His terse answer told them only that he had not abandoned his quest.

Chapter 13

"What truth did you find at Regalis?" This question, also in the common tongue of the surface tribes, came from the woman-fairy seated at the far end of the council table. Naydie had been an admirer of Kuntza for some time, finding his scientific research and reports consistently enlightening. Once she had even toyed with the idea of attempting personal correspondence with him; now she regretted her decision not to.

"The surface fairies remain in tribes." Kuntza answered the question carefully. Knowing that this would be followed by other, longer meetings, complete with a full gallery, he saved his eloquence for the next time that question would be asked. "Their lives are very diff-er-ent from ours, it is true. But the chaos and law-less-ness we were told of is false." The pirates had painted a dire picture of oppression and confusion above the surface that horrified him. Naturally he included that information in his reports to Cachora. Now he knew that the pirates were the primary source of those ills and looked forward to telling the council about it in greater detail.

"How did you learn this?" Naydie asked.

"By ob-ser…" Kuntza regretted his choice of words even before he began stumbling. Unable to recall how the word was pronounced, he substituted, "By spen-ding time with them. Talking to them. Their hist-or-ies, too, I read." He chastened himself for his poor pronunciation, and comforted himself that it was his impression on the council, not the councilwoman, that concerned him.

The speaker looked to his right, at his senior colleagues, then to his left, at the junior council members. When they all nodded agreement, he looked again at Kuntza.

"Please, introduce our guests."

Naydie came close to dropping her pencil when Kuntza smiled. The sheer warmth radiating from him left her a little jealous of the woman-fairy standing behind him. Was that warmth for her?

Delighted when the speaker said 'our' instead of 'your,' Kuntza bowed with a flourish before beginning the presentations. Even a tacit acceptance was a victory. In a carefully considered move, he began with Rolf instead of Prince Cambrian or Admiral Kimberlite.

"Honored council, permit me to make known to you Rolf Warner: son of Princess Arabella; nephew to the king and queen of the Silver Fairy Tribe; observer of a great battle with the pirates; and official kaga of his tribe." Kuntza's voice rang with pride as he listed Rolf's relations and honors. His enthusiasm for the introduction rolled him through even the difficult words without faltering. "He brings not only greetings from his own king and queen, but gifts for our tribe, and a letter of recommendation from Julene of Kendu."

The Kendu family was also of the Mugan region, so her story was well-known. The murmur of surprise that the council gave satisfied him that he had sufficiently impressed them with Rolf's worth.

A slightly red-faced Rolf bowed in the best fashion of the Silver Fairy court. While Kuntza had warned him that it would be necessary to make him sound extraordinary, he never expected to come out sounding like a hero or anything. While he could make sure he remained a mere footnote in his history book when he made his own record later, if any of his acquaintances ever got ahold of the minutes from this council meeting, he was going to have to move.

"If it please the council," Rolf pulled Ambassador Julene's letter 'from the air' in a bit of sleight of hand that his uncle had recently taught him. "Ambassador Julene was unavoidably detained at Castlemain, and begs that you receive this letter with her compliments." When the speaker indicated for him to come forward, Rolf obeyed. "My king and queen also send their warmest felicitations, along with a set of our history books." Unsure of exactly what to do next, he bowed to the speaker, then to the council members on the speaker's right hand, then to the remaining members before returning to his place with the others. Doing his best to appear calm the entire time, he was greatly relieved to fade into the background when Kuntza began the next presentation.

Kuntza, sensing that he had succeeded with Rolf's presentation, rolled smoothly on to Cambrian, deciding to save Constance for his big finish. Like Rolf, her qualifications needed to be firmly established right at the beginning.

"Honored council, permit me to make known to you Prince Cambrian Bijou: second son of the royal house of the Sky Fairy Tribe; protector of the laws of his tribe; defeater of the pirate Bane; and promise maker for his tribe."

Cambrian was hard pressed not to show his amusement at Kuntza's efforts. The grand gestures, the dramatic tones…it was all just so unlike the reticent man-fairy he had come to know. Stepping briskly forward, he bowed and took a chance.

"Honored council," he made eye contact with each of them, his hands forward, palms up in the same gesture of peace he had observed Kuntza use with the group that surprised them at the border. "I offer you the sincere regrets of my father, King Jasper, who wishes circumstances permitted him to come himself. With your kind permission, I, too, bear gifts from my tribe to yours. A select sample of our medicines, for your study and use," he could not help noticing the interested expressions on several of their faces. "And a one hundred twelve pound chest of sugar for your enjoyment."

Kuntza was surreptitiously watching the council for their reaction to Cambrian's remarks when he made eye contact with Naydie. Most distracting.

"Honored council." Kuntza paused for a fraction of a second, like the actors in the Sky Fairy play he attended last week. "Permit me to make known to you Admiral Constance Kimberlite," he indicated her without taking his eyes off the council. "August traveler of the skies; defender of the weak; trusted officer of her king; princess by marriage to her husband, Prince Cambrian; and defeater, in single combat, of the outlaw Bullierd." The sound of a water droplet striking the ground could have been heard in the silence that followed this presentation.

Constance took a self-conscious half-step forward. Snapping to attention, she saluted crisply. She was trying to think of something profound to say when she realized that she was still holding her salute. The speaker, apparently deciding that she must expect some sort of response, tipped his head forward just as she was wondering how to get out of it without looking foolish. Lowering her hand to her side, she dress-stepped back to her place in line, and assumed a relaxed parade rest position. She did not even notice when her hand settled on her sword hilt.

"Deceiver!" An irate woman-fairy, distinctive as the only fairy present with silver hair, barged in through the bilera's opening. Pointing at Kuntza, she challenged, "You dare to tell me my father is dead? Slain by that puny creature?" She flung one hand in Constance's general direction. She would rather have flung a knife.

Constance surprised them all by smiling. Several acerbic remarks sprang to mind, but she ignored them. Really, she should have deduced that Bullierd's dying words had been to his daughter.

"Your father died sword in hand," she told Amber, by way of consolation. That was understandable, given how he had lived. Again she disciplined herself to keep her thoughts to herself.

"Deceiver!" Amber screamed. She wanted to crush this arrogant officer, to erase her from existence. Dedication to her mission, her father's dream of Fairydom domination, was all that held her, shaking with rage, at the mouth of the bilera. "I will have your name."

Constance felt the unspoken challenge and it took all the strength of character she could muster not to respond. Dueling in the bilera would be a poor diplomatic move.

"I am Admiral Constance Kimberlite, princess-by-marriage of the Sky Fairy Tribe." She kept her tone even by thinking of the last time she checked windship's stores with Miss Dunn, as tedious a task as ever she hoped to complete.

Standing at Constance's side, Cambrian was rocked to his core by the insanity boiling in Amber's liquid silver eyes. This was their *diplomatic* enemy? He considered sending for

Jennings right then. *You can stop unpacking, the job of convincing the Water Fairies to side against the pirates has been done for us.* A sick feeling settled in his stomach, however, when he saw that some of the council members had emotionally iced over. Now what?

Kuntza inserted himself between Amber and Constance to bow to the council. He had not expected to present their evidence at the first council meeting; however, neither had he anticipated such a volatile encounter.

"We have come far to bring you evi-dence from the surface. Bid us to rest now, will you not?" He smiled as he reminded them of the ancient custom of traveler's rest.

The council speaker, disturbed at the turn of events, nodded slowly. "We will resume with the morning tide." Frowning at Constance, he warned, "When we will hear more of this single-combat."

Constance nodded, her face a picture of serenity. She wanted them to remember her poise while they thought things over later. Unfortunately, and unbeknownst to the others, there were those on the council who were sympathetic to Amber. Their principles were planted in shifting sand, which conveniently allowed the desire to venture to the surface to take precedence over their sworn duty to protect and guide their tribe.

Cambrian, watching the council members file out, observed the looks Amber gave to the last three as they moved past her. His former inclination to dismiss Amber was clearly incorrect.

Constance, comfortable in the knowledge that she had done no more than duty required, slipped her hand into Cambrian's, sensing that he was not at ease. He looked down at her and the rest of the world faded away.

Kuntza happened to look in their direction just in time to see the not-so-imaginary sparks flying between them.

"Well." He coughed. Looked away. "That was tire-ing! Come." He wrapped his arm around Rolf's shoulder to help him keep track of the lad. "It is the cust-om to assign guest quarters up-on arri-val." His haste to get them safely out of public areas and somewhere that they could all relax manifested itself in his increased difficulty with pronouncing their language. Rolf's stomach rumbled, prompting Kuntza to chuckle. "And to-night, your first meal in Cachora!"

Constance and Cambrian followed along obediently, not wanting to get lost their first night there. After they had taken a couple of turns, the foot traffic in the tunnels faded out until it was just their group. Nevertheless, when Cambrian made as if to call ahead to Kuntza, Constance squeezed his arm and shook her head. Something told her that they were still being observed.

"These tunnels are reserve-ed for impor-tant

guests," Kuntza told Rolf, his speech improving as his tension eased. "So late in the season, we should have them to ourselves."

"What of the Lady Amber?" Cambrian erred on the side of respect when he called her a 'lady.' Meeting her unawares could have very nasty results.

"No." Kuntza shook his head. "We treat-ed her with res-pect and com-passion when she first arrived. Now her status here is almost that of an inter-lo-per." He shrugged self-deprecatingly. "However, you, as the guests of a truth seeker…"

"Who is also from the Mugan region," Rolf inserted, demonstrating the depth of his understanding, shallow as it was. He could not explain the significance of the term, but it clearly carried weight.

"Yes, that also," Kuntza brushed off the reference as quickly as he could. He liked these fairies, enjoyed their company, and did not want to risk the formalities that so frequently came with the mention of his region. Mugan was the region of Water Fairy territory nearest the edge of the sea floor, settled by the richest and most powerful families in the early days. Now his and other families, like Julene's, stood guard between their world and the surface, as well as leading the way in science and philosophy. But he found it wearisome to have so few friends.

"And here we are." Kuntza beamed at Constance and Cambrian as he slid open the door to their quarters. The room had one bed and one long, waist-high dresser. It was lit by one lightning globe and a clear, circular pane of volcanic glass that would allow them to observe the ocean. "It is not large, but I hope you will be com-for-table." He paused in the doorway, puzzled by the set of unopened luggage on one side of the room. "Set your trunks outside the door when you are ready. They will be taken and stored for you. Oh, dinner will be served at seven tonight." Kuntza indicated the spring-driven clock that stood in one corner of the room. The languages had evolved separately, but the numbers were the same. "A page will come to fetch you."

Rolf coughed slightly, ready to give them their space as well as eager to see his own. He had no valet, but he did have a lot of things to record, and a snack to wheedle. If he had to wait until seven—a good two hours—he was going to starve.

"And you." Kuntza chuckled at Rolf's innocent expression. "You, I will give a gui-ded tour of our kitch-en." They all laughed at Rolf's wide-eyed interest. "Jennings, too, if we can find him. I think the chef may even let you samp-le the dishes. It could be crab cakes," his mouth watered at the thought of his favorite dish. "Or grilled shrimp with a dabberlock salad." He had Rolf's complete attention.

Cambrian gently slipped one arm around

Constance's waist and lifted her over the threshold, shutting the door behind them while Kuntza walked Rolf away. Resting his cheek against Constance's hair, he inhaled deeply. For the next several months, the closest he would come to home was smelling her daffodil-scented shampoo and holding her close.

"I see Jennings chose discretion over invasion of my privacy," Constance chuckled, eyeing her unopened trunks. A practical packer, she separated her things so that at least one complete set of clothing was in each trunk. In short, she appreciated that her husband's valet had not rummaged through them.

"A wise choice." Cambrian kissed her cheek. The clock's single pointer was almost to the five. "We should probably get you unpacked before dinner." He slipped his other arm around her waist, the action belying his words.

"Hmm." Constance felt warm for the first time since their arrival. "Later."

"In that case," he turned her to face him, "I have a surprise for you."

She felt a touch of disappointment when he did not resume kissing her.

"This," he reached into his pocket and withdrew the paper he had carried with him from the *Seeker's Wind*, "is a poem I have written for you." Unfolding it, he drew her closer so that she could read it with him.

I take quill in hand—
Words mine to command—
And they hasten to obey.

My darling, my own,
Its fire yet unknown,
My heart at your feet I lay.

And how sweet t'will be,
When two becomes three,
When with life's dearest joys we play.

Our way lies before…
A day? A year? More!
Forever, starting today.

Before he had quite finished, Constance hid her face against his chest, still listening, but unable to continue reading the words—the lovely, powerful words—of his poem. Her emotions were so high that she remained there, in the protective circle of his arms, while she tried to accept that he wrote those words for her.

Unsure what else to do, Cambrian slipped the poem back into his pocket, and began gently stroking her hair. The lump in his throat prevented further speech, anyway. After several moments, he noticed a subtle shift in her posture. He no longer felt like he was being crushed by a hands-free bear hug; now he could feel the slight dampness on his shirt front, as though she had been crying.

Constance peeked up at him, feeling a little foolish for overreacting the way she had. Perhaps it was because she so rarely stopped to think of herself, beyond her identity as a daughter or an officer, that she found the experience of being cherished so utterly overwhelming. She smiled when he winked down at her, relieved that he was not upset by her behavior.

Looking around the room again, Cambrian spotted the small, framed picture of the Crystal Castle that he always took along on his travels. Scooping Constance up, he deposited her gently on the bedspread. From his other pocket, he produced their marriage contract, shook it out, and fitted its top edge under the picture frame.

"What do you think?" he asked, stepping back to observe it critically. Pretentiously raising his thumb as if to assess the lines of a work of art, he frowned. "My suites at the castle are all done in overstuffed and comfortable," he announced with all the pomposity of someone dropping the name of a famous interior designer.

"Perhaps, between diplomatic meetings," she rose, slipped her arms about his waist, "and state dinners, we might be able to arrange to have the room redecorated." Going up on her toes, she kissed his jaw, smiling at the stubble she found there. "We could insist on a mother-of-pearl shaving mug, studded with their rarest gems." The diamonds and other stones that they mined above paled in comparison with the jewelry the female council members wore.

Cambrian became instantly serious. Pulling her tightly against him, he murmured, "So long as you are here, I will have what is most precious to me in all of Fairydom, above or beneath the sea." His gaze dropped to her lips, so soft and appealing.

To her surprise, Constance did not blush. He spoke in earnest, and she believed him. She even met him halfway when he bent to kiss her.

Chapter 14

Constance, who had never really enjoyed seafood before, was delighted to find that the clam chowder served at dinner was delicious.

"I do not understand," she told Cambrian for the second time, "how this can be clam chowder."

"Probably the ingredients are fresher," Cambrian remarked, only half of his mind on the conversation. He had done his best to dress appropriately for a state dinner, choosing his charcoal gray barkcloth suit as it was not a tribal color. After Constance's mention of the gems worn to the council meeting, he had gone to pains to polish his crown—much to Constance's amusement.

"Disappointed?" Constance, aware that her husband's mind was elsewhere, smiled at him because she could. Dinner, as it turned out, was served in a private dining area at a table set for five. She and Jennings had both promptly removed their dress jackets when they saw it was going to be just them. With no formalities to observe, Jennings and Kuntza were reviewing the rules for Stratagem, again, while Rolf laughed at their efforts at reproducing the Stratagem board with utensils.

"No, I..." Cambrian's voice trailed off when he looked her in the eyes. "Yes, a little. I expected to use this time to get to know the council and their culture better."

Constance reached for an herbed biscuit, frowning thoughtfully. They had discussed being surprised at the border while they dressed for dinner, finally agreeing that they should assume the best of Kuntza until it was no longer an option. He had certainly done his part at the council meeting.

"It does make me feel a lot like I am on trial instead of a guest," she said at last. Popping a bit of biscuit into her mouth, her eyes half-closed as she savored it. "These are impossibly tasty."

Cambrian smiled mischievously at her. "I think I could probably fit a few into my jacket pockets," he offered in a conspiratorially-lowered tone.

Constance pretended to consider the idea, then shook her head regretfully. "Better not." She was thinking of her tailored wardrobe.

"Do not be shy," Kuntza instructed without looking up from the goblets they had substituted for Stratagem pieces. "Win-ter is much the same to us here as any other season."

Constance looked at the table—the half-full tureen of chowder, the pats of an unusual sweet spread, the dozen or so small crocks with their different flavors of water—and had difficulty swallowing. Winter shut everything down above the surface. A few of the wealthier Plant Fairies had private greenhouses. Even fewer members of other tribes hired skilled Plant Fairies to maintain greenhouses for them. Other than those extreme exceptions, what could not be bottled, salted, or dried was slowly eliminated from the menu.

Cambrian was still trying to digest the concept of year-round plenty when the servers returned. Quietly, quickly, they replaced the main course with plates of dabberlock salad.

Kuntza maintained his position, still studying the makeshift Stratagem board, until the servers had exited, sliding the door shut behind them.

"Please under-stand." Kuntza looked around the table at his guests, reminding himself that their culture was very different. "Our sit-ua-tion is still unknown, even to me. To us, the meal is for friends and fam-ily, not for bus-iness. If two council mem-bers share the meal, they do not discuss the bilera."

Cambrian felt as if a weight had been lifted from his chest.

"You should know," Kuntza warned before the four relieved faces could begin speaking all at once, as they had a perplexing propensity towards doing, "Am-ber came here woun-ded, the wea-pon still in her chest. The wea-pon was as silver as her hair."

Constance leaned forward. "Was it an arrow?" This sounded vaguely familiar. A woman-fairy of the Silver Fairy Tribe, wounded with a silver arrow and...*the attempted assassination of Princess Rebecca.* Now she understood why Rolf was white as a seagull's wing. In fact, she felt ill herself. How much damage had the Bullierd family done?

"Yes," Kuntza nodded. "You know of this?" He rather hoped they did not. Violence was looked down upon among his tribe.

"A bit," Cambrian nodded. Glancing at Rolf he clarified, "It happened at Castlemain." Reaching under the table, he took Constance's hand in his.

Rolf took a deep breath. This was not his favorite bit of recent history. Nevertheless, it was more his story than theirs. "It was discovered, earlier this year, that a group of rebels was trying to force my grandfather, who was King Nathaniel at the time, to," remembering Kuntza's limited vocabulary, Rolf traded 'abdicate' for, "yield his throne to another fairy of their choosing. They were defeated." He summarized weeks of details. "But we learned that Count Bullierd," he nodded when Kuntza raised an eyebrow in Constance's direction, "was leading the rebellion. He was banished and Amber, his daughter, tried to assassinate my aunt, who is now Queen Rebecca. That arrow was meant to kill Amber." Despite his youth, Rolf was sadly aware that there were those who would never voluntarily stop their evil-doing. "Our senior guard will be devastated when he learns that he missed." He added this last bit without heat, as a simple statement of fact.

Kuntza shook his head, astounded at the story. "She told us it was the doing of evil law prot-ect-ors. Pres-ented herself as am-bass-ador of the opp-ressed."

"Kuntza."   Constance had lost too many friends to pirates to mince words.   "Law protectors, fairies like myself," she tapped the insignia on her shirt collar with her free hand, "fight pirates because they will kill and plunder whenever they can. Wherever they are stronger, they hurt those who are weaker."

"Am-ber is a pir-ate?"

"Worse."   Cambrian fielded that question. "She and her father used the pirates to try to force the surface tribes to yield to them. When that did not work, they thought of the snowstorm you helped us to defeat."   He leaned forward deliberately. "Now, she is here, trying to make friends with a tribe that is capable of crippling the rest of Fairydom by denying us water. And I am very worried that she has persuaded three of your council members to somehow help her take over your tribe."

They all recoiled in shock when Kuntza lunged to his feet. The force of his abrupt movement sent some of the flavored water sloshing over the rim of a crock and onto the bare clamshell table. Without a word, Kuntza spun on his heel and exited the room, the door slamming behind him.

Glances were exchanged around the table, with Cambrian sighing when all of the others ended up looking at him.

"As the council left the bilera today," he began to explain his observation to the others.

Kuntza, meanwhile, had waved off a startled servant and was flying swiftly down a deserted hallway. He moved more and more rapidly until he suddenly opened his wings to their full extent. Hovering there, in the mouth of the darkened bilera, he struggled with what he had just been told. To a Water Fairy, a bilera was a special place. Liars were few and far between in their tribe of scholars, but here even a liar would bow to the weight of generations and tell the truth.

Lowering himself softly to the floor, Kuntza walked inside. Approaching the speaker's chair, he thought back to the first bilera he had ever entered. His second grandfather, his first grandfather's father, occupied the speaker's chair at that meeting. A young student, guilty of taking public supplies for a private experiment, had sheepishly acknowledged his guilt before the council and learned the better way. Resting his hands on the back of this speaker's chair, Kuntza groaned softly.

"Who is lying now?" He had seen Bane's pirate stronghold once, while operating on a badly injured pirate. A victim, they told him, of the chaos that reigned above the surface. Then Captain Trevaille brought him Prince Cambrian, Constance, and Jennings, along with many others who said they had to escape from the pirates or be harmed. They insisted that the pirates were the chaos-makers. And he had believed them. Then tonight they accused council members of treachery? Lifting the speaker's chair from the ground, Kuntza slammed it back down in frustration.

"Careful." Naydie spoke from where she was sitting in the empty gallery. "That chair is nearly five hundred years old, you know." She used Margua and kept a friendly tone, having been aware of him from the moment he arrived.

"Forgive me." Kuntza bowed humbly towards the voice, unsure of who was speaking so kindly to him after his fit of temper. "I have no right even to touch the chair."

"Then perhaps you will sit over here with me," Naydie invited hopefully. Kuntza was the first Water Fairy to voluntarily visit the surface in over a thousand years. Young officers were tasked with river and stream assessments, general maintenance, etc., and avoided the other tribes at all cost.

"You are too kind," Kuntza protested, his eyes still searching the darkened seating for the voice's owner. His curiosity led him to venture a few paces further into the bilera. "Councilor Naydie!"

She laughed softly at his obvious astonishment. "Come," she invited again. "Sit with me."

Kuntza complied, telling himself it would be discourteous to refuse.

"You are angry." She shook her head, a side braid falling over one shoulder when he tried to dismiss his mood with a hand shrug. "The truth."

Kuntza, caught neatly by his own recent thoughts, bowed his head. "It is a weakness of mine, to be angry when I cannot find an answer."

Naydie watched him silently for several heartbeats before saying gently, "This is not a council meeting, Kuntza. Did you tell me the truth because I am Councilor Naydie?"

"I," he hesitated. "My family had a speaker only three generations ago. I try always not to lie, but especially never in the bilera."

Naydie smiled despite herself. Kuntza was older than she was, the pink fading from his hair, his first wife dead nearly two hundred years. For the first time since her appointment to the council, Naydie found herself wishing she was free of the responsibility. If she was just herself, she could tell Kuntza how wonderful his introductions had been. She could ask him what it was like to visit the Sky Fairy Tribe. Had he actually ridden on one of their windships? Oh, at least a dozen more questions. To do so now, however, might color her perception of the forthcoming proceedings.

"I should go." She paused, taking a final look at the council table, reminding herself how it looked from the gallery, then rose. "Stay," she put her hand on his shoulder, pressing him back onto the seat when he attempted to rise with her. "The bilera is a good place to think."

Kuntza watched her go, admiring her grace and youth. He had not forgotten what drove him from the company of his friends, but could not help wondering if, under different circumstances, he might not have tried to persuade her to remain there a little longer. Rubbing his face with both hands, he forced his thoughts back to the situation at hand. Treason. The worst kind of treason a Water Fairy could commit, using a council seat to further chaos and destruction. He dismissed the whisper of a thought that Cambrian might have been referring to Naydie. That was absolutely ridiculous.

Still in the dining room, Constance took another stab at the salad. It was oddly tangy. Oops—she quickly speared the sea grape that was trying to roll off her plate. She might even say pleasantly tangy, most likely the result of a vinaigrette dressing on the sea lettuce, dabberlock, and dulse salad. But not right now, when everyone else in the room was gloomily pushing their salad around their plates.

"Trust me," she said at last. "I was as upset as you are when Kuntza did not tell us what was going to happen at the border. But now…"

"You think we should trust him," interrupted Jennings, dropping his tiny salad fork beside his plate and producing the larger one he had accidentally hidden in his napkin earlier.

"To trust us," finished Rolf, his chin coming to rest on the palm of one hand. *Brown*, the other half of his brain sighed. *Why is my salad brown?*

"We hope you are right." Cambrian picked up the conversational thread. "Nevertheless, we really should at least try to prepare in case I have permanently upset him."

"Well said." Kuntza watched them all start guiltily. Shutting the door behind him, he resumed his seat. He did a double-take when he saw the size of the fork Jennings was using, then shrugged it off as relatively unimportant. For a valet, Jennings had never seemed to have a polished sense of etiquette. "It is our prac-tice to be cautious of cocheta. Sur-prise tells us much."

"Cocheta," Cambrian echoed. "Strangers?" he guessed. At Kuntza's nod, Cambrian felt a little foolish. "I have used that tactic myself," he had to admit. "During my investigations."

"What about when you were kneeling by that first lava tube?" Rolf asked, seizing the opportunity.

"I asked for them to come and bring us here."

"So they *were* watching us," Constance inserted before Rolf could launch a barrage of questions. Forking another mouthful of salad, she chewed and tried not to blush as she remembered how easily rattled she had been back at the border.

"Yes." Kuntza nodded. Deciding he had answered enough of their questions, he looked directly at Cambrian and posed one of his own. "Which three?"

"The last ones to leave the bilera." Cambrian could have sworn he saw a flicker of satisfaction in Kuntza's eyes.

"The new mem-bers." Kuntza scowled. "To

be app-oint-ed to the council is a great compliment of character."

"I would like to understand." Cambrian slid his plate aside and leaned forward, his best listening expression on his face.

"Ev-ery city has a council. Ev-ery council has a speak-er. On their right, sit the long-time mem-bers. On their left, the new ones." Kuntza scowled again. "They work to find the truth, some-times of liars or crimes, but most-ly of ex-per-iments. Scientific ex-per-iments."

"You said they have to be fairies of good character?" Constance inserted, wanting to get that cleared up.

"The best." Kuntza sidelined the image of Naydie that suddenly popped, unbidden, to the front of his mind. "They must show wis-dom, intell-i-gence, judge-ment." He slammed his fist down on the table, his anger getting the better of him again.

"And if fairies like that can be persuaded by Amber," Cambrian kept his tone as mellow and as conjectural as he could, "then we are even more suspect."

Kuntza had the grace to look embarrassed. "It would be easy to be-lieve," he conceded at last.

"Historians do not lie." Rolf stated firmly.

"Neither do council members." Cambrian fixed Rolf with a steady look that pierced the lad's bubble and let in a healthy dose of reality.

"Forgive me, Kuntza," Rolf was instantly contrite. "That was foolish of me."

Kuntza waved it away. "It is a night for mis-
takes." He looked around the circle. That was as
close to an apology as he was going to get in this
particular instance, for he considered his leaving
the dining room earlier to be an action of
remarkable self-control.

Chapter 15

Constance slept-ate her way through breakfast the next morning. If not for the page that Kuntza had sent to awaken them, she might have slept all…day? Night? She shook her head and took another nibble of the baked cod. Fish for breakfast. It was going to be a long, long winter.

Cambrian was having the same internal dilemma. Accustomed to the seeing the sun, basking in its warmth, automatically using it as an indicator of time of day, he might even have said the lack of it left him downright disgruntled. Except that he could not afford to be disgruntled right now. They were meeting with the council in less than half an hour and his bad moods were notoriously tenacious. Rare, thankfully, but difficult to overcome.

Rolf and Jennings, seated on the other side of the same table, were commiserating silently via yawns. Their mattresses, like every other mattress in Cachora, were stuffed with dried seawrack, a type of seaweed. The odor, while not overpowering, was unusual enough that they had difficulty falling asleep even after staying up late talking with Kuntza.

Kuntza arrived shortly after breakfast was served and stuck to smiling at the lass who brought in his plate. Even Constance looked out of sorts this morning. Hopefully, his news would cheer them up.

"Good news," he announced as soon as he was sure the door had slid securely shut behind the lass. "My cousin has agreed to visit Prince Isaac and send back a re-port as soon as she can." She was accompanied by her assistant, a trunkful of 'indispensable' surgical tools, and a letter of introduction from Prince Cambrian to the Wood Fairy Royal Family.

"Kuntza." Cambrian shook his head, at a loss for words. "Thank you," was the full sum of his eloquence. He felt one of the knots in his stomach shudder, then ease itself out of existence at the update. Kuntza's cousin, Cassidy, was a highly skilled Water Fairy reconstructive surgeon. Prince Isaac, of the Wood Fairy Tribe, had sustained life-threatening injuries during the pirate offensive. In fact, some of the whisperers at Regalis hinted that he would rather have lost his life than be doomed to a bed for the rest of his life.

Kuntza smiled back, comforted by the depth of emotion in Cambrian's voice. Spending an entire winter in the Deep Woods seemed to him an enormous thing to ask Cassidy to do; but if Prince Isaac had been injured in a battle with pirates, and would add his testimony that of Cambrian and the others, that would be three out of the four surface tribes bearing witness of the same thing. The council would be convinced that Amber and her supporters were liars and it would mete out a just punishment.

Constance was glad for the good news, naturally. However, she still had to look away when Kuntza paused to savor his cod. Taking a fourth piece of toasted 'bread,' she chewed it slowly. After eating so much at dinner last night, her now-empty stomach was registering serious protests against picky eaters, each noise duly stifled by clenching her abdominal muscles.

A mournful wail echoed down the hallway outside, causing the peculiar, upside down fork in the table's center to vibrate sympathetically.

"It is time." Kuntza wiped his mouth and fingers on his napkin and rose. "They are calling for the gallery," he added before Rolf could reconfirm what Kuntza had explained last night. "Today we have an aud-ience."

"At least we have a few days before Amber can accuse us." Cambrian grinned a little.

"Hmm." Constance paused to button Cambrian's jacket cuffs, then allowed him to help her with the collar of her jacket. "I would feel better if I did not know she would be in the gallery, plotting the whole time." She added that last softly, not wanting Jennings or Rolf to overhear.

"Pity they will not interview us separately," Rolf sighed. Ever since Kuntza mentioned the word 'library' last night, Rolf had found thinking of anything else terribly difficult.

"Perhaps they will work you over first." Jennings threw his wadded-up napkin at Rolf, hitting him lightly on the shoulder. His job was pretty straightforward. During the council meetings, keep an eye on the gallery. Between council meetings, keep an eye on Rolf. What Jennings wanted to know was who was going keep an eye on *him*? This was new territory for him, too, after all. He forked a final bit of cod into his mouth. At least the food was good.

Their little group arrived at the bilera just in time for the scholar on duty to wave them over to where they stood the day before. Jennings ducked past them and hurried up to the top row of the gallery. All he could see were backs of heads at the moment, but he figured once things got started, he would be in good shape.

The council members were the last to enter the room, their ceremonial robes swishing softly the only sound as they took their seats. The speaker looked steadily at the witnesses before him while he waited for his fellow members to finish arranging themselves, or more accurately, their robes.

"Guests of the bilera," he began when the chamber had fallen silent. "We are pleased that you have chosen to join us today for this most important truth seeking session." Fully aware that Amber was just arriving, two overgrown men-fairies in tow, he warned, "We ask only that you refrain from disrupting or otherwise disturbing the proceedings." His eyes traveled over the gallery, passed lightly over an oddly demure-looking Amber, and landed on the scholar to his far right. At his nod, the scholar lightly rapped his knuckles against the clamshell gong. The meeting had begun.

"Historian Rolf Warner, of the Silver Fairy Tribe." The stout councilmember on the speaker's far left pretended to consult the pages before him. "Tell us how your tribe is governed."

Rolf shuffled through his thoughts for a moment, his education having been somewhat more thorough than the average Silver Fairy's due to his close relation to the crown.

"The Silver Fairy Tribe is primarily governed by the king and queen, with a citizen's council to advise them and regional judges to interpret the laws."

Neither Rolf nor Jennings saw how displeased Amber was when he answered so well. She had assumed that, as the youngest, he would be the easiest mark, and instructed her friends on the council accordingly. But Naydie, watching Amber from under her fringe of uselessly long lashes, saw and took note, it striking her as a peculiar reaction.

"Is it not true," the councilmember was drawing on Amber's official testimony, "that members of your tribe recently tried to rebel against this government and were ruthlessly put down?"

Rolf's jaw dropped. A laugh might have escaped him if the councilor's glare had not frozen it in his throat.

"You speak of Bullierd's rebellion." It was not a question and Rolf did not wait for him to answer. "You speak of a group of greedy cutthroats who tried to remove my," he swallowed *grandfather*, "king and replace him with a crowned puppet." His professor of orations would have been proud to see Rolf's chin come up as he spoke, his shoulders already thrown back and voice ringing through the bilera. "Bullierd's rebellion was successfully defeated, it is true. Defeated with the help of his own son, Edward Bullierd, who has since accepted the title of King's Champion, the title his father spurned." Unintentionally, Rolf took a step forward. "King Hugh Lawson also played a part in defeating Bullierd, eschewing his offer to become a puppet, then swearing an oath to defend the Silver Fairy Tribe with his every breath."

Naydie stared, wide-eyed, at the passionate youth. Was this fierce loyalty a trait common among surface fairies? Ardor was almost a thing of the past here in her sedate, underwater world. It could not be quantified, after all. Amber looked at least as excited as Rolf. Actually, it was more than that. In Naydie's opinion, Amber looked angry.

Kuntza's nails dug deeper into his arms as he waited with the others for the council to respond to Rolf's fervent testimony.

"Thank you." The speaker intervened when he thought the silence had stretched out thin enough. "We may call on you for further testimony later."

Rolf acknowledged the speaker with a stiff bow, barely inclining his shoulders to the ground before coming ramrod straight again.

"Admiral Kimberlite." The speaker called.

Constance moved forward, her lips twitching at the completely irrelevant thought that she was now Constance Bijou, or would be once she retired.

"You admit to having killed Count Bullierd."

Her smile vanished. "Count *Edward* Bullierd is alive and well. I dueled his father and survived, yes. The alternative was not at all acceptable to me."

"Do you mean to say that," the speaker tripped over the incorrect title and settled on, "Bullierd would have killed you?"

"He was an outlaw, banished by his own tribe. And yes, he did his best to do just that," she replied tightly. "However, had I not been there, I am confident he would have been satisfied to slay some blood member of the Sky Fairy Royal Family." A mental image of Ian holding Cambrian back sprang to mind. Both she and Ian had sworn to protect the royal family whatever the cost. She had been unable to do so when Cambrian dueled Bane, and was grateful that this recent incident had turned out the way it did.

"Can you prove what you say?" It was the only other question the speaker could think of.

Being responsible for someone else's death was surely punishment enough for the crime; assuming that other fairy had, in actuality, refused to desist otherwise.

Constance hesitated. "I can." Looking at Kuntza, she raised an eyebrow. When he nodded, she removed her jacket and handed it to Cambrian. Unbuttoning her left shirt sleeve, she lifted it to above her elbow, so that the blade-width scar was visible. A few more days of treatment and even that would be gone. "A few inches to his left and I would have been done for." Feeling vulnerable and angry at the same time, she re-buttoned her sleeve. At Cambrian's insistence, she allowed him to help her back into her jacket.

Rolf used that time to add his testimony. "I witnessed the last of the duel." Despite his best efforts, he could feel his stomach starting to turn at the memory. "The outlaw missed her heart only because she moved in time, causing him to bury his sword in her arm up to the hilt."

"Thank you for explaining." The speaker was experiencing his own bout of queasiness. Exercising his right as speaker, he continued, "Admiral Kimberlite, we have no duels here. Please remember that." He felt torn between their testimonies and the story Amber told, which had spent weeks settling itself firmly in his mind. There would have to be an investigation, of course, but since Amber was already under discreet surveillance, the natural result of her complicated status as a guest-advena, he was not overly concerned.

Naydie witnessed the baleful expression on Amber's face, for the heartbeat that it was visible, and was reasonably certain that Amber was one who would cavalierly ignore the speaker's understated warning.

"Prince Cambrian." The middle-aged councilor to Naydie's left broke the silence. "Please explain to us why you have come here."

Cambrian, feeling more than ever the weight of Fairydom on his shoulders, began his answer with what he hoped was a charming smile.

"We have come for a number of reasons." He stepped forward so that he was slightly out of line with the others. In a way, even though Rolf was a Silver Fairy, Cambrian was the leader of their group. "First and foremost, we have come to answer questions that Kuntza did not have time to ask before winter set in." That was true, but it also sounded good. They wanted to help the Water Fairies however they could, even at great personal sacrifice. "Secondly, and no less importantly," he focused his energy on eye-contact with the councilors to his left and the speaker, "it is our understanding that we have encroached on territory that rightfully belongs to the Water Fairies." A slight exaggeration—or an excellent opportunity for them to contradict him and remove that cloud from the horizon. "For that we apologize." He tipped his head to the council, waiting hopefully.

"The boundaries of our tribe have been lost to history by your tribe," the speaker inserted. "As they should have."

Cambrian kept smiling. He was going to have to ask Kuntza later, though, whether he won that point or not.

"The surface tribes are still guilty of sending their spies among us." This came from a thin, reed-like fairy to the speaker's left. Coincidentally, his voice was rather thin and reedy as well. "Or did you think we would be so easily fooled?"

Constance's heart constricted painfully. Every time a windship went down over the West Sea, the fleets tried to locate it. Just finding the wreckage would be enough to convince them that there were no survivors scanning the skies for rescue. How many times had the windships inexplicably disappeared, without leaving so much as a shred of sail for a clue? Stepping slowly forward, until she was even with Cambrian, she took a deep breath.

"These whom you call spies," she began. "One group arrived two hundred years ago, and claimed they were from a windship called the *Farren*."

The thin councilor slammed his palm against the table. It hurt, but Amber had been emphatic in her insistence that such actions would incite the gallery to action.

"You admit it!"

"No!" Constance's answer cut his accusation off at the knees. "I spent months searching the skies and shoals for that windship. Months of dying inside while I hoped to find survivors." Her tone was dangerously calm when she addressed the speaker next. "I should very much like to know what happened to them."

The speaker was at a loss as to how he should answer her. It was common practice to detain all who wandered into Water Fairy territory, especially those found on their small, island hunting grounds; but he was not foolish enough to believe that she would take that answer calmly.

Kuntza solved the problem by turning to face Constance. Waiting until she finally turned from the speaker to him, he answered for his tribe.

"We kept them."

Constance blinked back the tears as best as she could. Hundreds, perhaps thousands of survivors, kept from their families and friends by an irrational fear of...of what? What were the Water Fairies so afraid of, anyway? The tears clogged her throat so that she could not speak.

"We strongly desire to negotiate their release." Cambrian, hurting as much for Constance as for the captives, spoke quietly.

"Speaking for the Silver Fairy Tribe," Rolf came up even with them, "we feel the same way." His approach having brought him right up next to Constance's left side, he gave her near hand a quick squeeze of support.

Brief as his gesture was, it was not lost on the council. The speaker actually felt a tinge of guilt when he thought of the dozen or more supposed spies he personally had interviewed and decided to detain. This was not going the way he had expected. Perhaps that was why he failed to notice the faint whispering in the gallery and did not call them to order.

"Your request has been noted." Naydie met Constance's gaze directly. "It will be considered."

What might have sounded like empty words from someone else filled Constance with optimism. She liked what she saw when she looked at Naydie, and not just because of her orderly appearance. Self-confidence radiated from the woman-fairy like warmth from the sun. Satisfied, Constance stepped back. She smiled when Rolf came with her, leaving Cambrian where he had started, waiting for the council's questions.

Kuntza spent the next two hours watching as the newer council members glanced furtively in Amber's direction, taking her half-nods and headshakes and translating them into rapid-fire accusations or word traps. He found it surprisingly amusing when his guests began functioning as a team to counter the attacks, deferring each to the other as the council members tried and failed to confuse or anger them. Cambrian neatly intercepted and deflected all questions aimed at defaming the royal families. Rolf astutely intervened when a point of history came into question, and wisely yielded to Constance on the finer points of military procedure. They all understood the Water Fairies were coming from the background of nearly a score of millennia on their own, receiving sporadic snippets of information from the 'spies" who had the misfortune to fall into their hands.

The council tried twice to object to their tactic, stating that they wanted answers from the fairy they were addressing. The trio held their ground, however, insisting that they were deferring to each other in the interest of providing the best and most correct answer. The gallery chuckled at that, and scowling a little, the council subsided. Finally, the clamshell gong rang twice, signaling mid-day recess.

Jennings stayed where he was, cursing his poor choice of seating as every other fairy in the back row rose to leave. He could not see beyond arm's length in the crush. Sure enough, Amber was nowhere in the bilera by the time the crowd cleared. Disappointed, he kept his eyes down while he made his way, hovering just above the stairs, towards his friends. If it had been otherwise, he would never have noticed the tiny slip of paper on the row where Amber had been seated with her lads.

Kuntza, exhausted from the mental exercise of weighing how every answer might be interpreted, decided it was time for them to leave the public area.

"If all is well," he began once Jennings had reached them, "our lunch waits for us."

The shared condition of reflection left them all quite sober as they followed Kuntza from the bilera. Except for Cambrian, who fell easily into his old role of witty observer, remarking on this as they passed it or that cluster of gems the woman-fairy near the front had been wearing—six or seven stunning rubies, each as large as a tachinid egg.

Constance, recognizing the act from a previous adventure, took it for what it was and winked at Rolf when he shot her a puzzled look. Cambrian's cheerful patter occasionally required a response from one of them and carried them from the bilera to their dining room without pause.

Constance, feeling a bit guilty for letting Cambrian bear the whole burden of conversation, made a point of remarking on their meal.

"Mmmm," she inhaled deeply as soon as she entered their dining room. "Is that…" It was! The grilled shrimp coiled in the center of the table was dripping with butter! "But where do you get it from?" she asked Kuntza without thinking.

Kuntza pulled her chair out for her, inviting her to be seated. The servers were nearly done placing the trays of jackfruit bread and would be gone in a moment. He was not sure what she was talking about, he just assumed that it was better discussed in private. Even though the servers *probably* did not know the surface tongue, until things were settled with the council it was wiser to assume otherwise.

"Where do we get what?" he asked after checking the door.

"Butter," Jennings answered for her, already spreading a liberal amount on a piece of the bread.

Kuntza smiled at Jennings' enthusiasm in devouring the bread. "Sometimes the windship surv-ivors had domes-tica-ted ani-mals and seeds with them." He took care to speak of them as survivors instead of spies.

"And you have developed the herds here, underwater?" Cambrian chose to focus on the practical side of the situation. "Astonishing."

"Yes." Constance did her best to smile at Kuntza.

"They feed on seaweed," Kuntza smiled back, grateful for their effort at pleasantries. "Rinsed, of course."

"Of course. What are these other dishes?" Constance asked, indicating the large silver bowl of…something. Anything to change the subject.

"Jack-fruit." Kuntza used one hand to draw the steam from the bowl towards him. "Boiled with garlic," he identified easily. "On-ion…and ses-ame oil." Taking up the heavy knife and fork the servers left near the shrimp, he proceeded to carve. "The jack-fruit is spread on the plate," he paused long enough for Constance to put a small helping on her plate, "with shrimp on top." As the others helped themselves to the jackfruit, Kuntza continued carving the shrimp until they were all served. Since Constance had already seen the need and transferred a not-quite-Jennings' size helping of jackfruit on his plate, Kuntza only had to add a piping hot cut of shrimp. Taking a nibble of the shrimp, his smile widened. "Lem-on!"

The shrimp was delectable and made eating the unfamiliar jackfruit easier. The diced, boiled jackfruit was reminiscent of rice, with a different texture. None of them had quite gotten used to it before they finished, but they could all agree that it was a satisfying meal.

"My cousins, Daniel and Steven, will never believe me when I tell them about this jackfruit," Rolf chuckled as he chased the last of his down with his fork and a slice of bread.

Chapter 16

"Kuntza," Constance hated herself for asking a third time, "are you *sure* this is alright?" She dearly regretted leaving her sword in her quarters, but as Kuntza pointed out, survivors—advena— were not permitted to carry weapons. The note Jennings spotted in the bilera contained a vague reference to Amber meeting with the advena during lunch that day, and Constance's suspicions had instantly gone on high alert. So their plan was to visit the survivors with the hope of catching Amber in the act of something criminal, but at the very least, they had to get back in time for the afternoon council meeting. And even though Kuntza had procured a set of plain workwear for her from somewhere, hats were not worn here, so there was a chance that she and her blue hair could be spotted before they reached the advena market.

"This is with-in my role as truth seeker," Kuntza reminded her. "Besides, the note implied Amber has supp-ort among the surv-ivors." Finding evidence that Amber was conspiring with survivors against his tribe would suit Kuntza fine. He would take any leverage he could get to convince the council that it was time to rejoin Fairydom.

Constance, frustrated at being given word-for-word the same answer as the two previous times, lapsed into silence. She had been startled to learn that there were communities of survivors scattered around the tiny islands of the sea, complete with herds of domesticated animals, gardens, and markets. They were not allowed buildings on the surface, which explained why they were able to hide from the routine patrols and merchant vessels. This being market day in Cachora, she hoped to blend in. Her pulse quickened when she realized that the faint sounds she was hearing was the clamor of voices hawking their wares.

"Carrots! Get azenario here!" Sang out one vendor from his stall. Like all the advena gathered there, he used the common surface tongue and the Margua word so he could be sure folks knew where to find what they were looking for.

"Butter!" cried another, a wiry-looking fellow with green hair and brown eyes. "Gurina for sale."

The fellows running the stalls just down the row from him were offering milk and cheese at the top of their lungs, and looked quite a bit like him, probably a family resemblance. The rest of the stalls in that section were much the same, their counters crowded with a limited variety of vegetables.

"Hello."

Constance turned towards the sound of the one soothing voice in the whole, jam-packed cavern. Two huge, hazel eyes stared up at her out from under thick blue hair.

"Hello." She answered without thinking.

"Are you new from the surface?" the girl-fairy asked.

"I…guess so." Constance ordered up a smile. "Why do you ask?" *And why do you look so familiar?*

"I am Neska, and my grandfather would like to meet you."

Constance found herself being led through the jumble of stalls, carts, and outlying tents to one particularly plain tent. She hesitated at the entrance to the tent, her fingers slipping out of Neska's grasp when the girl-fairy darted inside.

"Do we have time?" she asked, looking over her shoulder at Kuntza.

"Very little," he answered, frowning at the pocket watch he had brought along for just this reason. The lunch period was nearly over.

Constance ducked under the tent flap. There were no lightning globes here, only the oil lanterns that she had grown up with, so she paused to let her eyes adjust.

"Welcome."

A deep voice spoke to her from the far left, prompting her to turn towards it, fists clenched. It could be a trap, a ploy of Amber's to have her kidnapped so as to cast the others in a suspicious shadow. In an enclosed area like this, like most of the underwater world, flying could do more harm than good.

"Welcome," the voice repeated. A shadow

moved, turning up the wick on the lantern next to it. In the somewhat brighter light, an older man-fairy became visible, his faded blue beard touching his knees in his seated position. "You are new to this world," he observed. "Your face still carries the sun's blush. Please, sit and talk with me. Tell me," he leaned forward, "about my world." Advena farmers had tan skin, also, but she was no farmer. Her posture, her stance…no, he felt certain she was fresh off a military windship.

Constance's eyes widened in disbelief. "Uncle Wynston?"

The old man-fairy came slowly to his feet. "Who calls me uncle?"

"The eldest daughter of Alexander Kimberlite." Constance wanted to run to him as she had whenever he came to visit, tireless wanderer that he was. But after two hundred years apart, they both needed a moment.

Kuntza, who had turned to a nearby tent to keep himself occupied, was wishing he had gone into the tent with Constance. He was one Water Fairy among the dozens who routinely shopped in this market. In fact, the vast majority of the fairies present today were of mixed heritage, so silver, blue, green, brown, and pink heads dotted the market. What was it about the silver head to his left that was causing his stomach muscles to contract painfully?

"You have them?" asked Naydie's voice from his left.

Kuntza, caught in the act of holding up a comforter for inspection, continued looking it over from left to right for no better reason than that it was casual. His head kept moving, a regrettable course of action as the surprisingly familiar voice had come from his left. From roughly the same vicinity as the silver head that had been worrying him, which he now feared was Amber. What was she up to? Why was Naydie here?

"She is in the tent with Wynston, the book trader," Amber nodded across the narrow track that separated the rows of vendors. The advena (which Amber would have defined as any surface fairy besides herself) were allowed to keep the books they brought with them, but the law prevented them from making any more. As a result, a captain's log had once been traded for a week's supply of garlic. "And has been for some time." Amber deliberately implied a longer time than was actually the case. Five minutes could be a lifetime, under the right circumstances. Like while planning the advena's mass escape, a crime with severe consequences. Amber would have happily dispatched Constance herself, but this strategy was tidier. It would also serve to distract the local authorities, a fact Amber planned to use to her own advantage.

Naydie watched the back of Kuntza's head with detachment. Her plans for lunch had been interrupted and she was not happy about it. In fact, she was miffed. During her service as a tribal councilor—a position of enormous trust— she had always been privy to sensitive information, given assignments that required discretion and sensitivity. And yet here was Kuntza, loitering about the market between sessions in the bilera as if he had nothing better to do. Whatever he was *really* doing, he should have trusted her. Now she was left with no option but to suspect him of collusion in the plot Amber claimed to have uncovered.

"Kuntza." Naydie saw his shoulders rise and fall with what she assumed was a deep breath, then finally he turned to face her. "Did you think we would not find out?" She switched to Margua because her distrust of Amber outweighed her annoyance with Kuntza. Not that she could afford to ignore Amber's accusation that Constance was plotting to return the advena to the surface, ludicrous as it seemed in light of the stated diplomatic mission. A revolt like that would wreak havoc throughout their realm. It would also inevitably result in the surface tribes being aware of the Water Fairy Tribe again.

"Or are you here to catch the conspirators?" Naydie continued when Kuntza did not speak, a trace amount of sarcasm seeping into her tone.

Kuntza took a short step forward, bringing himself within arm's reach of Naydie. Illogically, she looked even more beautiful to him when she was upset than she had before, the color in her cheeks and spark in her eyes befuddling him terribly.

"I am here as a truth seeker," he answered tersely.

"With the admiral?" Naydie took a step forward as well. This was ridiculous. She was here as a councilor, that was all. She could count the chocolate brown specks in Kuntza's eyes some other time. Understandably, that thought brought the color even higher into her cheeks.

Kuntza paused to stare. The picture Naydie was presenting reminded him of Constance with Cambrian, a completely absurd comparison.

"Yes." His tone was anything but neutral. "With the admiral, princess by marriage of the Sky Fairy Tribe. A woman-fairy possessed of integrity of character and a valiant heart." He searched Naydie's eyes for betrayal to her oath as a councilor. Finding none, he dared continue. "If you are here at her behest," he indicated Amber with a barely perceptible nod of his head, "so are we, following a clue she left in the bilera."

Amber's smugness was fading quickly. She had learned a maximum of twenty words of Margua in her months underwater, but she knew anger when she saw it. And she was not seeing it. Her plan was going awry. By now they should have been arguing.

Inside the tent, Constance was just finishing explaining how she had come to be there when Neska reappeared from the kitchen, empty-handed. Constance was puzzled but not displeased. If they were out of the sweets Neska had been sent for, it was just as well. She really did not have time to sit and socialize right now, despite her uncle's urging.

"Neska, what is it?" Uncle Wynston frowned.

"Officers."

"Where?"

Constance looked sharply at her uncle. Had she brought trouble to them?

"They surround our tent," Neska replied succinctly.

"Here," Wynston held out his arms to his granddaughter. "It will be alright," he assured her with a hug. His efforts, early on in his captivity, to escape to the surface, made him suspect in the eyes of every officer underwater. The faintest whiff of a conspiracy brought them round to collect the 'known troublemakers.' And unfortunately they were not in Sikya, the region he usually traded in. The officers there were willing to give him the benefit of the doubt after over a hundred years of conformity.

"What do you sell here?" Constance asked abruptly. "And for how much?"

"I sell nothing," he answered, confused. "I trade books."

"Then trade one to me. Anything." She was reaching for her money pocket when she remembered that she was in borrowed clothes. Angry words boiled to the top of her mind, but she forced them down again. Getting angry was an early form of surrender.

"Here," he pressed a book into her hands, a thin volume of poetry that he snatched up off the nearest stack. "No, please," he took her arm and escorted her towards the tent flap. "Find me later," he muttered under his breath, determined to get her out of his tent before the trouble started. "Accept it as a gift from a poor, wandering book trader," he said jovially.

Constance exited the tent and came face to face with a beautifully flushed Naydie. Looking sideways at Kuntza, whom Constance knew to be a widower, she was astonished to find him exhibiting similar symptoms.

"Bring them." Naydie stepped back, putting one hand on Kuntza's arm and drawing him away before he could attempt to intervene on Constance's behalf. To her surprise, the book trader did something similar with Constance, who looked mad enough to fight. An oddly peaceful gesture for two fairies accused of treason. "Leave the child." Naydie looked at the frightened expression on the girl-fairy's face and sighed inwardly. Most said that frightened advena were the most trustworthy. Having been raised in one of the few families to ever hire advena to work in their house, Naydie disagreed from the depths of her heart.

"Have you broken our laws?" Naydie asked the girl-fairy gently. As expected, the thick pigtails bounced from side to side with the energy of her denying headshakes. "Then do not be afraid." Putting her hand on the girl-fairy's shoulder, Naydie looked at the merchant from the blanket tent. "Do you know him?" she asked the girl-fairy, nodding at the plump man-fairy across the aisle. "Would you be safe with him?"

Neska nodded vigorously.

"Good. Then stay with him until the book trader returns."

"You promise?" Neska asked sweetly in Margua.

Naydie's heart twisted painfully when she had to hesitate. Her plan at the moment was simply to question Constance and the book trader. However, the fact that he was so far from his usual trading route, his history of attempted escapes, added to the admittedly questionable accusation…it might all prove a little too coincidental for the council.

Kuntza stepped forward from where he had been forgotten, touched by Naydie's obvious concern for the child.

"I do." Together with Naydie, Kuntza watched Neska scurry across the aisle to where the blanket merchant greeted her like an old friend. Kuntza resolved even more firmly to keep his promise to the child-fairy and return the book trader to her. "Now." He turned to face Naydie. "What is this all about?"

"Why should I tell you?" Naydie asked spiritedly. "You are only a truth seeker; not even a council member in your own region."

Kuntza looked away in exasperation, then looked in the other direction. Finally, he looked directly over Naydie's head.

"Amber is gone," he announced quietly.

Naydie looked everywhere he had and even flew up a few flaps to be sure.

"But why? And where did she go?" Naydie asked as she dropped back to the ground.

"Why should I tell you?" Kuntza teased, folding his arms across his chest. "You are not even an advena." Her pout was adorable, especially since it was so short-lived. "Wait." He put one hand lightly on her shoulder when she started to turn away. "I am of the Botere clan," he reminded her.

His clan was the oldest and most powerful clan in the tribe, their sovereignty acknowledged by each of the six regions that rippled out from Cachora. Of course, part of the reason others supported his clan willingly was that they ruled with an open hand, preferring to live quietly in their libraries and laboratories. Also, they consulted the other regions on decisions that would impact the entire tribe. Decisions like whether or not to resume diplomatic relations with the surface tribes. He found it quite fitting, in a way. His ancestor played a key role in severing diplomatic ties with the rest of Fairydom, deeming them violent and ignorant, unfit companions. And now, Kuntza was doing his best to reconnect his tribe to the surface world.

Naydie wilted a little. Then, looking around at the subdued marketplace, filled with wondering, staring, and *listening* advena, she slipped her arm through Kuntza's. It was time to get back to the bilera, anyway.

"Come." Since they could not possibly draw any more attention to themselves, they wasted no time trying to act as though nothing was wrong. "Things have been…odd ever since Amber's arrival." Briefly, she summarized the events she had noted, like finding one of Amber's surface cohorts snooping around the hall where the lightning chamber was hidden. "Knowledge of the lightning chambers is strictly guarded and absolutely forbidden to be made known to the advena."

"For their own safety," Kuntza agreed, and immediately felt a twinge of guilt. When he taught the surface fairies to build rudimentary lightning machines, he had not only broken that law, he had disproved the reasoning behind it. Surface fairies were curiously ignorant of the properties of lightning, relying on the sun as they did. However, their histories and medical advancements convinced him they were perfectly capable of learning about lightning just as his tribe had.

"So naturally she was restricted from bringing any more fairies here from the surface," Naydie went on, oblivious to the side track Kuntza's train of thought had taken in the middle of her explanation. "Except that by then, the damage was done."

Kuntza mentally regrouped. "Who else knows about this?" He caught the part about *damage*, and given that it was Amber they were speaking of, he skipped past asking Naydie to repeat herself in favor of locating a pre-laid plan to stop her. He was already aware of the efforts to cut Amber off from her surface support.

"No one." Naydie blinked up at him when he stopped and pulled her into an alcove of the hallway they had taken. "I had no concrete evidence," she protested when he seemed about to chasten her for not having Amber restrained sooner.

Kuntza shut his mouth and eyes. "No," he agreed, laughing at himself for not listening to her the first time she explained. His eyes popped open. "Quickly. Take me to Constance."

Since it was just the two of them, they were able to slip through a series of narrow shortcuts, Naydie leading the way.

"Halt!" Kuntza landed between the guards and…the bilera? Why were they bringing prisoners straight to the bilera?

"Continue," Naydie countermanded him. Tugging on his arm, she led him into the temporarily empty chamber. "This is the last place anyone will look for us," she shrugged. "At least until the council returns." Hopefully that would be enough time to figure out exactly what was going on.

"And the guards?" Kuntza was flabbergasted at this turn of events.

"Friends." Naydie smiled at them. "We worked together a few years ago to uncover a plot to…oh, never mind. I trust them, that is the point."

"Kuntza?" Constance had to stand on her tiptoes to see them over the fairly solid wall of Water Fairy guards surrounding her. "A little help?"

"You never ask me for help," Cambrian objected, he and Rolf entering the chamber with Jennings. Eying the guards, he reflected that he would probably ask for Kuntza's help, too, under those circumstances. "I guess things did not go as planned." They had agreed to rendezvous at the bilera early to discuss what Kuntza and Constance had found.

"Save your ban-ter," Kuntza ordered crisply in their tongue. He was pleased when, at Naydie's nod, the guards withdrew, forming up in one of the bilera's many shadows. "We have perhaps half an hour be-fore the council meeting resumes."

"Amber is missing."

Cambrian and the others looked at Naydie in surprise.

"Who?" Wynston met their looks when they turned to him and saw confusion to match his own.

"Uncle Wynston," Constance began, "Amber

is a dangerous woman-fairy of the Silver Tribe.
She is fearless and capable of doing anything she
thinks will further her goal of dominating
Fairydom."

Wynston nodded briskly. "Then we must stop
her."

"Stop her from doing what?" Cambrian asked,
looking back and forth between Kuntza and
Constance. He knew he should have been the one
to go with Kuntza.

"Dominating." Kuntza looked at Naydie.
"She knows of the lightning chamber, you said?"

All color drained from Naydie's face, so that
she looked like a chalk drawing. Her terror was
answer enough.

"Amber may be trying to steal lightning for
herself." Kuntza glossed over the how and where
of it. "Naydie," he took her small, cold hands in
his large ones. "There is still time. A swiftly-
made search could still stop her in time."

"While you do what?" The words were out
before Naydie knew she was going to speak them.
"It will take hours to search Cachora, even with
every available guard. She might have left."

"Gone to the surface for re-inforce-ments?"
Kuntza suggested, knowing in his heart that was
not the case. The rest stop he and his friends had
enjoyed on the way down from the surface was
also a place to stop advena who were trying to
escape. Amber was crazy, not stupid. She would
be stopped and turned around, by force if

necessary, if she tried to return to the surface. Her temporary freedom to come and go as she pleased, granted mostly out of sympathy for her initially wounded state, was terminated weeks ago. Kuntza should know. He had signed the papers restricting her to travel below the surface himself.

"You know she will not do that," Naydie deduced, watching him closely. "You know more than you have revealed."

"I spent more time with the pi-rates than any other Water Fairy." Kuntza knew he was still holding her hands and had no intention of releasing them.

"You knew all along." Cambrian eased himself into the nearest chair, the shock having taken most of the stiffening out of his knees.

"I had bits of infor-mation only," Kuntza shook his head. He retained his light hold on Naydie's hands even as he turned a little more towards Cambrian and the others. "They spoke deceit-fully of their role on the surface, telling tales of opp-ression and blood-shed. Alas, I learned this too late."

Constance collapsed into the seat next to Cambrian when her brain caught up with what Kuntza was saying. "You told them about lightning machines." Her mind began following two trains of thought simultaneously: The pirates know about lightning machines. *He showed us the lightning machines, too.* They are savages.

He thought he knew them. Pirates with lightning machines would be unstoppable. All of Fairydom would fall to them. The pirates were finally going to win…because Amber would have control of lightning.

"I told them." Kuntza agreed guiltily.

"But she learned more here," Naydie inserted quickly. "Three council members have proven themselves false."

Chapter 17

"Councilor!" The speaker, returning early from his lunch, stared in dismay. "You forget yourself." The proper procedure for accusing councilors of wrongdoing was to bring the evidence to the speaker. Not to mention the impropriety of holding hands in the bilera with someone involved in an active proceeding!

"Your pardon, speaker." Naydie tipped her head humbly towards him and finally succeeded in retrieving her hands. Not that she had been trying very hard until the speaker flew in. "I request permission to explain myself."

"No time for that," Kuntza intervened. Lifting the collar of his shirt, he revealed his clan's emblem. The startled expression on the speaker's face exceeded his former surprise. "A situ-ation has dev-el-oped around the advena Amber."

Constance noticed her uncle flinch at the word *advena* and decided she did not like the word, either.

"Post guards at the exit tunnels and sig-nal ahead to the train oper-ators that she has deadly intent." Kuntza waited just until the speaker moved to obey, then turned to Naydie. Recapturing her soft hands, he instructed her, "Search her quar-ters. There may be some scrap of evi-dence to tell us her plans."

"And her friends?" Naydie knew that some of the younger, richer men-fairies had taken to including Amber in their activities.

"Yes, but carefully," Kuntza admonished her. "To be kind is no crime." He realized it was unlikely that Amber would be friendly with anyone she could not use, but there was still hope that she was just duping them.

Naydie smiled, nodded, and left with the group of guards she called friends. She made eye contact with Constance and Jennings as she left, pleading silently with them to protect Kuntza from the guilt he displayed earlier. Because he was of the Botere clan, it was unclear as to whether he had broken the law against teaching advena about lightning or not. They were all in danger now, thanks to Amber and what she had learned about lightning. There would be time enough later to worry about the legal repercussions of his decision to reveal the lightning machines. In fact, Naydie resolved that if they all survived this, she was going to give Kuntza a piece of her mind—and the large chunk of her heart he had claimed with his expressive eyes—but until then, she saw no recourse save sharing as much of the current risk as she could with him.

"Kuntza." Rolf, recognizing the signs of romance and guilt flaring up all around him, spoke before the others could. Allowing Kuntza to take an active role in undoing any damage he had caused was the surest means of allaying his guilt. Letting him do it alone was out of the question. "My tribe failed to stop her. I will not rest until Fairydom is beyond her reach."

Constance swallowed hard, moved by Rolf's short, but effective speech. Action was the word, then.

"So, are you some sort of prince?" Jennings grinned unrepentantly back at Kuntza's reproachful glare. After they reached Regalis, Jennings had spent quite a bit of time with Kuntza, fetching this or that, trying to explain colloquialisms along the way—enough time to have reached his own conclusions about the mysterious truth seeker.

"Not a prince." Kuntza, faced with the knowing smiles of the others, surrendered. "But a keeper of the tribe's honor and guar-dian of her safe-ty," he cast about for the right word, then finally settled on the Margua term. "A zaldun." He shared those responsibilities with the rest of his tribesfairies, but understood that his family publicly accepted that role eons ago.

Cambrian bowed from the waist, acknowledging his peer.

"How shall we proceed?" Constance, defaulting to military procedure, effectively gave Kuntza command of the situation.

"While the others seek to catch her esc-aping or plot-ting with friends, I fear the worst." Kuntza lifted off. "Come. We will procure wea-pons first and meet outside their dining room. Also gloves, if you have them." Anticipating

Jennings' question, he explained, "The dining room is the closest point to each of our quar-ters." Or at least, the closest one they could all find on their own.

Constance was still buckling her sword belt when she and Cambrian joined Rolf and Jennings in the hallway outside the dining room. It had taken her a few minutes to find the soft, kid gloves that were a requisite piece of her dress uniform, so now she was out of breath from hurrying to make up the time. But Kuntza was nowhere to be seen. As it turned out, they heard him first, in the form of a rhythmic clanking sound. When he came around the corner, their chins dropped in unison.

Kuntza was sheathed in armor, from his feet to the crown of his head, where he wore a mask currently pushed up off his face. As he walked towards them, they saw leather peeking through the joint connections of his armor, while what looked like a high, silk collar came a few inches up from his breastplate. When he was still several twigs away from the group, he brought his right arm up and forward, sending a length of highly flexible, razor-sharp steel snaking out in the air before him. As soon as it was fully extended, Kuntza snapped the suge, or metal whip, back towards him. For demonstration purposes, he allowed it to contact the bone serving table beside him, slicing off a fragment. Before the fragment could hit the floor, he had reversed the whip's direction. The weighted end of the whip struck the fragment, shattering it. Re-coiling the suge, Kuntza held it up for them to see.

"We value discipline, and mas-tery of the suge demands it." He looked at their unshielded bodies and warned, "Our enemies will use these. You must work in pairs, so your risk will be less."

Jennings clamped one hand on Rolf's shoulder, claiming him as his partner. He was more than fond of the lad, and felt a keen responsibility for his safety. No more so than Constance or Cambrian, but Jennings expected they were better off watching each other's backs.

That left Uncle Wynston, as Constance called him, as a loose end. He grinned at Kuntza and gripped his heavy walking staff, which was made of carved bone, a little tighter. He had seen a suge before and was looking forward to finally testing the defensive moves he had been practicing for so long.

Kuntza, noting Wynston's heavily muscled torso and the height of his staff, nodded his agreement. They would fight together. His own weapon hanging within easy reach on his belt, Kuntza took one of Constance's gloves from her and examined it.

"You can fight wearing this?" he asked, holding up the thin article.

"Yes," she affirmed.

"It is too thin." Handing it back, he showed her the hilt of his suge. "Though the blade is made of met-al, the hilt is thick-ly coated with the sap of the hevea tree, to pro-tect from the smallest light-ning wires." He frowned. "We must go to the light-ning chamber," he explained. "If Amber wish-es to rule with light-ning, she must con-trol that."

In turn Constance and the others showed him their grips, each of which were wrapped with thick leather.

"Better," Kuntza agreed. At any rate, it was the best they could do. The heavy leather gloves that waited on a lightning chamber table for the workers would never do for sword fighting. And against a suge, one might as well be barehanded as wearing even those gloves. They all followed when Kuntza moved off.

"What kind of security do you have there?" Cambrian asked, studying the back plate on Kuntza's armor uneasily. He would not know himself without his wings. "Guards, locks?" The tunnels were strangely empty, a fact he attributed to the Speaker. Once he had gotten over his surprise, there was no telling what precautionary measures the Speaker might order. An excellent idea, too. It would prevent Amber from taking hostages.

Kuntza shook his head. "Light-ning chambers are guard-ed by se-crecy. Their exis-tence is hidden from all advena and most Water Fairies."

"You mean there is more than one of these things?" Jennings grimaced.

"One per city," Kuntza corrected the obvious misconception that they were going to have to defend multiple chambers here and now.

"I suppose councilors know of it," Constance noted unhappily.

"They a-ssign the work-ers and app-rove re-pairs." Kuntza's grim tone made it clear that he also believed it was the council members who had betrayed them. He held up a hand when they reached a cross tunnel. "You see those?" he pointed at the bundles of sap-coated lightning wires that ran along the top of the wall. "Those chan-nel the light-ning from where it is gen-erated to where it is used." They all nodded, but Jennings looked particularly disturbed.

"What is wrong with you?" Rolf asked Jennings, genuinely concerned at how pale the windfairy's face had become.

"I have been using those wires in my quarters to hang things on," Jennings spluttered. "I could have died!"

"They are safe, un-less cut op-en." Kuntza indicated their weapons. "Light-ning loves met-al and will surge up your swords so quick-ly that you will not have time to re-lease them. If we fight," and they probably would, "do not strike the lightning wires." He knew they had a healthy respect for lightning already, so he did not belabor the point. Touching a finger to his lips, he nodded at the cross tunnel. "We go in sil-ence now."

Rolf was starting to recognize the area when Kuntza came to a stop in front of the hidden doors Rolf remembered from his first day. He watched eagerly as Kuntza tried to open it. After the first two failed attempts, Rolf's smile began to fade.

They all looked on in surprise as Rolf tapped Kuntza lightly on the shoulder. Cambrian shrugged a little when Kuntza looked at him before stepping back. Curious, they gathered up a bit around Rolf to see what he did.

Rolf ran his fingertips around the doorframe, eyes half-closed in concentration. Tunnel diggers and builders, like everyone else, had their patterns, things that they had learned worked and they rarely deviated from those patterns. As he expected, the main difference between this door and the other doors in Cachora was that this one had no visible handle. Locating a faintly rounded edge on one side, he stooped so that his eyes were roughly waist level and examined the door on the other side. Unsheathing his belt knife, he carefully dug the tip of it into an odd spot on the door. Abruptly, the 'stone' gave way and the blade of his knife slid up to its hilt into the slit in the door. His knife blade was a smidgen narrower than the typical Water Fairy counterpart, judging by the bit of wiggle room he detected.

Gripping the hilt of his knife like a door handle, Rolf pointed at the far side of the door and gestured for someone else to push against it. When Kuntza was in position, Rolf held up three fingers, lowering them in sequence so that Kuntza's push was timed exactly with his own. The stone door, while significantly heavier than the doors to their quarters, responded to their united efforts. Kuntza's side of the door sank a finger's width into the wall-frame and a barely audible click was heard. The door, now properly aligned on its grooved track, yielded to Rolf's sideways push. It opened so swiftly and so smoothly, in fact, that Rolf ran right into Kuntza, landing in his arms with a grunt of surprise.

Kuntza, his shoulders shaking with silent laughter, righted the lad and patted his shoulder. The hidden doors worked differently in each city, another layer of secrecy for protection, and he was impressed at how quickly Rolf had solved the puzzle.

Rolf, who was having difficulty retrieving his knife, graciously endured the successive shoulder pats as Cambrian and Constance slipped past him into the tunnel beyond the door, but scowled at Jennings, who playfully patted him on the head. Reluctantly, Rolf left the knife behind, wondering if it was a safety mechanism that kept the door open while the workers were inside, designed to prevent them from getting trapped. But he had already forgotten that this was a secret door in his haste to catch up with the others. A single glance at the back side of the door would have revealed the switch that would have released his knife and sent the door sliding closed via a spring mechanism.

The access tunnel opened out into an enormous chamber, its left side filled with three large, horizontally-placed cylinders with lightning wires coming out the near end. The lightning globes dispersed along the walls and dangling from an artificially lowered ceiling of cords made the chamber almost as bright as full daylight. A persistent whirring sound filled their ears as they entered, and their noses were instantly assaulted by a strong, oily smell reminiscent of burned fish. Constance quickly came to the conclusion that both the sound and the smell were coming from the cylinders.

Kuntza motioned for them to fan out. Amber and her cohorts could easily be hiding somewhere between the lightning generators. Gripping his suge loosely, and keeping Wynston on his left, Kuntza struck off to his right. Stepping carefully over the larger lightning wire where the three generator wires merged, he went toward the distribution web, which was how the lightning generated here was dispersed throughout Cachora.

Cambrian and Constance maintained an instinctual awareness of each other as they made their way through the shadows. Constance flexed her hands, wishing she could take off her gloves and wipe her palms on her trousers. The heat in the chamber rose the further they went, and she could see by the beads of sweat forming on Cambrian's forehead that it was affecting him, as well.

They were approaching the far end of the two cylinders they were scouting between when something made the hair rise on the back of Constance's neck. Grabbing Cambrian's arm, she pulled him with her into the shadow cast by the cylinder on her left. To his credit, he came without protest. Still guided by an inexplicable compulsion, Constance changed her mind. Moving out of the shadow, she slowly began heading back the way they had come. An awful feeling of dread began in her stomach, then rose until it squeezed her heart, stopping her in her tracks.

Looking up suddenly, she peered at the top of the cylinder. It was at least twice her height, probably more. Her mouth tightened. They had forgotten to look up, having already grown accustomed to Cachora's low tunnels, neglecting a critical point in their search. Propelled by the same feeling that had guided her thus far, she flew up to check. She was about to land when she realized the humming sound was louder up there. Deciding hovering would be safer, she looked over in the direction that Jennings and Rolf had taken. Rolf was hovering over a cylinder of his own, his attention focused somewhere below. Probably talking to Jennings, Constance decided, noticing that his mouth was moving.

Cambrian, having followed Constance to the top of the cylinder, saw Rolf, too. Then his attention was drawn to his left by a series of flashes.

"Kuntza!" Cambrian shouted the word at the top of his lungs, bringing Constance whirling about to face him. But he was already gone, zipping towards Kuntza at breakneck speed. A hanging wire scraped a wingtip, slowing him fractionally. He could not help Kuntza if he was snagged on the wires.

Constance, spotting the flashes also, chose to go straight up. Her heart constricted painfully when she saw that Kuntza and Wynston were busy fending off four armed Water Fairies while Amber and someone else—a councilor?—bent over one of the thicker lightning wires. Still mindful of the dangers surrounding her, she made a mental note of the fact that the lightning wire was not hurting her enemies before tucking her wings for a controlled dive. She thought she heard a shout behind her, but had no time to look back. Careening through the labyrinth of support cords and guide wires was no trick at all for her, their pattern sorting itself out as she neared them, the result of centuries spent keeping track of the sheets and halyards of windship rigging.

Wingtip course corrections kept her from getting carved up and she hit Amber going just shy of full tilt. Backhanding the councilor, who was trying to remove heavy leather gloves so that he could use the elaborate-looking suge hanging from his belt, she scratched him off her list of concerns and turned to face Amber. From the corner of her eye, she caught a glimpse of five figures in armor and wielding suges. Their face masks were down but she assumed that the one fighting side-by-side with her uncle was Kuntza. Cambrian was just landing when Constance sensed Amber's intent. Bringing her attention back to her own fight, she raised her sword to block Amber's wild overhand swing.

"I never welcomed you to Cachora properly." Amber smiled evilly at her over their crossed blades. Swooping her wings forward, she threw herself back, reversed course and lunged.

Constance, at first not sure what to expect, brought her sword in and down, forcing Amber's blade out of line with Constance's body. Following through with the motion, she stepped forward on her left leg and drove her right knee into Amber's midsection.

Amber staggered clear of Constance's reach, struggling for air. When she got her breath back, Amber began to laugh.

"You arrived just in time," she gasped. "Winter setting in on the surface means there is nowhere for them to go. They will have to accept me as their ruler."

Sensing motion behind her, Constance propelled herself several twigs into the air. She was confused to find that it was just the councilor, resuming whatever he had been doing when she arrived. It involved what looked like a large, ceramic pot, but that was all that she had time to see before Amber was upon her.

Fencing in the air was especially dangerous, for one's wings were exposed to their enemy's razor sharp sword. In the lightning chamber, it was far worse. It required Constance's complete concentration to avoid Amber's blade and the wires at the same time. Sweat stung her eyes as she retreated before Amber's completely unorthodox attacks. Lunges became slashes, making dodging nearly impossible. Backhand swings dipped clear of Constance's blocks to transition into upward or downward cuts. The jacket Constance had considered discarding earlier because of the heat in the lightning chamber saved her life repeatedly even as it was reduced to shreds. One by one, her buttons fell away until the jacket hung open.

Breathing hard, Constance swiped at the sweat on her forehead and landed. Amber, driven by excitement and revenge, seemed to grow stronger with each attack, while Constance could feel her strength waning. Shrugging out of her useless jacket, she threw it at Amber, who laughed and deflected it with her sword tip.

Amber stopped laughing when she realized that Constance had used her jacket as a distraction while she brought the rounded metal hilt of her sword down on the back of the councilor's head. Amber screamed like an enraged falcon when he slumped to the ground.

Constance was driven back by a brutal, bewildering onslaught, finally tripping and falling, exhausted, to the ground. Her sword clattered off somewhere into the shadows.

"You think you have won?" Amber was still screaming, oblivious to the fact that she alone remained uncaptured. "You will lie there," she pressed the point of her sword into Constance's shoulder until a stain of blood appeared and began spreading outward, "and watch me become ruler of Cachora!"

"No!" Naydie's scream was the sound of true fear. She and her guards, finding the door to the lightning chamber still ajar, arrived just in time to watch in horror as Amber reached down into the bundle of wires where the councilor lay unconscious.

Amber, assuming that she had already begun to achieve her goal, demonstrated her complete ignorance of the lightning wires when she sliced one free from the outer wall and plunged it into the ceramic pot's opening. Sparks of lightning flew, uncontrolled, from the rapidly overloaded storage container.

Summoning up her last reserves of strength, Constance got her hands under her. Pushing herself off the floor, she stumbled forward, her eyes on Amber, who was already succumbing to the devastating effects of lightning exposure. Reaching the councilor, Constance tugged his suge free. It uncoiled beneath her as she unsteadily lifted off, reflexively relying on flight because she was in a hurry. She aimed herself towards the lightning wire behind Amber, reasoning that the lightning was streaming through the thickest wire from the cylinders towards the wall, like water through a funnel. It might be too late, but…

"Wait!" Kuntza, having silenced his last opponent, was too late. The suge in Constance's hand snapped forward, slicing cleanly through the primary chamber wire behind Amber. Constance's body gave a tremendous jerk as the force of the lightning caused her muscles to contract, then tossed her like a rag doll across the chamber.

Chapter 18

Constance thought that being held by her husband was her favorite part of being shocked. Her bruises were still forming, so it did not even hurt much. Of course, after a few hours of snuggling, she was ready to be up and about, but Cambrian was being stubborn.

"You were thrown across the lightning chamber." Cambrian reminded her. "You were unconscious for several minutes." He tucked her closer to him, hoping she would just put her head back against his shoulder and let him go on savoring the peace of holding her, alive, in his arms. "Kuntza said that, even with the extra protection from the suge's in-sulated," he tripped a little over the unfamiliar word, "hilt, he has no idea how you are still alive."

"I know I *was* unconscious," she decided to skip over her near-death experience. "It is just that I am awake now." Much to her surprise, Cambrian took her chin in his right hand, turned her face towards him, and kissed her breathless.

"Humor me."

Unable to think of an argument for that, Constance shifted a little further onto her side and nestled even closer. She hoped they had brought along a powerful pain potion; she could tell by the dull ache in her wingtips that tomorrow was going to be awful. Her eyes were drifting closed when she realized what was on the little table by the bed.

Cambrian, who had just placed his chin on the top of her head, was thoroughly rattled when she sat up.

"What is it?" He gripped her hands in his. "Are you in pain?"

Constance's indignation cooled quickly in the face of his concern. "No, I am not in pain." Bruises aside, of course. Pointing one of his hands, which was still holding hers, towards the end table, she asked, "Is that what I think it is?" It looked remarkably like the resignation papers she brought from Regalis.

When he saw what she meant, his curiosity regarding the packet of papers redoubled. "That depends, I suppose." He turned so that he was facing her again. "On what you think it is."

Constance deliberately plumped a pillow and set it against the headboard. When she had gingerly arranged herself, leaning back on the pillow, she cocked her head to one side and batted her eyelashes at him.

"Could you repeat the question?" she asked, intentionally stalling for time. Now that the moment of her resignation was upon her, she felt a little nervous.

Cambrian reached over and picked up the papers, plopping them into her lap.

"I believe you asked me if I knew what those are." It was not a direct quote, but he was pretty sure he had the right question behind the question.

Constance, seeing that the seals were

unbroken, felt an odd rush of relief. Of course she had hoped he would not pry, but there had been a moment of niggling doubt when she saw the papers just now. She did not even bother to ask where he had found them because—unless the papers had grown wings and moved themselves—they would have been in the bottom of her small vanity trunk where she left them.

"I was looking for smelling salts," Cambrian tried to anticipate her next question. He supposed he would be just as disturbed to find that she had been in his things. He trusted her, he loved her, but he was not yet accustomed to sharing his private space—or secrets—with her.

"Did you find any?" Constance had a hazy memory of being hauled, semi-conscious, down a tunnel before she blacked out again.

"No." Cambrian slid closer to her, not liking the distance between them. "You woke up on your own."

"Did I miss much?" she asked, still not ready to discuss her resignation papers.

"Well," Cambrian laced his fingers through hers. "The councilors that were working with Amber have been dismissed and imprisoned to await a full investigation and trial. They are already working to repair the lightning chamber." Much to his surprise, Constance's actions had triggered a massive malfunction, something about too much lightning for the remaining lightning wires. He did not understand the technical side of it, but apparently a third of Cachora's lightning globes were dark right now.

"Amber?"

Cambrian took a deep breath and exhaled slowly. "She thought she could put all of the lightning in that one, small pot. Then she would trade the lightning for the Water Fairy crown." He shook his head, caught between marveling that lightning could be stored in a pot at all and that Amber had been so foolish as to tamper with anything so powerful. "If she had confided in any one of her co-conspirators, they could have told her it would not work, but she did not. There was just too much lightning and it escaped from the pot into her." He rubbed the inside of her wrist comfortingly with his thumb while he tried to clear his mind of the sights and sounds of Amber's demise. "There was nothing they could do for her."

Constance closed the gap between them, her knee coming up and dumping the papers into Cambrian's lap as she buried her face in his chest.

Silently, Cambrian rocked her while she wept. He had purposefully diverted her from talking about it when she first regained consciousness, wanting to wait until he was sure she had her strength back. She had just…seemed so fragile, lying there, unconscious on their bed. He smoothed her hair and began slowly rubbing the base of her right wing, careful not to move the wing itself. Too much. They had been through far too much in too short a time.

"Strange, is it not?" he asked, when her sobbing had eased a little. "Bullierd's father served with distinction for nearly five hundred years. He never aspired to titles," Cambrian knew that from his time at Castlemain, "but was an honest and well-liked marine. And now Bullierd's son, Edward, serves as king's champion to King Hugh."

"Do you know Edward?" Constance asked, her emotional storm reduced to a few remaining tears that were currently trickling down her face.

"Yes." Cambrian had seen very little of Edward since Joanna's death, but they had become reacquainted during Cambrian's recent visit to Castlemain for the combination coronation and wedding. *Triple* wedding. Edward and Alfred, another quasi-friend from Cambrian's youth, had married their wives in the same ceremony as King Hugh and Queen Rebecca.

"Is he truly a good man-fairy?"

"Oh yes. And if he was content with merely not being bad, his wife, Helen, would certainly require more of him." Cambrian dug a handkerchief out of his vest pocket and dabbed at her eyes. He kissed her forehead, then her eyelids, still warm from crying. "Now," he cuddled her close, mindful of the bruises on her arms and legs from where she landed on the hard chamber floor, and tapped the papers on his knees. "These may be none of my business, I am not sure." The fresh, unbroken seals told him that they were of recent date, but nothing else. "But I will not press you to tell me about them."

Constance, her ear pressed against his chest, lay there and listened to his heartbeat while her mind finished wading through the recent events.

"Have we accomplished our mission?" she asked, reaching out to nudge the papers closer to her.

Cambrian frowned thoughtfully. "An excellent question. Let me think. We have successfully met with the Water Fairy Tribe." He pressed a kiss to the tip of her little finger. "We have established, by the speaker's own admission," this had happened in the chaos following the globes going dark, "that the surface tribes are not a threat to the Water Fairies." He kissed her next fingertip. "Kuntza has proposed that they welcome diplomats from each of the other tribes," he continued making his way around her fingers. "The council is drafting letters to the regional representatives, inviting them here to discuss it. Also, they have agreed to release the advena to return to the surface, and they have agreed to let us spend the winter here." He kissed her thumb and her palm. "So, yes. I would say our primary mission is complete." He had just kissed the inside of her wrist and was about to make his way down her arm when he realized she was shaking her head.

"No. Not *here*," she looked intently up at him. "Cambrian, I just learned that I have an uncle and cousins here."

Cambrian did not have to think very hard to know he would rather spend the winter getting to know her family than making his way awkwardly through the main tunnels of Cachora while the locals gawked at him. Or at least, at Constance. He had not yet figured out how he was going to tell her that she was a local hero. Public opinion had dismissed her involvement in the blackout and was praising her for her actions in apprehending the treasonous councilors. The rest of them got a little credit, too—more than any of them were comfortable with, really—but she was the one carried unconscious through the tunnels; she was also the one who went to visit the advena; and yes, she was the one who slew the evil Count Bullierd at Regalis.

"If Uncle Wynston has room," Cambrian smiled down at her. "And if he does not, we could always leave a few trunks behind in storage." They chuckled together, remembering how Cambrian's former valet, Roberts, stranded him aboard the *Nadauld* with only his most formal suits, taking the other trunks aboard the *Kimuxwe* with him. Then they had all wound up wearing slops after Bane threw their trunks overboard in a fit of rage.

Constance blushed when Cambrian stopped chuckling and resumed kissing. "Darling?" She freed her hand so that she could pick up the papers. "Could you bring me my hat?"

Bewildered, Cambrian just stared at her. "Kuntza warned me that you might suffer some ill effects from the lightning shock…"

She laughed. "Please."

Cambrian studied her face a few seconds longer, then got up and retrieved her tricorn from the pegs by the door.

"Wait," she stopped him when he was about to sit back down. "You need your hat, too."

Translating 'hat' to 'crown,' Cambrian walked over to where he had hung it by hers.

"Anything else?"

She nodded. "Ink and a quill."

Fortunately, all of the guest rooms at Cachora were stocked with such items, or else Cambrian might have had to go find Rolf. Setting the ink bottle on the end table, Cambrian deftly trimmed the fresh quill tip into writing shape before setting it down as well.

"Anything else?" He wanted to be sure. She might need a…oh, a bottle of bootblack or something else equally logical.

She patted the spot on the bed beside her. Waiting until he was comfortably situated, she put her tricorn on and saluted him.

"Prince Cambrian," despite the oddly informal setting, she felt no desire to laugh, "Admiral Kimberlite begs to present you with her resignation papers."

Cambrian, his hand already extended to receive the packet, froze in place. Her words rang in his ears. *Resignation papers…resignation…*

"Constance," he took the papers with one

hand and caught her wrist with his other. "Are you sure?"

She smiled. "Yes."

Releasing her, he held onto the papers with both hands.

"Will you tell me why?" he asked. He had no objections whatsoever. Truthfully, he remembered hearing her tell Watts something to the effect that she planned to retire. He simply had never found the right time to discuss it with her.

Constance had been trying to put it into words for days. Now that the time had come, she found that all she was able to do was speak from her heart.

"I joined the fleet because I watched my father serve and thought it would be a very fine career for me. I wanted to do it and I quickly learned that I was quite good at it." She took off her tricorn and set it aside. "I know that I am young to retire; however, I have found a career that I want even more. One that I want to give my whole strength to, one that is full of new experiences and opportunities for me. I will be able to travel, really travel, not just stop long enough to replenish supplies. I will meet new people, learn their customs, teach them to others..."

Cambrian interrupted to ask, "And what is this wonderful career?" His puzzlement faded as he watched the pink creep up her neck.

"That of wife," she answered, trying awfully hard to stop blushing. "And someday, mother."

Cambrian would have leaned over and kissed her, but his crown slipped off, landing in her hands. When she had replaced it on his head, he disciplined himself to the task at hand—breaking open the seals on her resignation papers. Opening them, he read them carefully to be sure everything was in order. Usually at least one witness was required for the signing of official papers. He reached for the quill anyway. Who was going to protest? Certainly neither of them. Besides, Admiral Waban had witnessed Constance's initial request for resignation, so there were technically two.

Laying the papers out on the table so that the ink could dry, Cambrian leaned back against the headboard.

"Are you disappointed?" Constance asked when he did not speak.

"Hmm? What, no!" Cambrian shook his head vehemently. "Not at all." He smoothed the hairs that the tricorn had mussed. "I was only thinking." Looking deep into her eyes, he murmured softly, "I love you so much."

Constance, held fast by the fervor in his voice, listened quietly, for he had more to say.

"For fifty years my broken heart was held together by false pride. I thought I had to keep going or I would prove everyone right, prove that I was weak and spineless, half a man-fairy." He was angry now, angry at those who whispered loudly enough for his quick ears to catch their words, angry with himself for believing them. "I looked at the fairies around me and I did not realize that I was seeing elaborately-crafted façades. It tore me up inside to lose Joanna." He realized too late that he was speaking of his first love to his bride. Again. "I began to believe I would never be whole again, that the rest of Fairydom had moved on, even though they had not, not as completely as they pretended. I could not pretend, so I buried it. I buried my pain, my anger, my fears...I was fading into a life devoid of emotion. Until I saw you."

Constance was listening with her whole self this time, not with just her heart or just her head. Her very soul vibrated in sympathy with his as he spoke. Unwilling to deceive himself, he had endured decades of self-inflicted torture instead of allowing himself to grieve in peace. All because he mistakenly believed his grief was wrong somehow, too consuming perhaps. If only he had taken into account the fact that his heart had broken more than anyone else's at her death, save those of her family members. Then he might have been more patient with his pain, more forgiving of what he had instead condemned as weakness.

"I learned, from being with you, that my heart had healed without my being aware of it. I saw that I was using my former pain as a crutch, leaning on it whenever I encountered something I did not want to accept. Worse, I had let my past shape my vision for my future. Only the hope of being with you was strong enough for me to break free."

Reaching up, Constance removed his crown and set it beside her tricorn. Pressing both hands to his chest above his heart, she leaned close enough to rest her head against the side of her husband's jaw.

"I am free," Cambrian continued hoarsely. "I have chosen a path with you that may take me up or down at any given time, but I am willing to follow it. For moments become hours, and hours build days, and days are what we measure our lives in." He lifted her away from him, needing to see her face, to be certain he was not inadvertently hurting her.

Constance smiled at him through her tears, happy tears this time. "Courage," she told him, her hands still over his heart, "is doing the right thing even when one is afraid." Taking the handkerchief up from where he had dropped it, she dried first her eyes, which were damper, then blotted the single tear that had slipped past his defenses. She was just getting ready to lean close again when someone knocked on the door.

Cambrian, emotionally exhausted, leaned back against his pillow and groaned aloud. That done, he adjusted his façade enough to be socially presentable.

"Who is it?" Constance called, assuming correctly that she was the more composed of the two, though not by much.

"Jennings, reporting by the surgeon's orders, ma'am!"

That made them both laugh a little. Rising, Cambrian went over to the door and opened it.

"If you are looking for Admiral Kimberlite," Cambrian told Jennings, who was trying to see around him into the room, "she is not here."

Astonished, Jennings nearly dropped the pitcher he was carrying. "What, you let her leave? In her condition? Why you great clod! You incompetent oaf!" He might have gone on reciting the insults officers had bandied about over the years, if Constance had not started laughing.

"However," Cambrian jumped at the chance to interrupt, "if you would like to speak with Princess Constance Bijou," he drew back so that Jennings could see Constance clearly. "She awaits within."

Jennings sniffed his disapproval of Cambrian's joke and entered without further invitation. "Surgeon's compliments, ma'am," he threw a withering glance at Cambrian, who remained singularly un-withered as he leaned against the wall next to their still half-packed trunks. "Says to take half a glass of this every two hours," he plunked the pitcher down on the end table, then sat down hard on the bed.

"Jennings!" Cambrian and Constance yelped his name in protest at the same time. A windfairy should never casually seat themselves on their captain's bed, nor a valet on his boss', but Jennings just went on sitting there.

"You resigned?" Jennings said at last, twisting at the waist so that he could see her better. When she nodded, he nodded, too. "Resigned, she has," he muttered to himself, oblivious to the awkward circumstance of his proximity to her. "What will become of the fleet? We need good officers!"

Constance sighed in relief as that brought him to his feet. "*We?*" she scoffed. "You resigned first!"

Cambrian watched the byplay with a generous amusement, more confident than ever that hiring Jennings as his valet had been an excellent decision. Cautiously, he slipped his hand into the heavy dress jacket he had worn the first day. Cachora had turned out to be much drier and comfortable than he originally anticipated, but the jacket was the perfect place to hide a certain surprise for Constance.

"To be sure, but I…but I…" He tried without success to bluster on about why he could and she should not, then threw his hands up in despair. "Of all the…"

Cambrian, deciding he had had enough of Jennings' invasion, caught him by the upper arm and propelled him from the room.

"You can tell us all about it, later," he said as

he slid the door firmly shut.

The couple grinned at each other. There seemed to be a great deal of silence for the next several seconds while they both digested their first marital lump. Constance felt that her resignation had gone off rather well, all things considered. And she desperately hoped that Cambrian would not mention Joanna to her again for the next few hundred years. A woman-fairy's understanding had its limits, after all.

Cambrian, in contrast, was full of peace, for his memories of Joanna had finally been set to rest. There was, though, one more thing he needed to share with Constance. Walking over to their bed, he seated himself approximately where Jennings had been.

"Princess Constance Bijou," he recited. "No middle name?" Under ordinary circumstances there would have been a formal crowning ceremony to accompany their wedding. Since that was out of the question, he had come prepared.

Constance smiled and shook her head. "Father was very practical when it came to things like that."

"In that case." He brought his hand out from where he had been hiding it under his jacket, revealing a delicate crown. "Accept this crown, Princess Constance Bijou." Gently, he placed the crown on her head, the diamonds and sapphires catching the light from the lightning globes and flinging it around the room like flowers at a coronation.

"On one condition." Constance leaned forward. "That every time you put it on me, you kiss me."

Cambrian was happy to oblige.

Epilogue

Watts looked longingly at the helm, but it only took a deep breath to remind him that his collarbone was still more broken than healed. That re-decided, he lifted his glass again. The terrain ahead was steep, rocky, and nearly devoid of dwellings. Finding Takoda without Dixon's help would have been impossible if not for the creek they had spotted an hour ago. And it was still hard to believe that the single warehouse and accompanying shack rated the designation of 'city' on the royal Sky Fairy maps.

"Check with the lookout," Watts instructed Miss Dunn, needing an update on the storm. They had parted ways with it after accounting for the other chasers, but at their current altitude it was barely in range of a good glass. He scanned the deck, counting the number of heavy, spare spars that the crew had brought up from below decks to be used in propping the *Sorter* up once they landed. If she listed far enough either way to rest on her wings, her odds of ever flying again would be cut to less than half.

"Good news," Dunn answered as the lookout finished signaling.

"Another patch of clouds has split off. That makes seven confirmed clouds."

"And the lightning?" Watts agreed that was good news. However, now that the lightning had done its work, causing the original storm cloud to leave half its snow at the edge of the canyon where they found it, he would just as soon have the lighting dissipate as well.

Miss Dunn's smile widened. "Completely out," she announced cheerfully. The lightning was sporadic at first, but with this last split-off, the lookout reported the lightning was completely finished.

"Excellent." Watts shipped his glass and nodded. "Sideboats away," Watts commanded as they began their final approach. In an effort to lighten the *Wind Sorter*, and thereby minimize damage to her hull, he had ordered the ballistae crews and craftsfairies into the small, emergency craft his chaser carried, along with any and all supplies they could safely cram aboard. With any luck, they would be able to land the sideboats much closer to the only visible shelter than the *Sorter*, bringing those same supplies that much nearer their end goal.

"Furl all sails. Secure the deck
for weather! Flaps down full."
    The crew sprang to obey,
anticipation lending a dash of
nervous energy to the mundane tasks.
They were running barely ahead of a
smaller storm cloud, which,
diminished as it was, would still
blanket the area with a thick layer
of damp snow.
    "Brace for crash landing!" The
cry echoed down the deck as the *Wind
Sorter* slowed to a hover. The
remaining crew members not actively
engaged in flying the chaser were all
huddled forward of the waists with
the intent of bringing her nose down
fractionally before the rest of her.
Those still in the rigging held on
for dear life.
    Watts forced himself to breathe as
the *Sorter*'s nose caressed the
mountainside. He had run her in
nose-down, reasoning that if she
were ever to fly again, it would be
easiest if she was already pointing
the right direction.
    "Over the side!" he bellowed as
she began to settle, wincing
inwardly at the scraping sounds as
she ground to a halt. "Get those
props in place!"
    Windfairies swarmed over the side,
hauling the heavy spars with them.

The bo'sun dove over one side to supervise while Miss Dunn, who protested that her previous injury amounted to a headache, took the other side. Correctly positioned, the spars would prop the *Sorter* in an upright position.

The order already given for the ship to be battened down, Watts took the helmsfairy and Toby, the cabin lad, and hurried towards the buildings.

"Strange n'body out ta meet us," muttered the helmsfairy, a tall, gangly fellow commonly known as Gasket because his appearance was so similar to that of the lengths of rope used to hold the sails in place after furling them.

"Indeed." Watts, feeling the urgency and wishing he could fly, waved Gasket ahead. "The warehouse, and be careful," he ordered. That left just him and the cabin lad, running as quickly as their legs could carry them towards the shack. The lad moved ahead at the end, his young lungs powering him forward and through the rickety door.

"Empty!"

Watts huffed his way through shortly after the lad. Leaning against the doorframe, trying to catch his breath without aggravating his still-mending collarbone, he swept the room with a glance. Empty. Bare. Stripped of everything that was not built into the shack's original design. Wincing his way further in, Watts sat down on the desk that protruded from one wall. The dust lay thick, but he did not bother wiping it away first.

"Where is everybody?" The lad's voice, high-pitched already due to his youth, was almost a squeak now. "What are we going to do?"

Watts lifted a hand and waved it at the lad to hush him. "Look under the desk. Look in that cabinet. I do not care how small it is, tell me if you find anything at all."

Obediently the lad dropped to his knees, then scurried over to the cabinet. Having caught the sense of the order, he took it further and examined everywhere anything might have gone overlooked when the previous occupants packed up and left.

"Sir!" Gasket's voice made them both jump. "Sir," he repeated as he came into view. "The warehouse. It has a tunnel."

Watts hesitated. He had to make a decision and do it quickly. And it had to be the right decision.

"How big is it?"

Gasket shook his head. "Tall enough to get into easy, sir, but too deep for me to see into."

"Toby, go find Miss Dunn. Get everything into the warehouse that they can carry, food and blankets first."

"Aye, sir!" Toby did not have far to go, for Miss Dunn had started the crew unloading the *Sorter* and begun checking on the sideboats, most of which were able to land next to the warehouse.

"You and I," Watts tore a loose wallboard free and yanked down the lone, ratty curtain, "are going exploring."

The empty warehouse was rapidly filling with supplies when they entered it. Watts signaled for Miss Dunn to join him while Gasket expertly manipulated flint and steel.

"Gasket and I are going below," he jerked his head in the direction of the tunnel's mouth. "Keep things going up here until the storm arrives." His eyes widened slightly when he saw two ballista crews carrying an entire sideboat up the hill to the warehouse. "If we are not back by then, come in after us and close it up behind you. We can wait out the storm down there."

Miss Dunn nodded, then resumed her task. "You!" she hailed a craftsfairy. "Ever taken a shack apart before?"

"Put a few up," the fellow responded, his hands straying to his ever-present tool belt.

"Good enough." She jerked her thumb towards the door. "That thing out there is useless to us except as firewood."

The last thing Watts saw before entering the tunnel was Dixon being carried into the warehouse on a stretcher.

"Careful, sir." Gasket pointed at the ground with the makeshift torch, revealing a veritable graveyard of old, broken tools.

"Mining equipment," Watts muttered, kicking enough aside to clear a path. Squinting in the uncertain light, he picked up what looked like an old ax handle. Unless he was mistaken, he thought, as he forced a knot of frayed rope into the crack that ran halfway down the ax handle, there was water down here. He could hear something dripping.

Gasket obligingly lowered the torch so Watts could light his. Then, both of them armed with spluttering, smoking lights, they advanced into the tunnel.

"What d'ye suppose they were mining, sir?" Gasket asked to fill the relative silence. The sounds of the lads hauling loads above had faded too quickly for his liking.

"Ore, maybe." Watts toed an empty bucket aside and smiled faintly when he saw that one side was stove in. "Gems." He shrugged. All he could say for sure was that they were not wasteful. Anything and everything of any practical value, under ordinary circumstances, had left with them. "Go back up top and tell Miss Dunn to focus everyone on transferring what is in the warehouse into here."

Gasket hesitated, whether out of reluctance to go off by himself or to leave Watts by himself, it was hard to say.

"Hurry!" Watts watched Gasket go, faintly amused at the large fellow's obvious fear of the dark. The tunnel was deserted, save for themselves. The chamber they had just entered was large enough to hold his crew, the craftsfairies, and the ballistae crews uncomfortably for at least the next several hours. Since he would be no use hauling boxes and Miss Dunn was more than enough officer for the job, Watts jammed his torch into a

crack in the wall and set about
trying to scrape all of the litter
to one side, starting about halfway
to the tunnel mouth and working his
way back towards the chamber.
Finding a few more broken bits of
wood and other combustibles, he put
together a small, hot fire in the
center of the chamber.

"Captain." Dixon's voice carried
clearly over the sound of his
bearers. "Where do you want me?"

Surprised, Watts indicated a low
shelf he had discovered earlier. He
coughed a few times, trying to get
the lump out of his throat, then
pointed at a random branch tunnel.

"You take charge here," Watts
ignored the scowl on the surgeon's
face, "while I scout further in. We
will need more room than this if we
are going to winter here." When Dixon
saluted him, Watts, for the first
time, questioned the absoluteness of
rank. The only reason Dixon was not
zipping about under his own power was
because he had done what none of the
rest of them could, or—at bare
minimum—before any of the rest of them
could. The lump was back in his
throat when he returned the salute.
"The chamber is yours, Mister," was
all he managed to get out before he
turned and retrieved his torch.

A few hasty steps into the tunnel, Watts slowed, then stopped. Was it instinct or accident that made him choose the tunnel that led towards the dripping sound he heard earlier? Either way, he proceeded more carefully. Slipping and breaking something else would set a very poor example for the crew.

Adjusting his grip on the smoldering ax handle, the rope having completely burned out by now, Watts bent close to the tunnel floor, hunting for something else combustible. He would never have spotted the broken shard of glass if not for the reflection. The…green reflection? Lowering his useless torch, Watts waited for his eyes to adjust to this new light. He had heard of cold fire, he had just never seen it before.

Several twigs further down the tunnel was a handful of glowing mushrooms. They were growing, as he had expected, inside a log, one no doubt trimmed and transferred here from the surface by the miners for this purpose. It was an old trick, one ideally suited to this area as there was a small, subterranean stream for them to rest one end of the log in.

"Saves air," Watts mused aloud as

he stood, admiring their ingenuity and thinking of how quickly he would tire of the stale air down there. "Saves fuel. Saves energy, too, once you got the blamed thing down here." The further he went, the brighter the light became until he realized it was not a single log with a handful of glowing mushrooms. Watts shook his head, baffled. "What is this place?" he wondered aloud.

There were a dozen, perhaps two dozen, such logs scattered along the bank of the stream. By the light they gave off, he could see that his tunnel emptied out into a large cavern. A cavern relatively well-lit on his side of the stream. As he paused for a moment, to take in the beauty of the scene, he became aware of a…presence. It was as if there was something—living, breathing…watching—just beyond his ability to sense it. He scanned the area as far as he could see, but the far side of the stream lay in darkness.

Ordering himself to focus on one side of the stream at a time, he turned to face the wall behind him. A low shelf ran along it, just like the one where Dixon was lying. Excellent. Plenty of room to store their supplies. He grinned for the first time in hours while he wondered how they would sleep with so much natural light.

The sensation that he was not alone, however, would not leave him. He eased one hand down to his sword hilt and listened more carefully. On the distant edges of his hearing, there was a…whisper. Turning to face the far side of the stream again, Watts began moving closer, walking because it was quieter. He stopped and silently cursed himself for a fool when the toe of his boot sent a rock skittering down the bank to splash into the water. Whatever he had been hearing, or thought he heard, faded. It was replaced by an even more uncomfortable sensation that he was being stared at.

"Come out." Watts hesitated, then added, "Please." Removing his hand from his sword hilt, he reminded himself that he was the interloper there. "Your pardon," he held his hands out, palms up to show he was not concealing anything. "We found your tunnel in the warehouse." As long as he was guessing, he might as well guess he had found a citizen of Takoda. A shadow moved to his right, prompting him to turn towards it. "I…hello."

"Hello." A woman-fairy leaned on an intricately carved staff, her shoulders bent with age. "You startled me, you know."

Watts smiled, liking her instinctively. "Forgive me." He shook his head. "I did not realize anyone else was down here."

"Just me," she smiled back. "I often come here to practice, ever since I was little."

Mesmerized by her sing-song tone, Watts looked around the cave when she did, wondering what she saw.

"Of course, that was back before they came with their picks and their noise," she waved at the tunnel with a frown. Sighing, she selected a mushroom log to sit down on. That was how she came to know their language so well, from years of listening to it, then speaking it with herself. "I told my grandson, Kuntza, about them. He liked to hear the stories of how they would come here at the end of the day, to cook and eat and rest."

Watts sat down, too, wondering how long she had been coming there to watch the miners. Now that she was so close to a light source, he could see clearly that her hair was not blue like his own. Neither was it brown or green or silver. The greenish tint of the mushroom light made him question himself, but her hair appeared pink.

She chuckled a little when she saw how closely he was watching her. "Well, go ahead." She leaned towards him. "Ask."

Sheepishly, Watts rubbed his palms on his knees.

"Who are you? Where are you from? How," he gestured at the huge cavern, "did you get here?"

She laughed aloud this time, a warm, pleasant sound. "Curiosity is a good sign," she nodded, pleased with him. Especially at a time when her clan was trying to determine if the surface fairies had broken the terms of their treaty. "Now. I will tell you, if you will tell me. Agreed?"

"Agreed," Watts answered immediately. His mission was no secret. Also, she was far too relaxed for him to believe she was truly alone. Better to start off as friends.

"I am Damaris Botere, of the Water Fairy Tribe."

Watts opened his mouth to respond but nothing came out. *The Water Fairy Tribe?* He closed his mouth, swallowed, and tried again.

"I am Captain David Watts," his promotion had come with the news that Constance would not be commanding the *Wind Sorter*. "Of the Sky Fairy Tribe."

"You do not seem surprised to hear of my tribe, Captain," Damaris observed shrewdly.

"I would have been a few weeks ago," Watts answered impulsively. "But I was captured by pirates. Their other prisoners spoke of a tribe with pink hair and hazel eyes." He shook his head. "I thought they were mad."

"Then you did not know you could find us here?" While she had always taken care to avoid the place during the warmer months, when the miners came to work, there was always the chance that they had discovered some clue and passed it on to their military.

"Here?" Watts barked a short laugh. "We came here to shelter from a thundersnow storm. We expected to find a town. A small town but, a town." He gestured around him at the empty shelves and bare ground. "With supplies and fairies and..." He shrugged helplessly. "We will be lucky not to starve this winter."

Damaris frowned, her compassion

aroused. "What a dilemma," she murmured, as much to herself as to him.

Watts took a moment to collect himself, glad that none of his crew had been present to hear his dire prediction. "Of course," he rose, folding his arms across his chest. "The stream might provide some sort of food. Plenty of fresh water, too, so we can turn our salt meat into soup. That will help stretch things."

She smiled with him, perceiving the false note in his cheerfulness. But how could she, Damaris Botere, help advena who did not even *know* they were advena, infiltrators from the surface? What would her family think? There was a great deal to consider.

"Are there so very many of you?" she asked, careful not to commit herself.

"Nearly three hundred." Watts glanced back over his shoulder at the tunnel. The storm was probably overhead by now, dropping house-sized snowflakes on the world. While still aboard the *Wind Sorter* they had a close shave or two with graupels before really getting clear of the storm, and he supposed it was possible that the violence of the storm might even knock the rickety warehouse flat.

Damaris' hope of slipping a handful of advena into her private home evaporated and she sighed. The potential benefit of having almost three hundred advena to talk to for the whole winter weighed on her mind. How could she let that slip away? She could hardly continue visiting them while they grew leaner and leaner, either. She shook her head impatiently. There had to be a solution.

Watts turned to face her. "Forgive me, but I must ask. Can you help us?"

Damaris did not answer immediately. "I will speak with my son, Dilan. It is all I can promise."

"Thank you. If there is any way we can repay you," Watts shrugged eloquently. He was not the something-for-nothing type.

Damaris perked up visibly at his offer. She was a zaldun, was she not? Responsible for protecting and guiding her tribe? Whatever was decided about the intent of the surface tribes, things were definitely building towards direct communication with them. That meant her tribe would need to be able to communicate with them, fluently. They would need to know the customs, the recent events, the diplomatic and power structure of the surface world.

"Well," she smiled thoughtfully. "Perhaps there is one thing."

Advena: Fairies from the surface detained by the Water Fairies after stumbling into their lands; also their descendants, many of mixed tribal heritage
Origin: <u>Advenæ</u>: Latin: foreigners
Bijou, King Jasper: leader of the Sky Fairy tribe; husband of Marta; father of Oliver, Cambrian, Lesley, Laura, and Lila.
Bijou, Prince Cambrian: the younger son of King Jasper Bijou.
Origin: "The Cambrian Period marks an important point in the history of life on Earth; it is the time when most of the major groups of animals first appear in the fossil record. This event is sometimes called the "Cambrian Explosion," because of the relatively short time over which this diversity of forms appears."
http://www.ucmp.berkeley.edu/cambrian/cambrian.php
Bilera: Water Fairy place of meeting; where the city's council convenes to hear evidence and make decisions impacting an entire city
Origin: Basque: meeting
Botere clan: Oldest and most powerful Water Fairy clan
Origin: Basque: one definition is "potential"
Botere, Kuntza: a Water Fairy introduced in *Troubled Skies*. Scientist and truth-seeker for his tribe. Also a Water Fairy zaldun, or knight; a resident of the Mugan region, which borders the surface.
Origin: (Basque) verbal suffix signifying an abstract act or action. *(Basque-English Dictionary* by Gorka Aulestia)
Cachora: the capitol city of the Water Fairy Tribe. *(Pronounced Cash-ora)*
Origin: Cachoeira, Portuguese for *waterfall*
Cassidy: Kuntza's cousin and a skilled physician, specializing in reconstructive surgery
Origin: Irish surname,
http://www.babynamesofireland.com/cassidy

Cloud Chaser: Sky Fairy windship class, specifically designed for versatility and maneuverability in every kind of weather a windfairy can survive. Used to wrangle storm clouds.

Dabberlock: "Dabberlocks, Badderlocks or Winged Kelp is one of the easiest seaweeds to identify. But it is a low-shore variety and rarely seems to get stranded."
Source: http://www.ispotnature.org/node/637599

Domesticated animals: I have imagined a world where there are cows, goats, etc., that are small enough for farmers roughly one-quarter inch tall to raise and tend.

Farren: Sky Fairy windship lost on the wind two hundred years ago; her passengers were deemed spies and detained in Water Fairy territory
Origin: English first name meaning "adventurous"

Kendu: The family name of Ambassador Julene's distinguished Water Fairy relatives
Origin: Basque: Distant or remote:

Kimberlite, Admiral Constance: first seen as the captain of the windship *Falcon* in Silver Verity (Silver Sagas Book 3).
Origin: "Diamonds are brought to the surface from the mantle in a rare type of magma called kimberlite and erupted at a rare type of volcanic vent called a diatreme or pipe."
Source: http://volcano.oregonstate.edu/diamonds

Kimberlite, Norah Izar Niyol: Admiral Constance Kimberlite's mother
       Izar: Origin: Basque, feminine name for star
       Niyol: Origin: Navajo: "Wind"
Source: www.snowwowl.com/swolfNAnamesandmeanings.html

Kimberlite, Wyanet: Constance's younger sister
Origin: Native American: Beautiful
http://www.warpaths2peacepipes.com/native-american-indian-names/native-american-names-w.htm

Kimberlite, Wynston: Uncle of Constance Kimberlite, believed to have died two hundred years previously when

the *Farren* was lost on the wind
Origin: English first name for wanderer
Kiwidinok: Cloud chaser flagship
Origin: Chippewa: "woman of the wind"
Source:
http://www.snowwowl.com/swolfNAnamesandmeanings.html
Mugan region: The seventh Water Fairy region, nearest the exits to the surface; settled anciently by the wealthiest and most powerful clans. Water Fairy territory is arranged in circles, going out like ripples from the central point of Cachora.
Origin: Basque: Border.
Naydie: Prominent Water Fairy Councilwoman
Origin: Algonquian: Wise
Sanuye: Cloud chaser
Origin: Miwok : " red cloud at sundown."
Source:
http://www.snowwowl.com/swolfNAnamesandmeanings.html
Seawrack: "Seawrack is an algae which grows to a height of 100 cm or more."
Source: http://www.herbsguide.net/seawrack.html
Sikya: Water Fairy city where Wynston Kimberlite usually travels and trades books
Origin: Hopi: Small canyon
Suge: Water Fairy weapon of choice, requiring incredible discipline to master; a whip-like sword; three or four feet (human measurement) of double-bladed, razor-sharp flexible steel with a handle insulated in rubber tree sap and a weighted sword tip. Modeled after the Indian *umusi*.
Origin: Basque: snake
Sumendi: Area dotted with lava tubes near Port Herio
Origin: Basque: Volcano
Takoda: Sky Fairy city where the *Wind Sorter*'s crew will be sheltering for the winter
Origin: Sioux: Friend to everyone
Zaldun: Water Fairy for guardian and protector
Origin: Basque: Knight

Zorion: Traditional Water Fairy greeting
Origin: Basque: Happiness

https://thedailyomnivore.net/2011/10/31/irony-mark/ The
'punctus interrogativus' and the 'punctus percontativus'
together form the general seal of the Botere clan, denoting
their deep interest in science and learning.